BANNER OF DAWN

BANNER OF DAWN

FRANCIS PIO

Library of Congress Cataloging-in-Publication Data is available.

ISBN: 978-0-9722231-0-2 (Paperback)
ISBN: 978-0-9722231-2-6 (Hardback)
ISBN: 978-0-9722231-3-3 (Ebook-Kindle)
ISBN: 978-0-9722231-4-0 (Audio)

PRINTED IN THE UNITED STATES OF AMERICA

For all inquiries, email: Contact@BannerOfDawn.com

"I discovered the secret of the sea in meditation upon a dewdrop."

- Kahlil Gibran

To My Father

TABLE OF CONTENTS

MONDAY

TUESDAY

WEDNESDAY

THURSDAY

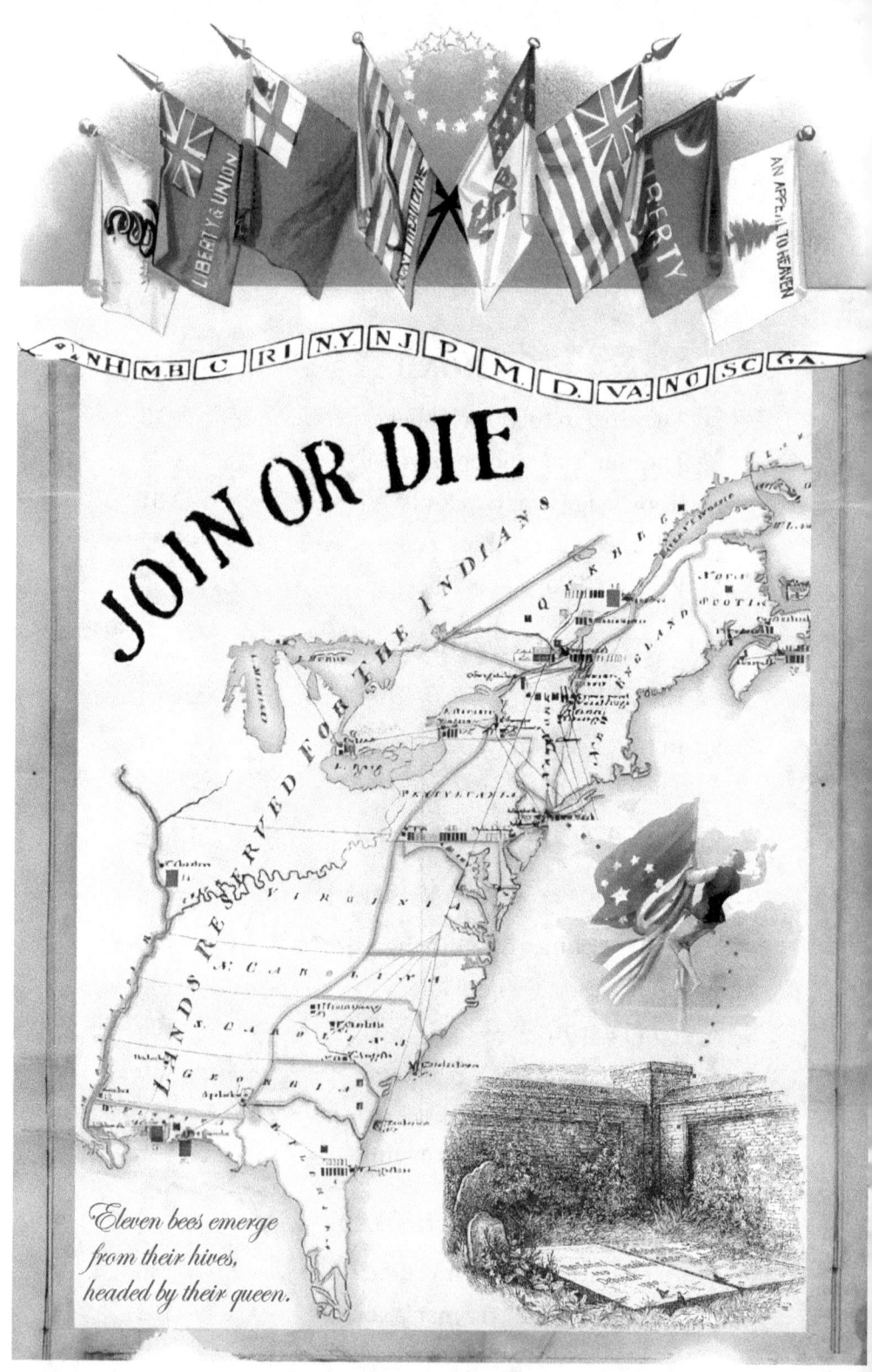

JOIN OR DIE

Eleven bees emerge
from their hives,
headed by their queen.

"... and she handed me the old map." (page 85)

Landing of the Pilgrims at Plymouth Rock, 1620 (Detail) — by Joseph Andrews

MONDAY

Dear Professor Redmand,

Attached is a curious account of the recent events—a daily journal Hackworth wrote on his phone and saved as a draft email.

We have not been able to locate him or Pepper since that Sunday morning.

Hack tells a remarkable tale about a missing flag and stolen diaries (and other sensitive matters of which you may be aware).

Only you have seen this; we await your instructions. We want to send a copy to the new training hall once it is completed.

Always & sincerely yours,

Capt. Morgan Stonewall, USN

Chapter One

"These people have neither King, nor Lord, nor do they yield obedience to any one, for they live in their own liberty."

– Amerigo Vespucci in a letter to Pier Soderini 1497, writing about the people who lived in what would be named America.

You know that person you hit it off with the minute you meet them—who radiates so much light, freedom, and happiness that you become one with them? That was Pepper to me. Until my first day of kindergarten, I didn't know other kids even existed besides my brothers and sisters.

Walking up the steps to the school hand-in-hand with my mother, I was blinded by the sight of her—this happy, beautiful, smiling, radiant girl with black hair and shining blue eyes.

And those eyes were staring at me!

She wasn't shy like I was.

"Hi, I'm Pepper," she declared, boldly walking towards me as I retreated behind my mother.

My mother gently pulled me around to her front.

"Go ahead, tell Pepper your name."

I stammered, and my face started blushing. Pepper was like an angel, wrapped in light and beaming. And I was embarrassed.

"I'm....mm...umm..."

I couldn't get the words out.

"Hack, my name is HHHHack."

"Hackworth."

She burst into laughter and grabbed my arm.

"Hackworth Lancaster."

"We're going to be best friends, Hack," she said as we walked together to the school door.

Suddenly, I realized my mom wasn't with me and turned to see her standing back, her hands covering her face. Mom told me years later that she couldn't stop crying that day.

Pepper and I were best friends up to the third grade, when she would write notes like: *Hi Hack, I like you. Do you like me?*

And then she offered several box selections, including *Yes, Maybe, and Don't Know.*

She didn't give the option of "No."

I checked "Yes" every time.

Third grade would be the last time we saw each other, as her father was in the military and they had to move. My last memory was her waving good-bye to me with a tear running down her cheek.

Then came Brown University's freshman orientation, ten years later. Imagine the thrill of spotting her across the room! It was like we were meant to be together. And, indeed, we were together for three of those college years until we broke up and, like before, she went away.

Pepper was a top student and ended up at a leading publishing house. I was a C student and ended up at a not-so-leading trade magazine publisher. To make ends meet, I was also a part-time sales clerk at the Franklin Antiques Bookstore.

Ironically, we ended up working in the same place—The City of Brotherly Love, Philadelphia—founded by William Penn after peacefully negotiating with the Lenape natives. My best friend

Tory told me that the Quaker Oats man is an image of William Penn. He also preferred calling the Lenape the "Delawares" because they lived along the Delaware River.

Years after last seeing her, out of the blue, Pepper sends me an urgent text on Sunday to meet her.

You can imagine my thrill to see her once again; our paths had barely crossed since we left college.

"Hi. Must see u. 7am tomorrow (Monday). Alfreds."

Alfreds, a little café of warmth, happiness, and grunginess for the weary, is just off Washington Square.

"Hack, Oh My! My!" she said, her bright smile beaming as she walked up to my booth. She was dressed in a smart business suit.

We hugged, and she held me for a moment and then whispered in my ear, "Act chummy, but follow me to the back."

The serious tone of her voice did not match her demeanor.

"When was the last time we saw each other?" I asked, standing and looking straight into her blue eyes.

"It was Tory's Christmas party," she replied. And then, under her breath, "I don't have much time. Follow me."

We walked to the back table.

"Pretend we like each other," she said, grabbing my hand.

"Pepper, what is going on?"

"I am in trouble, big trouble, and you are the only one I knew who would understand," she said.

"Yes, of course, I will help."

"We don't have much time to talk, so I need you to listen."

Just as she said these words, she looked over her shoulder at two men in business suits who entered the café.

"Take this key," she said, turning to me. "And listen."

"Have you ever been in an earthquake?" she started.

"No, I ..."

She stopped me from answering.

"Just listen to me. Of course, you haven't been in an earthquake, but imagine if you were. Imagine the San Francisco Quake of 1906, where the ground splits in two and everything is destroyed, including you."

"You are making no sense," I said.

She looked again at the men who had walked in. Then she grabbed my hand, placed a small key in my palm, and closed my fingers around it.

"This key is to a parcel locker at the bus station. What is inside is an earthquake, Hack, except what it will destroy is not just a city."

"Pepper, what are you ..."

"Listen, Hack. What is in that parcel locker will destroy not just a city but the whole country."

She looked right at me, her eyes frighteningly serious.

"Destroy the whole country," she said.

"Destroy? What?"

"Not literally destroy. Awaken destroy. Shatter the lies."

As if on cue, with her repeating those words, another man entered the café and immediately went to the table where the first two men sat. In a flash, he knocked one of the suits to the ground and punched the other.

"We have to get out of here!" Pepper exclaimed, pointing to the back door.

The men were now arguing with each other, but as we got to the door, I heard the one who was punched yell at us.

"Hey, wait. STOP!" he yelled.

"STOP NOW!"

I froze. The way he said it sounded like a cop, and I don't run from the police.

"Now, Hack, Now!" Pepper pulled me into the alley. She started running, and I quickly followed. We stayed in the back alleys behind the buildings for what seemed like five blocks when, finally, I grabbed her arm.

"What is going on, Pepper? Who are those men? Why are they after you?"

She stopped. And turned to me.

"Hack, I can't tell you everything because I don't know everything. But some of the answers are in that locker."

Her eyes and voice now started pleading with me. I thought she was going to cry.

"I don't mean to put you in harm's way, but you were the only one I knew who would help."

"It's them," she said, pointing down the alley. We pressed ourselves against the building wall.

There the two men were, hurriedly looking down the alley and then moving to the next one.

They didn't see us.

"I have to go," she said.

And just like that, Pepper disappeared into the building through the fire door, and it clicked shut. There was no door handle on the outside; she must have planned this and propped it open for her escape.

I stood in the alley for about an hour. The men had disappeared, too.

My mind raced.

Everything happened so fast.

Pepper was beautiful.

I loved Pepper. Still did.

But what had she gotten me into?

Figuring out what to do next wasn't easy because I sensed that the men who were after Pepper would now be after me. I also remembered that I had a four-hour shift at the Franklin Antiques Bookstore.

And then I remembered the key she had given me.

Looking down at my hand, I slowly extended my fingers. And there it was, a parcel locker key with "#76" stamped on it. Something inside me said I should get the locker's contents now. Pepper was obviously in some serious trouble, and whatever was in the locker would make it all clear.

I called the Franklin Antiques Bookstore and told Tory's father I was sick.

"Stay away until you're better!" Mr. Russoff said in a gruff voice. And then he hung up the only phone he uses—the one that's tied to the wall.

The bus station was just a few blocks from where Pepper had vanished.

"Boy, she really thought this out," I muttered to myself.

In college, she was super popular, and guys of all kinds chased her for dates. She had such an easy way about her and was very friendly. But she was not naive. She had a tongue that was as sharp as a knife and could cut you up and make you feel like an idiot.

She always sat in the front of the classroom. I always sat in the back. Let's just say that not only was I not as popular as Pepper, but

I wasn't as interested in studying and sucking up to the professors as she was.

My memories of her abruptly ended when I came to the bus station. I had been careful not to walk on the street for fear of being seen by those two men. The side street entrance had a couple of homeless people sitting next to the steps, and things seemed safe and normal.

I took a deep breath, walked in, and headed straight to the locker. The place was mostly empty. An old woman with a suitcase sat eating a hot dog. The place smelled like hot dogs.

Then a terrifying thought went through my head.

Pepper said that what was in the locker would destroy "not just a city, but the whole country."

"It's not a bomb, obviously, but is it nuclear?" I wondered.

"Not literally destroy. Awaken destroy. Shatter the lies." That's what she said.

I was scared and started to turn back, then stopped dead in my tracks. There, in front of the bus station, was the guy who fought the two men in business suits. I didn't have a second to waste and quickly put the key into the rusty locker and opened it, nuclear bomb or not.

A cardboard box was inside—a box like the kind books are shipped in. I grabbed it and headed for the side door. Outside, I looked for the man but didn't see him.

A taxi stand was just around the corner, and I got in line.

When my taxi pulled up, I jumped in.

And on the other side, so did the man from the cafe.

He had a young man's face but was older.

He had a sincere, earnest look about him.

He didn't scare me.

"Give me the box," he demanded.

I froze, but then did something so strange, so out of character, but so brilliant.

I calmly told the cab driver to wait one moment, and then, sticking my hand in my blazer's pocket, I lifted the pocket up and pointed it at the man, pretending to have a gun.

"You have three seconds to leave, or I will kill you."

He looked shocked and stared at my blazer, slowly looking up at me.

I stared at him and gritted my teeth.

The cab driver had the most terrifying look as he stared at the both of us.

"My friend, I know this man. Please. Please. He means business. Please leave now," the cabbie said, his voice rising.

Before the cabbie could finish, the man darted from the car, and the cab screeched off so fast that his door slammed shut automatically.

I told the cabbie where to take me and that I really didn't have a gun. He never spoke or looked at me again.

Back at my apartment, I carefully placed the cardboard box on the table.

And I stared at it. My mind was racing. Pepper. The two men looking for us in the alley. The young man who fought with them in the coffee shop. The bus station.

The earthquake.

"Have you ever been in an earthquake?" she had asked. "Where the ground splits in two and everything is destroyed, including you."

"What is inside is an earthquake, except what it will destroy is not just a city."

"Awaken destroy. Shatter the lies."

I went to the kitchen, found a sharp knife, then carefully cut the tape that sealed the cardboard box, slowly opened the top, and looked inside.

I gasped, which I would have done no matter what was inside because of the pressure this morning's episode had stirred in me.

And then I pulled it out.

It was a slim, old wooden box in the shape of a triangle, about three inches thick.

It was a mahogany flag box. I pulled it open to reveal an old American flag, folded in a triangle.

I could tell it was very old because the red and white stripes were hand-sewn and fading.

I turned the cardboard box upside down and shook it.

Nothing else came out.

Chapter Two

I stared at the object on my kitchen table for what seemed to be an hour. The events of the morning were racing through my head. This was far from an ordinary day.

Get up, drink coffee, go to work at the business magazine, interview advertisers, and write and edit stories; that was my day. Making puff pieces is probably a better way of saying what I did for a living. Write articles that served the interests of the advertisers. My job was to separate the wheat from the chafe and throw away the wheat!

But the one thing the daily grind had not yet killed in me was curiosity. The longer I looked at this old flag and thought about seeing Pepper and running through the alleys, the bus stop, and the man who invaded my cab, the more curious I got.

At that moment, the lights went out.

Beeep. Beeep. Beeep. The alarm system was beeping to tell me the electricity had gone out.

As if my eyes couldn't have figured it out.

The alarm wanted me to punch in a code to let it know that I knew the power was out.

And the ringtone is so annoying, you do what the alarm tells you to do. And fast.

At the panel on the wall, I struggled to remember the pass code and punched in the last four digits of my social security number. It didn't work.

I then remembered that the code was written on the alarm keypad on a sticky note on the side. I punched that number in, and the ringing stopped.

Funny—you write down your secret passcode next to the alarm, where a burglar could easily find it.

The power had been going out a lot lately. At first, I thought it was because my landlord hadn't paid the electric bill. But when it happened at work two times in one week, it obviously was a city-wide issue.

I instinctively reached for my phone and turned it on. On top of holding the story of my life as told in emails, messages, photos, videos, and apps, it was the best pocket flashlight in the world.

It lit a path to the table. I sat down to check my email and noticed there was no cell service.

Great. Just me, no lights, and no connection.

I turned the light on the flag, which made it glow.

"What is this, Pepper?" I muttered.

You mutter a lot when you live by yourself.

"What is so important about this flag?"

Carefully, I unfolded it on the kitchen table. It was fraying around the edges. It smelled like every grandma's attic—that moldy, musty stink.

Now fully unfolded, I stared at it. Thirteen stripes of red and white, like any other flag.

But not as many stars.

What had Pepper involved me in? Why did she have what appeared to be a Revolutionary War artifact or antique? My eyes went to the stars.

There was one in the center, slightly larger than the others.

I had never seen an American flag where one star was slightly larger than the others.

Weird. And that wasn't the only odd thing.

I counted all of the stars again to double-check because it couldn't be right.

This flag had 11 stars circling the one in the middle. Everything I learned in school screamed in my head: *there should be 13 stars for the 13 states.*

Just then, the lights flickered on, and the buzz of the various appliances started whirring.

Power was back on!

Beeep. Beeep. Beeep. The alarm system was telling me the power was back on. Duh! And now the passcode had to be entered again to let it know that I knew the power was back on.

As I started to enter the code, a sharp tapping came from the door.

Three hard, firm knocks.

I quickly grabbed and folded the flag and stuffed it in the wooden box.

Beeep. Beeep. Beeep. The alarm was still ringing.

"Hackworth Lancaster," a deep voice rang out.

I panicked, took a few steps this way, then a few more that way, clutching the flag and not knowing what to do.

I was trapped.

"Hackworth Lancaster," the voice said again.

"Open up, sir. This is the police."

I had to hide the flag. Where could I put it?

"Hackworth Lancaster, this is the police. Open the door NOW." The voice was angry.

Not knowing what to do, I quickly ran into the kitchen and put the flag in the oven. The oven!

I took a deep breath and peered through the door peep hole.

Standing outside were the two men in business suits who first walked into the coffee shop.

Beeep. Beeep. Beeep.

I took another deep breath and opened the door just enough that the chain allowed.

"Y-e-s," I sputtered.

"Mr. Lancaster, we need to speak with you."

"Let me see some sort of identification," I said, my voice returning to its usual confidence.

The man closest to the door stuck the badge inches from my nose.

The words were unmistakable.

"U.S. Department of Homeland Security."

I quickly unchained the door.

Beeep. Beeep. Beeep.

That infernal alarm wouldn't stop ringing.

"The alarm needs to be silenced," I said to the men, the door now wide open.

After entering the passcode, I turned to see two serious federal agents in business suits standing at the door. They could have been advertising salesmen; they were dressed so sharply.

They were staring at me, stone-faced.

"May we come in?" the other agent asked, with a slight tone of sarcasm in his voice.

"Yes... yes," I said, gesturing them to the kitchen table.

And as they came in, my eyes quickly darted to the table.

Oh no, the empty box was still there!

"Mr. Lancaster, you're in serious trouble," the first agent began.

"What are you talking about?" I asked, walking into the kitchen. "Would you like some coffee?"

"No. Cut the crap," the first agent barked. "We know everything."

"Well then, good," I quickly replied, "maybe you can tell me what is going on."

I turned my back on them and activated the coffee machine. As the coffee dribbled into the cup, I shut my eyes and said to myself, "Calm down, Hack, calm down. Confidence, Hackworth, confidence."

I turned and looked directly at them. The second agent was holding the box.

"Mr. Hackworth, we know you met Pepper Stillwater at Alfred's coffee shop. We saw her text message to you."

I started to talk, but he wouldn't let me.

"And we know you were in the bus station and picked up a box. We saw the surveillance video of you coming and going."

I had to act quickly.

"Well, then you probably also know I haven't gone to the bathroom unless there are cameras there, too."

They looked at me awkwardly, startled that I would be such a wise guy just when they were pinning me down.

"Look, gentlemen, you are right about everything you say, but I still don't know what is going on."

I moved to the table and sat down. They did as well.

"You are correct. I met Pepper this morning, and she gave me a key. I went to the bus station and picked up this box."

I then stopped talking and grabbed the box for effect.

"This empty box."

The agents looked at each other for a moment, then turned and looked at me.

"Empty?"

"Well, do you see anything in it?" I asked.

They didn't take their eyes off of me.

"The strangest part of all of this is that some guy tried to steal an empty box from me."

They looked incredulous.

"The same guy who caused trouble with you and Pepper in the coffee shop."

Silence. They were sizing me up.

Then the second agent spoke.

"Lying to federal agents is a felony, just like stealing federal property."

"Wait just a minute," I said, pretending to become angry. "I haven't stolen anything, unless an empty box is federal property."

I grabbed the box and handed it to them.

"You can have it back."

The agents again looked at each other. They did not accept my offer.

"Mr. Lancaster, you and your college girlfriend are involved in a very dangerous game. This isn't a silly prank like you two would do at Brown University. This is serious. We will charge you as an accessory if you don't start cooperating."

I was becoming annoyed. Pepper and I once snuck into Professor Macsen Redmand's office and wrote inappropriate things on his whiteboard, and we were written up by security. That was the most trouble I got into at college. But how could they have known that?

"Good work, agents. So you've been through my texts, my posts, my Instagram, Reddit, TikTok, and Facebook pages? You found out everything about me and Pepper. Or so you think. Because if you really did your homework and checked my phone records and email, you would know I haven't seen Pepper in years until this morning."

"And you should also know I have never been in trouble with the law."

My voice was rising.

"So why don't you tell me what was stolen, and maybe we can figure it out?"

The agents looked at each other again.

"The box was empty?" the first agent asked.

"Look for yourself and keep it," I said, pushing it toward them. "Better yet, search my apartment. Search me!"

I raised my arms, feigning a pat-down.

"What was stolen?" I asked again.

They looked at each other and then at me.

"We are not going to discuss this any further," the first agent said. "There is a possibility Pepper used you as a decoy to throw us off the trail."

He reached inside his suit coat and took out a picture.

"Do you know who this is?" he asked, handing me a small photograph. It was a picture of that sincere-looking man in the cab.

"Yes," I said, pretending to be excited. "That's the guy who tried to steal the box from me."

They knew I was telling the truth. They probably had a video of him trying to get into the cab.

"Do you know who he is?" the agent asked again.

"No, I don't. Never saw him before. Who is he?"

"We don't know. But he is involved with all of this somehow."

"How can you not know him," I asked, "when you know everything about me?"

"He must be off the grid," the second agent said sarcastically, implying he knew more than he was letting on.

"Obviously," I repeated.

The meeting had come to a standstill. The agents were not interested in telling me anything and were forced to accept my explanation of the empty box. A strange silence hung in the air.

They rose from their seats.

"Here are our business cards, Mr. Lancaster. If either Pepper or this other guy contacts you, you are to call us immediately. Do you understand?"

I looked at the names on the cards.

Brian Trowbridge and Neuman Church. Both with the title "Senior Agent."

"Sir," I began, looking at the second agent. "I have never been in trouble with the law, and if Pepper has done something wrong, I want no part of it."

I led them to the door, then shut it behind them, then ran to the window to watch them get into a black SUV and drive away.

My heart was beating so fast. I had just lied to Homeland Security, and I had no intention of finking on Pepper.

But what was this all about?

Why was the old flag so important?

And why did it have 12 stars?

Chapter Three

"Knowledge is of two kinds. We know a subject ourselves,
or we know where we can find information upon it."

– Samuel Johnson, The Life of Samuel Johnson

"If other proofs than these and the plain letter of the
Constitution itself be necessary to ascertain the point
under consideration, they may be found in the Journals of
the General Convention, which I have deposited in the
office of the Department of State."

*– President George Washington, Letter to Congress, March 30,
1796. Not until 1839 would full debate records be released to
the public, with the publication of Madison's Notes.*

Two days before I received Pepper's text message, I was on my
Friday night shift at Russoff's Franklin Antiques Bookstore. It
was great to escape my "day job" and become immersed in the
leather-bound books, old statues, dusty golden objects—the smell
of antiquity.

But more valuable than the relics was the living, crazy personality who challenged anything "taken for granted."

The son of Mr. Russoff and my best friend.

Tory.

That's not his real name; it is Terrance. I learned that because
every now and then Mr. Russoff yells at him, "Terrance!"

His last name, Russoff, was shortened from a larger Eastern
European name. Tory was born here, but his parents weren't. They

were young children whose parents were fleeing communism. The family knew the book trade in the old country, learning to sell popular bestsellers but specializing in rare books, maps, letters, and other expressions of human communication like statues, stamps, and coins. They adopted Tory when they couldn't have children.

Tory's Grampa began the bookstore, passed it down to his father, and it was expected that soon Tory would take it over.

(Tory said he would sell it the second he could.)

If he did sell it, he would get a good price. It's a lucrative business, and the Russoff's seemed to do well.

The bookstore was something to behold. Grand murals depict historic events—the largest is a reproduction of Benjamin Franklin Drawing Electricity from the Sky by Benjamin West. Tory's grandfather took a picture of it at the Philadelphia Museum of Art, blew it up, and had it recreated on the fireplace wall in the 1920's.

On the opposite wall was a smaller mural named Pharos of Alexandria, Egypt—the ancient lighthouse overlooking the Library of Alexandria. A large fire roared at the top of the Pharos, illuminating the port and making it visible for miles out to sea. Captains could guide their ship by the great lantern, avoiding the shoals while navigating into the port.

The Library of Alexandria was the largest in antiquity precisely because of its port location on the Mediterranean Sea. Sailors from around the world would visit, often bringing books and maps from their home country to sell or trade with library officials.

Mr. Russoff told customers the Pharos symbolizes the beacon of truth, lighting up the library and the treasures it contains (and the way he told the story helped make the outrageously overpriced antiques seem worth it).

The oak bookcases were stained mahogany—rich, reddish, and luxurious. The cases were made into cabinets with wired and locked doors—cages for rare books and objects that were at once visible with their price yet inaccessible. Theft wasn't really why the cases were locked. Instead, it was to add to the perception of rarity and value.

My job was to open the case, let the customer see the item, and answer any questions.

Near the fireplace was the sales counter, with two barstools and several glass display stands. My job wasn't fun when Mr. Russoff occupied the other chair. It was spectacularly fantastic when Tory was there. There's nothing like working with your best friend.

Tory is a big boy with an even bigger smile, tucked under cherubic cheeks. He is always joking and laughing about nearly everything that comes within view.

I get on him about his weight, but he keeps telling me it's genetics and that his birth father was a "big boy." Or maybe it's the snacks and soda and sitting all day?

He knew it was and thought it was funny. He didn't care. The only thing that seemed to be on his mind was the next smart observation—enlightening or cynical, as the case may be, but usually ending in a hearty laugh.

That, and whistling to his little parakeet in the bird cage next to the fireplace. Tory would click his lips and whistle to the bird, who, in turn, would click and whistle back. You would swear they were communicating with each other.

Earlier, there was a protest in Washington Square, and after it was over, the protestors went to the coffee shop next door and then trickled into the bookstore. Protestors in general weren't really good customers for us because few of them actually had the kind of money our rarities demanded.

Tory didn't like them, and whatever the protest was about, Tory would take the other side—sort of a permanent Devil's Advocate. But if you were a paying customer, Tory would agree with everything you said.

The protestors who walked into the store today were a small group of college students holding signs that read "Stolen Land" and "Native Rights."

Tory ignored them as they walked past the cabinets, looking through the book cages and reading the small card with the price and description. One protestor nudged the arm of another and pointed at the price.

"Two thousand five hundred!" he exclaimed, but in a hushed whisper.

After the protestors left without buying anything, I baited Tory: "America is built on stolen land, you know?"

Tory put his index finger in the air and started laughing.

"If humans came out of Africa like the evolutionists say, then we're all living on stolen land," Tory began. "Take the Native Americans."

"You mean Indians, right?" I teased.

"Sure, OK, the Indians. Actually, that is the correct term. The In dios, the people in God," he said, waving his hand as he started pacing the floor. "There are no natives anywhere since we all originated in the same place. The Indians came from eastern Europe and Asia and trekked over the frozen land bridge into Alaska. They then headed south and east. Sometimes they encountered others, and sometimes they fought and killed for their territory and home."

I started thinking of my answer, but Tory kept on going.

"There is no such thing as indigenous, anywhere, ever! There's just now—the people who replaced the people before them."

We laughed. It was just banter, but Tory loved it. He loved being a contrarian, especially if he could crack a joke at the end. For Tory, the heartier he laughs, the more successful the observation.

"Wait, wait. One more thing. We are all indigenous people. We are all from the same place, with good and bad inside and among us. We're indigenous to the Earth!"

The sun shining through the front window onto the mahogany-stained trim told me my shift was almost over. I hopped off the stool and bent down to get my backpack.

When I stood up, a strange man entered the bookstore. (Calling him strange is saying something considering the assorted eccentrics and oddballs the Franklin Antiques Bookstore attracted.)

He was wearing a large, long black jacket in such a way that it was difficult to see his face, his hat cocked at an angle. He was a caricature of a spy. He had dark glasses on, obscuring his face.

Tory walked up to greet him, and the strange man spoke, but I couldn't make out what he said.

"Yes, I believe we do have it," Tory said, leading him over to a cage of books.

"It must be the First Edition," the strange man said.

Tory looked through the cage.

"I don't see it," he said, walking back to the counter. "Let me check the computer."

Tory sat down on the stool and started typing, and the computer screen promptly froze and stopped working. Tory violently clicked the enter button multiple times, frustrated.

"It's like my computer is slow exactly at the moment when I need it fast," Tory quipped. "And fast when it doesn't even matter."

We both laughed. The strange man didn't. He now seemed vaguely familiar.

"A couple of nights ago, I had a nightmare of this growing, giant Bill Gates Head laughing at me uncontrollably, enjoying my suffering from his mediocre products."

The strange man stepped forward.

Tory started typing the search query. He would oftentimes pretend to look up the book when he was really checking Google to see what the current price was online.

"It must be the First Edition," the strange man said. "By Commodore Byron McCandless and William Furlong."

Tory didn't have the first edition, but a pristine second edition for $245. On Amazon, you could get it for $4 in pretty good shape.

"It looks like the one copy we have is the second edition," Tory said.

"That won't do," the strange man said. He thanked Tory, turned, and walked out the door.

"What book did he want?" I asked, putting on my coat to leave.

Tory laughed. "A real exciting one."

"*So Proudly We Hail*, a book about the U.S. Flag."

Chapter Four

"It is through symbols that man consciously or
unconsciously lives, works, and has his being."

– Thomas Carlyle, Sartor Resartus, 1836

"Symbols and colors enabling nations to distinguish
themselves from each other, have from the most
remote periods exercised a powerful influence upon
mankind. It is a fact well established both by sacred and
profane history that a standard or ensign was borne in
the armies of all nations from the most distant era."

*– History of the Flag of the United States of America,
by George Henry Preble, Rear Admiral U.S.N., Boston, 1880*

I thought about the strange man at the bookstore wanting the
flag book. He seemed familiar. Three days later, an odd antique
flag lays hidden behind my refrigerator.

I looked out the window of my apartment for the next half
hour, certain the government agents were right around the corner.

But there was nothing unusual.

The significance of what was happening now penetrated my
mind. The agents were after Pepper. They were watching me. They
were monitoring my emails, texts, and phone calls.

And in my possession is the object of their pursuits.

An old, odd 12-star flag.

Pepper was the only one who could give me answers, but calling or texting her was out of the question.

She had to be found—and fast.

I left the apartment out the back door, walked to the street, and hailed a cab.

"Worthman Publishing on Market Street," I told the cabbie, not sure of the address.

I remember seeing a Facebook post with her sitting in her office at Worthman as assistant editor. Nowadays, she is a senior editor in charge of premium publishing projects. She worked with newly retired presidents, secretaries of state, football stars, and the like to publish their memoirs.

Her job in publishing was in a different league than mine. While I toiled working with corporate PR executives on a new product introduction, she worked with President Bush and President Obama.

While I interviewed the CEO of an ink company promoting his color of the month, she spent the day with Neil Armstrong going over his memories of being the first man on the moon.

Looking around to see if I had been followed and being convinced I had not, I walked into the Worthman lobby and grabbed an elevator to the 21st floor.

Getting off, I headed to the receptionist's desk.

"I don't have an appointment, but I need to see Pepper Stillwater," I told the young woman behind the counter.

She scrolled through her computer screen and looked up at me.

"As I told the man an hour ago, she is not on this floor."

"What floor is she on?"

She replied, "As I have said, she is not assigned an office in this building. Her name is in the directory, but she does not have an office."

"Does she work from home?" I asked.

"Beats me," the young woman responded. "I just know she does not work here."

Now this was strange because even if she did work from home, like many people did, she still would have an office in the building.

"Do you know how I can get in touch with her?"

The receptionist turned the computer screen toward me. There was Pepper's name, but contact details were blank.

"Can you describe the man who was looking for her?"

"Yes," she said. "He was a very nice guy, very sincere."

Hmmm. The taxi robber was trying to hunt her down as well. But interestingly enough, the government men weren't mentioned. They didn't have to come here. They must know where she is or was by monitoring her online.

Pepper was funny in that way. One moment at Brown, she was thick as thieves with you, partying the night away. The next morning, you would go to see her, but she was nowhere to be found. Only weeks later would you see her in a dumpy sweatshirt studying at the library.

She still looked great, even in that dumpy sweatshirt.

I was at a dead end and didn't dare call or text Pepper because Homeland Security was watching. She was no longer in the Worthman Building, and I didn't know where she lived. She could be on the crowded streets of Anywhere, USA. But where?

What was my next move?

I saw a coffee shop and headed in to think things over.

What did the government men say that was so curious? Ah, yes. It was the stuff about our college antics with Professor

Redmand. There was no way they could have known about this because there was no social media back then—there was no opportunity to post the wilder side of our lives.

Professor Macsen Redmand.

What a character! He looked the part of the crazy old professor with thick, bushy white eyebrows that matched his full head of white hair.

He was a genius and a great professor, one of the few who actually taught classes at Brown instead of handing them off to graduate students.

He was infatuated with Pepper for the same reason everyone else was. She called him Maximum Sun, a play on his first name, but he was known by everyone as "Professor Mac."

Pepper challenged him. He liked her because she questioned him. She earned her A's in that class. Just like I earned my C's.

Wait a minute, I thought. There is no coincidence here. Professor Redmand taught American history! Who better to ask about the 12-star flag than him?

I had to get to Providence. Now.

Calling my office, I whispered that I had a terrible stomach ache and may be out for the next couple of days. I can sound sicker than a dog when I have to. And after all, the article about the ink color of the month could wait, and I had plenty of sick days.

Getting to Providence was easy enough. Getting there without being detected was my challenge. I knew I had to take extra precautions not to be followed.

Instinctively, I reached for my phone to look up Amtrak train schedules. But as quick as I had clicked it on, I clicked it off. I got a cab back to the apartment and left the phone there.

"They can track you through your cell phone," a voice inside my head said. "Not only track you, but get inside your head and know what you are thinking."

Grabbing a small bag and some cash, I headed to the train station. The conveniences of the modern money world of credit cards and American Express travel points had to be left in the apartment as well.

But evading the authorities was not complete. In order to buy my ticket, I had to show identification. That didn't scare me considering how quickly the rotund Amtrak cashier looked at my driver's license and handed it back to me.

I looked over my shoulder. Everything seemed normal.

The trip felt long and tedious—five plus hours from Philadelphia to Providence, rocking back and forth on the tracks. It felt like we made a dozen stops along the way, but that's what you get when you take the cheaper local service. Taking it was a habit born of my college days; when the train pulled into the Providence station, it felt like I was coming home.

Visiting your old haunts brings back a flood of memories. I loved Brown, even if I wasn't the most serious student. I had gotten a writing scholarship there, whereas most of the others had the money to pay straight up or borrowed massively. Brown would see the end of my adolescent naiveté.

My very first day, I met Pepper in orientation, and our childhood romance was restarted. She captivated me in kindergarten, in third grade, and in college. And now she was drawing me back here.

Finding Professor Redmand's office was easy. I was concerned he wouldn't be there. He was an old man when I was at the university. By now, he must be an ancient man.

Sure enough, the old wheezer was still on the job!

I peaked into his office, where he was intently listening to a student. He was dedicated.

A thrill went through my body. I was going to find out what all of this was about.

When the student left, I strolled in.

"Well, hello, Professor Mac!"

He looked up from his bushy, white eyebrows. He was exactly the same as my memory of him.

"Hack! Hack, my boy," he said, jumping from his seat and rushing to greet me.

We embraced with a big hug, but then he walked past me and looked out the door.

"Stillwater runs deep," he laughed, looking up and down the hallway and then shutting the door.

"Where is Pepper?"

"That's a good question, Professor Mac."

"Why didn't you two ever get married?" he asked.

"I don't know."

"I can't believe you didn't, the way you two carried on."

"Actually, Professor, I am here in search of Pepper and to get some answers."

"Oh," he said. And the way he said it made it sound like he already knew.

"Well, come in, come in," he said, shutting and locking his door. He placed a sign on the door that read, "In Session. Do Not Disturb."

"Well, how have things been? Are you still working at..."

I cut him off.

"Professor Mac, I am in a bit of a difficult situation, and I need your help."

"What kind of situation?"

"A 12-star flag situation."

He stopped moving. He stopped talking. He just stared at me. And I stared back.

He sat down in his chair.

"What is a 12-star flag situation?"

I quickly relayed to him what had happened in the morning, how Pepper had met me, directed me to the locker, and its contents. I hesitated to tell him every detail, but figured he should know it all.

"And you lied to the Homeland Security agents?" he asked sternly. "That's a no-no."

"Of course it's a no-no, but I didn't have a choice. Pepper wanted me to have this. And she said something to me I will never forget."

"And what was that?" he asked.

She said, "Have you ever been in an earthquake, where the ground splits in two and everything is destroyed, including you?"

"What is inside the box is an earthquake, except what it will destroy is not just a city. But the whole country."

Professor Mac's hand moved to his mouth, and his finger started tapping his lips.

He swallowed—a big gulp of a swallow. His demeanor went from warm and friendly to concerned and nervous. It was a side of him I had never seen.

"Did anybody see you come here?" he asked.

I shook my head and said, "No."

"Are you sure?"

"As sure as I can be. And I have no cell phone, no EZ Pass, no credit cards—nothing to track me with."

There was a long silence. Kind of like the silence in the kitchen with the agents. He was thinking.

Then he spoke.

"Pepper has exposed you to grave danger," he began. "And now, you have exposed me to the same danger. We must leave here, but not together."

I didn't say a word.

"Do you know the park on the west side of the State Capitol in downtown Providence?"

I nodded. Of course I did. Pepper loved going there for picnics. It was one of our favorite spots.

"You are to leave now and never come back to this office. Meet me in that park when it gets dark, in about an hour. We can talk about everything there."

Professor Redmand was so serious and concerned that now I was beginning to understand this wasn't a game.

I got up and walked out of his office without saying a word.

Chapter Five

"The falsification of history has done more to impede human development than any one thing known to mankind."

– Jean-Jacques Rousseau

"Painters frequently take a poet's license, and are not always particular in the accuracy of the accessories of their paintings. Thus Leutze, in his 'Washington Crossing the Delaware', Dec. 25, 1776, conspicuously displays the American flag with the blue field and union of white stars, although the flag had no existence before the 14th of June, 1777, and not published until September, 1777."

– History of the Flag of the United States of America, by George Henry Preble, Rear Admiral U.S.N., Boston, 1880

I sat on the State Capitol lawn, admiring the magnificent building designed by McKim, Mead & White. My junior year, I took an architecture class and learned about them, a legendary architectural firm that renovated the White House and built many public buildings and museums.

The white marble of the capitol glistened, projecting the power and sovereignty of Rhode Island and Providence Plantations. That was the state's official name, though in recent years they dropped the "Providence Plantations" because some saw reference to slavery, even though there isn't any and it invokes the protective care of God.

I vaguely remember Tory ranting about this.

The sun was setting, but still enough of it was reflecting off the gold statue of a man atop the capitol dome. Called "The Independent Man," he is depicted in the wilderness holding a spear and covered only in a loincloth. Professor Mac said he lived in nature like the Native Americans, free from the dictates of society. A man who lived in a mountain cave who was removed from the shackles of custom that would make him dependent. In my life, I was the opposite and enjoyed technology's shackles.

A marker on the street said, "He represents men and women, young and old, times past and times present. He stands watch over our State Capitol as a protector of all Rhode Island citizens."

Pepper loved that statue.

I couldn't stop thinking about her and the mess she had apparently fallen into (and taken me with her).

And what about Professor Redmand? He knew more than he was letting on. Grave danger, he said. Because of an old flag that didn't even have enough stars? It didn't make sense.

From where I was sitting, I could check out anybody who came or went into the park. Not that far away, Pepper and I would go on long picnics.

The last rays of the sun struck the golden Independent Man. In a wink, the sun was gone and Twilight's purplish blue sky had arrived. Soon that color faded to black.

Still, no Professor Redmand.

I started to suspect something had happened to him when a figure sprang from the shadows.

It was him.

"Just keep looking at the building, Hackworth," he said. "I don't want anyone to see us talking."

No one was in the park except us. I couldn't take the cloak and dagger stuff. I turned to him and was startled. He was dressed completely in black, with even a black hat on his head. Only the whites of those bushy eyebrows stood out. Otherwise, I would not have known him.

It was difficult to determine where his body ended and the night began.

He started talking.

"That which is taken for the truth is often a lie, and that which is believed to be a lie is often the truth."

I started to interrupt him, but he stopped me.

"Hackworth, please just listen. You have to understand. Listen to what I say, and don't think about your response. Just let this sink in."

He was scolding me, like he occasionally did in the classroom. And he was right. I was thinking about my response before I heard what he said. That and interrupting people were my greatest faults.

"You know the history of the birth of the United States of America that you were taught?"

"Yes," I said with hesitation.

"Well, that was all fiction," he said.

Then he stared at me and said slowly, "It is a lie."

He paused.

"It is a lie, told to keep things the way they are," he said.

I interrupted him, this time more successfully.

"A lie about what? Give me an example."

He was becoming frustrated.

"Fine, I will do it your way," he said. "Tell me, Hack. Is July 4, 1776, the birthday of the United States of America?"

"Yes, of course it is," I responded. "I am not a fifth grader."

"No, it is not. That is a lie."

"What do you mean it is a lie?"

"I mean, it's a lie," he said. "It's not true."

He asked another question. "Was the Revolution a war for our nation's independence from Great Britain?"

"Yessss," I dragged out the words, waiting for him to contradict me.

He instantly did.

"No, that's a lie, too."

I did not feel like interrupting him again and felt my ignorance.

"Did the Constitution come from 'We, the people', who created the nation we have today?"

"Well, the answer is obviously no, since you..."

He interrupted me. "No, that is a lie, too."

"Did the Constitution even create a nation as we understand it today? No, that is a lie, too."

"Long ago, our American history was changed to be more useful to the government," he continued. "Lies were necessary to cover up wrongs that were committed. They became the norm in our schools to make the people think of the past the way the government wanted them to think."

I must have looked puzzled because his expression softened. I was being thrown into this bizarre conspiracy stuff by a history teacher. It wasn't leading anywhere, especially in relation to the flag matter at hand. He could sense my confusion.

"Let me put this another way," he started. "Your understanding of the past influences your conduct today and your plans for tomorrow."

"OK, I guess," was my reply.

"Each person has a personal past, full of fathers and mothers, brothers and sisters, grandfathers and grandmothers, going back hundreds, if not thousands, of years. From these people and the lands they lived in come the stories of who we are, or rather, who we believe we are," he said.

"What religion we believe in and how much we practice it. The kind of food we prefer. What we like on TV or at the movies. How we walk, how we talk. Even how we think is molded and defined by the past.

"Not only do we have a personal past, but a community past as well. The history of our community—this past also greatly influences us. This is our national past. Who we are as individuals and as a community is defined for us," he continued.

"Your parents teach you about your family's past. But it is the government school that teaches you about your nation's past."

I was beginning to understand.

"But what if we are not taught the true history but a version that has been written to serve the powers that be? Imagine being told your grandfather was the manager of the New York Opera House when you were young and that he was a person of accomplishment you could idolize. And you did, until years later you learned from Ancestry.com that his complete title was Manager of the Boot Jacks at the Opera House!

"Or consider the young man who is part of a cult like Jim Jones at Jonestown. Day after day, he practices drinking the Kool-Aid, and then, when commanded, he drinks the poisoned version—a brainless robot who operates from a manipulated worldview," he continued.

"So you see, Hackworth, what you are taught about your history can have a powerful impact on your life."

He paused, and there was a rustle in the trees near the Capitol.

We froze and turned to see a very large raccoon ramble into the bushes.

"Well, Professor Redmand, if July 4, 1776, isn't our nation's birthday, and if the Declaration of Independence and Revolutionary War were not fought for our nation's independence, then what's the truth?"

"Hackworth, everything in time. But you need to know something right now. That 12-star flag you have exposes the lie like nothing else could. Pepper is right. Its effect will be like an earthquake that will shake our nation."

It was all too much for me—this idea that an old flag and our history could have such an impact on our modern lives.

Professor Redmand could sense my skepticism.

"Do you doubt what I am saying, Hackworth? Then ask yourself, why are the government agents who came to your apartment so intent on retrieving it? Why would Pepper need to disappear?"

"More to the point, Hackworth," he said, drawing closer to me.

"As long as you have it, *you are in grave danger.*"

"You haven't answered my question," I replied. "If those things are lies, what is the truth?"

"If only it were that easy, Hackworth," the professor said, as if he were in front of the classroom. "You need to *feel* the reality. You need to *see* it. You need to *touch* it. You need to *discover* it. And then you will understand."

"See what? Pepper has disappeared, and the feds are trailing me. I have this special flag they want, but don't understand why."

"You will understand. Start here Tuesday morning; when the sun rises, look at this building. The answer is carved into the marble. Then go to Boston and see the truth like a senator would. Albany is next, and the 12-star flag will appear. Philadelphia's truth is right before your eyes. And in Washington, you will see the words as they were written and the myths in murals. By the time you get to Raleigh, the truth will become tangible. But you must do all of this. Not listen to empty words. *But feel the truth*," he said.

"And know this: flags are symbols of the truth. All flags tell in symbols truths that can be passed down through the generations. Know the symbols, and you have your answer.

"Then you can help Pepper."

He said all of this in rapid fire, like a professor reeling off at the end of class about next week's assignment.

Just then, a spotlight pierced through the black sky, focused solely on The Independent Man. My eyes looked up, and I was mesmerized by the sight. The Independent Man was clothed like a caveman, holding a stick and gazing into the future. I had seen him a thousand times, but right now, at this moment, he seemed so real to me as the gold shone brilliantly against the black night.

There was a rustle in the hedge. I watched to see if it was another raccoon. But the rustling stopped.

"Professor Mac," I began.

I turned to face him.

He was gone.

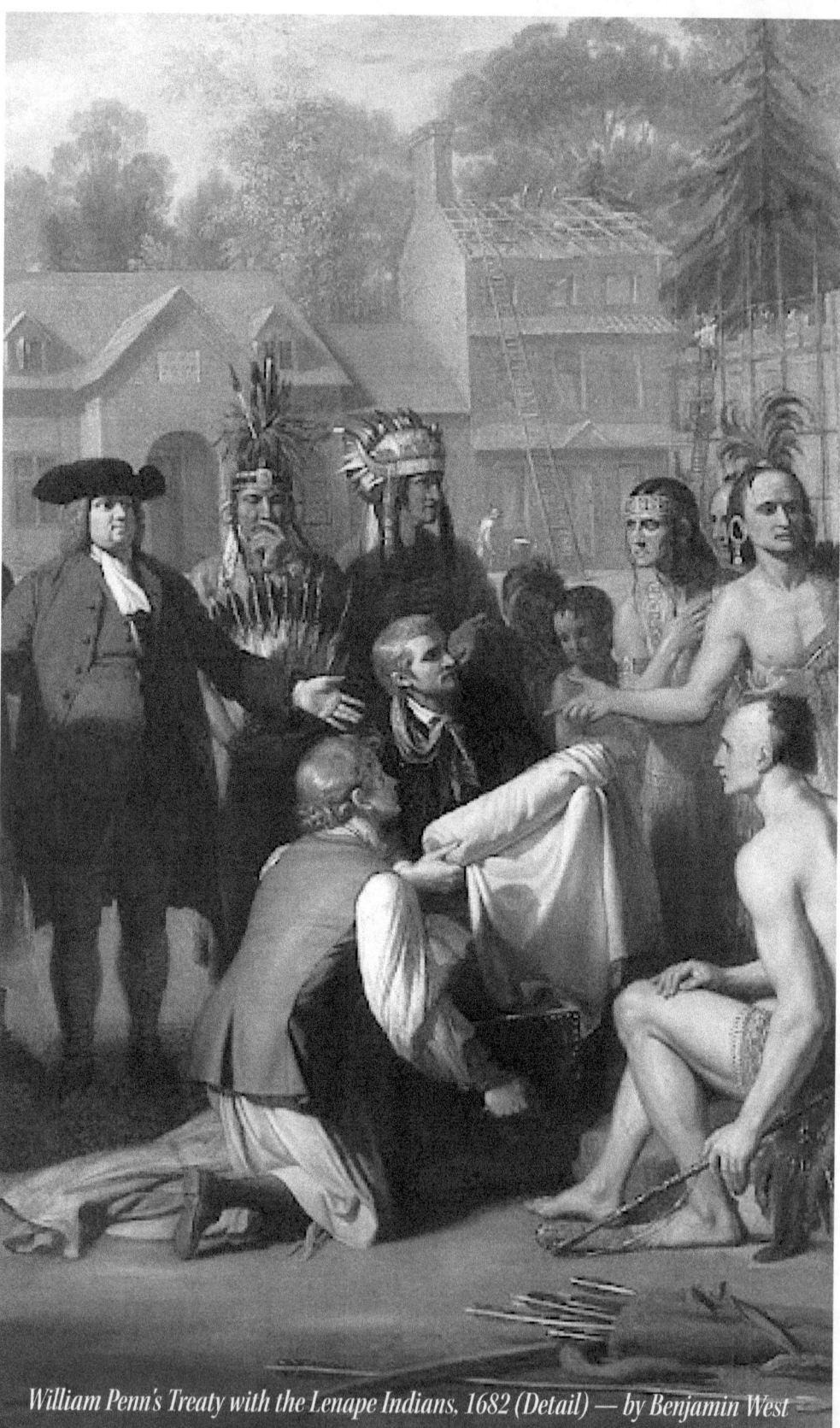

William Penn's Treaty with the Lenape Indians, 1682 (Detail) — by Benjamin West

AN APPEAL TO HEAVEN

TUESDAY

Chapter Six

Finding a place to stay in Providence that took cash without requiring you to fill out paperwork and provide a driver's license
was harder than I thought.

But I was determined not to leave a trail, especially after the
Homeland Security agents told me things my own mother didn't
know.

Credit cards are convenient, but they are also a great de-
stroyer of privacy. In their databases are every place I go and when,
where I eat and shop for food, the clothes I buy and wear, when and
where I bought gas, and what I buy online—information ready to
be reviewed by the government at anytime.

The agents spying really bugged me. I was determined not to
be easy prey.

Needless to say, the places that take cash without ID are
dumps located in the least desirable part of town.

I went to sleep the moment my body fell into bed and woke
up hours later, looking at the wall paper and thinking about Pepper. Then I noticed the wallpaper was moving! I quickly turned

the bedside lamp on and watched cockroaches scurry off the walls and ceiling. And when I looked closer, they were darting off the sheets!

Leaping up and grabbing my clothes, I left the room and wandered about looking for a cup of coffee. There was no attendant on, but there was a machine that made a cup of coffee, which turned out to be the worst I have ever had.

Later, I was able to grab a large coffee at a small breakfast nook on the corner next to the Capitol. I sat and drank it as the sun came up, exhausted but ready to get to the bottom of the mystery.

Professor Redmand said, "The answer is carved in marble," so I scoured every possible word that had been chiseled in the building.

It didn't take long to find what I think he wanted me to see.

There, on the north portico of the building, carved in letters big enough for a billboard, it read:

"Providence Plantations founded by Roger Williams, 1636; Providence, Portsmouth, Newport incorporated by Parliament, 1643; Rhode Island-Providence Plantations obtained Royal Charter, 1663; in general Assembly declared a Sovereign State, May 4, 1776."

Wait! How could that be? Rhode Island declared its independence from Great Britain two months before the Declaration of Independence?

I was sure this was a mistake because the United States declared its independence on July 4, 1776. But facts carved in marble on the side of a state capitol must be true.

How could little Rhode Island, the smallest state, do such a thing BY ITSELF?

Out of curiosity, I went inside and looked around. A janitor was busy opening the doors of a giant bank-like safe on the second floor. When he left, I went to it. On display were labeled "Rhode Island's Treasures." These included the actual Royal Charter of 1663 and a copy of the Declaration of Independence made in Philadelphia and sent to the state after it was signed.

There was a lot I didn't know, but I had to stay focused. Professor Redmand said the answer to the flag mystery could be found in other cities as well.

I had to get the next train to Boston and started heading to the station when a bus passed by with an advertisement on its side for the Providence Public Library. Yes, I thought, there was time to do some flag research.

The last time I was in a library was in college. Libraries lost their significance with the rise of the internet and, later, smartphones. With all the world's knowledge online, who needed dusty old books and scolding librarians reminding you to "be quiet?"

Or so I thought before Tory set me straight (and this flag mystery took hold of my life). The truth is, printed matter in libraries is a superior storage and research system than the non-printed digital world because it's private. The online world permits for centralization, which in turn enables monitoring and censorship by the authorities.

I walked in, and a very nice person helped me find every book that had to do with flags. There was no scolding.

What we found out is that there are many books on flags. And they all tell the same story, which, in its simplest form, goes like this:

After declaring independence on July 4, 1776, the Continental Congress passed a resolution on June 14, 1777 that the country's flag was to be thirteen stripes and thirteen stars—a stripe and a star for each state.

I searched and searched, but nothing could be found about 12 stars. Could it be that one of the states did not join with the others? No. Delegates from thirteen states signed the Declaration of Independence after each state authorized them to do so.

As I quickly scanned each of the books on the subject, I noticed something curious. They told the same story in the same style. It was cut and dry and seemed like it was written by the same person.

Now that is very odd, because at different times and places, people express themselves differently. And as time goes on, new facts are learned and incorporated into the story to give a more complete picture.

But not with this stack of books on the library table. They repeated the story like the Bible repeats stories—pretty much one version, the same through the ages.

I looked at the clock. It was time to go; there was nothing left to find here.

Just then, the power went out in the building. The lights flickered for a moment, then there was darkness. Some kids over in a corner let out a howl, and others started laughing.

Providence apparently has blackouts as well!

I left the library and headed for the train station. The funny thing is that when the power goes out, normal life stops. The traffic signals were off, and cars were driving haltingly. Workers had emptied their cubicles and gathered in the streets. Restaurants and coffee shops were at a standstill because you couldn't cook. Phones didn't work because towers were off.

It's like the whole city just stopped. But within 15 minutes, the power went back on, as did the ominous whirring sound, with everyone getting back to what they were doing.

The hive was buzzing again.

"It's a Twilight Zone episode," I thought. "When the power goes out, the earth stops spinning."

My experience in the Providence Library made me realize I desperately needed to be online—to at least be able to text Tory. But how? The government can track you on your phone or any services you use off the phone, like email, because that phone is registered to you at a specific number and billable address, loaded like a giant diary of everything you search for, see, take a picture of, call, text, read, and buy.

"No, you can't have your phone, your lifeline to the world." That's what the voice inside said as I walked down the street towards the train station. And then the solution appeared: an electronics store selling burner phones. I had to take the risk. The problem with being off the grid is that you're not on the grid.

I walked into the store and paid cash, also grabbing a copy of the *Boston Globe*. Every time I buy that paper, it seems thinner than the day before. Their online circulation is triple that of print, so I learned at my day job from the ink company.

The train station was across the street, and I soon settled into my seat. The front page story was about—you guessed it—the power outages that were plaguing the New England states. Some government officials said that for every hour there is no electricity, the economy suffers millions of dollars in losses.

I immediately called Tory, who didn't take the call, so I left a brief message, and in seconds he called me back.

"Whatcha doing with this number, Hackworth?"

"Long story, but I can't use my phone. Tory, dig through your books and find out about the symbols in the American flag and how it came into existence. Dig through the flag book the strange man wanted and let me know what the 12 stars symbolize. Better yet, find out the dirt on the revolution that gets to the bottom of this. Tell me what the symbols represent."

Tory paused and then said, "OK."

He paused again, said, "Gotta go," and hung up.

We did it like that—no long hi's or good-byes, no "good-byes" at all. Just hang up. There were no formalities between us.

An older woman in a smart business suit boarded the train, sat next to me, and opened her laptop.

I flipped the paper over to see the lower half of the front page. The train was now rocking forward, back, and forth. With just coffee in my stomach, I started to feel queasy.

And then I gasped. A gasp so loud, the people next to me turned to see if I was all right.

I wasn't.

There was a picture of Professor Redmand from 40 years ago. He had blonde hair then, and his eyebrows weren't so bushy.

The headline read:

BRUTAL MURDER TAKES LIFE OF NOTED ACADEMIC

My hands started shaking violently. I could barely read the next few words.

"Brown University Professor Macsen Redmand was shot and killed in an apparent robbery at his home in College Hill last night."

I was going to be sick. I jumped from my seat and ran down the aisle to the bathroom, stumbling as the train rocked back and forth.

Slamming the bathroom door shut, I fell to the toilet and threw up. The back-and-forth motion of the train was increasing. I was shaking so hard. Then I must have passed out.

A loud pounding on the wall pulled me in and out of consciousness. It kept pounding and pounding, and voices were yelling, louder and louder. Finally, I came to and sat up.

The pounding continued. And then I heard a voice on the other side of the wall.

"Ya been in there for an hour, for Crissakes," the voice said in a distinctly Rhode Island accent.

Embarrassed, I stood, cleaned myself up, and slid open the door. A stocky, bald man was in my way.

"Da toilet ain't your train seat," he said as I brushed past him.

I made my way down the aisle. Halfway to my seat, the guy yells, so the whole cabin hears him, "For Crissakkess, ya didn't clean up your puke... *you puke.*"

Every eye was on me, heads shaking back and forth in disapproval. As I sat down with my head spinning, the words kept swirling in my head.

"You are putting me in grave danger," the professor told me.

"You are in grave danger."

I sat down and read the news story again. It was short. There would probably be a longer obituary tomorrow.

"Redmand was a noted historian of America's past, having taught at Brown for over 45 years," the story read.

"In addition, he was a respected vexillologist."

I didn't know what that meant, and the burner phone was useless for searches.

I turned to the businesswoman next to me.

"My phone is out of power, and I need to look up a word."

She was standoffish, maybe because of the puking incident moments before.

"What word?" she asked.

"Vexillologist."

"I don't have to look that up; I know what it means," she said.

"Well, what does it mean?" I asked.

It was like pulling teeth.

"A vexillologist is a flag expert."

Chapter Seven

"In the earliest days of the Revolution each State
seems to have set up its own particular banner."

*– History of the Flag of the United States of America,
by George Henry Preble, Rear Admiral U.S.N., Boston, 1880*

The train rambled on its tracks, slowly rocking back and forth as we made our way to Boston. I still felt queasy and embarrassed about the scene in the bathroom. I had to go now but did not want to see the faces of disdain.

The newspaper sat folded on my lap. My mind was now fully comprehending what was happening. Just a day ago, I was living in my usual, repetitive, boring world and was excited to see a long-lost friend. But since seeing her face, that thrill of being with her once again has turned into a bizarre mess.

"You are in grave danger," is what the Professor said to me just hours before he was murdered.

"You are putting me in grave danger." In other words, am I responsible for what happened to him?

But how?

And why was he targeted in the first place?

I thought of the flag. In my haste to get to Providence, I hid it in my kitchen. When I first moved into the apartment, I purchased a smaller refrigerator than the hole it was to fill. So to make it look right, a false wall was built, and in it I had placed a small cabinet accessible only by removing the refrigerator from its hole. It was here that I kept my most valuable possessions.

And it is where I put the flag.

Now I was afraid the hiding spot wasn't good enough. That "they" would find it.

"Who are they?" I kept asking myself. "The government? The cab robber?"

Worse, I was afraid to go back home. Sooner or later, these people would come back and ask me more questions, beat me up, or kill me.

They could even be on this train right now.

My mind started racing, and paranoia was taking hold.

"No, they don't know where you are. Remember, you don't have your phone, and you are not using your credit cards. You are on the train, and there's no E-Z Pass." I couldn't stop thinking about it.

Then it occurred to me that Amtrak is owned by the government and that they do register names, and you did give your ID to the Amtrak representative.

Could they track me that way?

I thought again: THEY COULD BE ON THIS TRAIN RIGHT NOW, HACKWORTH.

Sitting up in my seat, I analyzed all of the passengers visible. There was a young couple directly in front of me with a small child. There was the businesswoman who wasn't really friendly. The seat across the aisle from me was empty, and the seat next to that held a young man listening to music and tapping his feet.

I couldn't really see anyone else. For all I knew, Professor Redmand's murderer was a few seats away, in either direction.

The train slowed, then stopped at the next station. We were still half an hour away from Boston. People came on the train as a few exited.

A man in a business suit sat in the empty seat across the aisle. I looked straight at him, and he smiled and nodded.

Something about the way he did it spooked me. He could be with the government or some other organization.

Why did he smile at me? Is he with them?

I jumped up and headed for the back of the train. I passed between cars, walked the length of the next car, and found myself in the café car. I quickly turned around to see if that man was following me. Nothing.

This was crazy, I thought. This whole thing is crazy.

"Can I help you?" A voice interrupted my thoughts.

It was the café host behind the counter. Without realizing it, I was standing in line, and it was my turn.

"Coffee, please," I said.

Taking it to the nearest table seat, I sat down. A panoramic window showed the countryside and played like a movie.

I started to calm down. Seeing trees, fields, water, horses, and barns out the window soothed me in a strange way. It gave me perspective.

"Get a hold of yourself, boy." That's what my father would say to me when I got upset and was on the verge of tears.

"Get a hold of yourself, boy." It was like he was saying it right now. And like then, it made me stronger.

Then I started to think of the most recent events.

Professor Redmand was a flag expert. Pepper came into possession of this old flag and then gave it to me.

Could Pepper have gotten it from Professor Redmand in the first place?

Was my return to Providence somehow revealing this fact to the government agents?

Why, when I asked him about the 12-star flag, did he say, "That which is taken for the truth is often a lie, and that which is believed to be a lie is often the truth?"

And then tell me the history of our country's birth was a lie?

And the mysterious flag proves this?

I had this intense desire to call Pepper. To break our silence. But how could I? Wouldn't they instantly know where I was by tracking the call? They were obviously watching her every movement.

Wouldn't they listen in on the call and find out where we were meeting? That is probably what happened when we saw them at Alfreds.

"Think, Hackworth. You can outsmart them," I thought.

As the train headed into Boston station, it passed a billboard with a giant lobster. And that got me thinking.

I hurriedly left the station and made my way to the James Hook & Co. lobster house. Pepper tried to get me to go to Boston back in our college days and would rave about how fresh the lobster was there. For whatever reason, I never went.

But that was exactly where I was headed.

When you walk in, you realize James Hook is more than a restaurant; it's also a thriving mail-order seafood company. Impressive, large tanks filled with freshly caught lobsters greet you as you enter.

I took a deep breath and then put my plan into action.

"Hi," I said to the man behind the counter. "I hope you can help me. I need to buy enough lobster for a party of one hundred fifty people."

"That's no problem at all," he replied, taking a greater interest in me. "When do you want to pick them up?"

"Next Monday afternoon," I said.

"Done," he answered. "You will have to pay for them now."

"Fine," I replied. "How much are they?"

"I can't say until we weigh them on Monday, but you can put down a deposit of $1000 now to hold them."

"OK, OK," I said. "But I need to figure out which credit card to use. May I use your phone?"

He looked at me for what seemed forever.

"Sure," he said. "Use the phone at the end of the counter."

I quickly took the phone and dialed Pepper's number. It rang, then went to voicemail.

"Hi, this is Pepper. You know what to do." Beep.

"Hello Pepper, this is the James Hook Company in Boston. Your lobsters were shipped, and you should receive them today by 4 p.m. Thank you."

It was a long shot, but she knew my voice, and she also knew she did not order any lobsters. She would also remember trying to get me to come here years ago.

I was pleased with myself because if they traced the call, it would indeed be from the James Hook Company in Boston. And what else could they learn? Heading for the door, a voice called out, "Hey, what about your order?"

"I need to get a different credit card," I replied. "I will be back tomorrow."

Grabbing a cab, I headed to the State Capitol. The Professor said something about seeing the truth like a senator would. Where else do you find Senators in Boston but at the Statehouse?

I had been there years ago and actually took a tour of the building. The Boston Statehouse is the oldest, continuously used State Capitol in the country. I remember the tour guide saying in his thick Boston accent:

"Built on Jawhn Hancawck's cow pasture, the building had its cawnahstone laid July 4, 1795, by Govahnaw Samuel Adams and Paul Reveeuh."

Sitting on a hill above Boston Common, its gold dome top makes the place look like a giant beacon.

"A beacon of liberty," I can remember the tour guide saying.

I got out of the cab and walked up the steps, but the entrance was locked.

Apparently, the main doors are only opened on special occasions, like the inauguration of the governor.

I followed the arrows to the public access, but a State Trooper stood in the way.

"I am sawry, the State House is closed to the public right now," he said.

"Why?" I asked. I could see a lot of people were inside.

"Official business," he said. "Come back tomawrow."

I thanked him and started walking through the Commons. It was a beautiful Tuesday afternoon, and, thinking that, I started humming the song by that name.

My stomach growled. I was starving and couldn't get the James Hook Company and those lobsters out of my mind. I headed back, deciding to walk it since it was so nice out.

Boston is like New York—old New York, downtown below Houston Street. Giant buildings soar near the water's edge, and some of the streets seem laid out by a drunken sailor.

I could smell the lobster rolls a block away, coming either from James Hook or another one of the little outlets along the waterfront that sell the best seafood takeout that you eat on nearby picnic tables.

What the heck? I thought, Why not go back to James Hook and get something to eat? I owe them for the phone call anyway.

Thankfully, the man who I had lied to about the credit card was not behind the counter. Instead, a guy who looked like Popeye the Sailor Man took my order.

"I don't know," I said to him. "Should I get the lobster roll or the tail dinner?"

A woman's voice answered my question from behind me.

"Get the lobster roll. They are the best."

I knew that voice, and my entire body felt a jolt of electricity.

"O-M-G, she got the message!"

I turned around.

"Hi, Hack," she said.

It was Pepper.

Chapter Eight

*"... men whose behaviour on many Occasions has caused
the Blood of those Sons of Liberty to recoil within them ..."*

*– Col. Isaac Barré speaking in Parliament in defense
of the Americans, February 1765*

We both froze in place. My jaw dropped. "Pepper," I said, and
we hugged. A tight hug. A full body hug. Not the kind your
sister gives you.

She was always in shape, and her whole body now attached to
mine in a vice grip.

Through the embrace, I could feel her quivering deep inside.

She was terrified, though you couldn't tell it by looking at her.

"Well, what is it going to be?" Popeye said in an exasperated
tone. I think he was jealous of me.

Pepper stepped forward.

"Two lobster rolls and two bottles of water," she told him.

There was an awkward silence as we waited for Popeye to get
the food. We both wanted to talk to each other but knew this was
not the place. So we assumed our position as hungry customers
looking for some grub.

We each took our plate and headed towards the picnic tables
outside.

"No, this way," she said, and now she led us behind James
Hook to this little patch of grass shielded by a concrete wall.

"We can talk here," she said, sitting down.

"You better start talking. You know Professor..."

She cut me off.

"Yes, I know," she said. Pepper looked down at her plate, holding back tears.

"I am responsible for all of this, Hackworth," she said, her voice starting to break. "And I don't want anything to happen to you, either."

I took a bite of the lobster roll. I was always extremely uncomfortable when a woman started to cry. And hearing her voice break and seeing her chin quiver told me it was only seconds away.

"Pepper, be strong," I said, grabbing her knee and squeezing. "Tell me everything."

She also took a bite of the lobster roll.

"Didn't I tell you this was the best?" she said, changing the subject so as to regain her composure.

She took another bite of the lobster roll.

"It all started about a year ago, Hackworth. I was assigned to work on the reprinting of a book by two famous admirals. The book was originally published by the Smithsonian Institution and titled, *So Proudly We Hail: the History of the United States Flag.*"

The word "flag" made me look up. That's the book the strange man was looking for at the bookstore.

"Anyway, the authors were Rear Admiral William Rea Furlong and Commodore Byron McCandless, and they..."

I interrupted her. "Commodore? The Navy stopped using that title years ago."

"Exactly," she said. "Commodore McCandless was an old navy veteran from the days when that title was used. He previously had written a book called *Flags of the World* in 1917 with the founder of the National Geographic Society, Gilbert Grosvenor."

"Both the Admiral and Commodore were the Navy's experts on flags. When Alaska and Hawaii were set to join the union in the 1950's, President Eisenhower asked Admiral Furlong to draw up the arrangement of the stars. He did, and his plan was accepted."

I interrupted her. "You mean the flag of today was designed by Admiral Furlong?"

"Yes, Hackworth. He was a vexillographer, a designer of flags. Keep in mind that the flag's birth is closely tied to the Navy, and with the Navy, its care has always been assigned."

She took another bite.

"After the new 50-star flag was approved, Admiral Furlong and Commodore McCandless agreed to work together to write the definitive history of the U.S. flag. All previous histories were long on myth and short on facts.

"The two of them went to the Smithsonian with their plan, got funding from the Ford Foundation in 1962, and commenced their work. They were extremely fortunate to have a woman named Lula Stephens aid their efforts. She had prepared the Navy's exhibit on the flag in 1926, the Sesqui-Centennial of the Declaration of Independence."

We both took another bite of the lobster roll.

"So they started this project in 1962, gathering thousands of records from various historical organizations," she continued. "Five years later, the book is still not published, and the Commodore dies. Six years after that, Admiral Furlong delivers a 1,000-page manuscript to the Smithsonian."

"Pepper, this is all fascinating and everything, but what does it have to do with..."

"I am getting there, Hackworth," she said. "You must hear me out on this."

I was out of water. "OK, but I need another one of these."

We both got up and retrieved two more bottles of water. Pepper wouldn't leave my side.

"Are you hearing me, Hackworth?" she said. "These two Navy men, with the resources of the U.S. government at their fingertips and both experts on flags, take 11 years to complete a book on the U.S. flag?"

"That seems like a long time," I agreed.

"But it gets better," she said. "It took another three years before the book was finally published. And only after Admiral Furlong had died."

There was a pause after the word "died." We both thought of Professor Redmand but did not say his name.

"So think about this," Pepper continued. "It takes two experts on the U.S. flag fourteen years to print the first edition. And neither of them is alive to see it through."

"It sounds like the Smithsonian intentionally printed the book after they were dead," I observed. "Why?"

"Why do you think, Hackworth? Because the book that was finally published was edited. And even after the first edition came out, there was still information that had to be removed."

"Can you prove that?" I asked.

"Of course," she said.

She took a big swig of water, tipping her head back and almost gulping it. "About a year ago, I got called into my boss' office. He tells me that Worthman is going to reprint *So Proudly We Hail* with a special introduction from a former president. He puts me in charge of the project."

"You lucky dog, Pepper, you lucky dog," I said.

She smiled, her eyes looking coy, like she had gotten away with something.

"Did you meet the President?" I asked, knowing she had met and worked with many famous people.

"Forget all of that," she replied. "Because what happened next is what led to all of this."

"The Smithsonian sent me the first printing of the book from which we were to prepare the reprint," she continued. "No sooner did I receive it, then I got a call from my boss. He tells me there has been a mistake, and I am not to use the first printing; they will send me a revised second printing."

"Now I start to wonder what is going on. It took these people 14 years to finally print the book, and now the one they printed is not good? And that I need to wait and receive an updated version?"

"But, Hackworth, the thing was that I already had read the first printing. So when the second printing came to me, I quickly found the differences between the two versions."

"What were the differences?"

She took another long drink of water.

"In the chapter about the flag in the 1780's, the authors included a very strange footnote in the first edition. It said that they could not determine what flag was used at the inauguration because Washington's diaries for this time period had vanished."

She stopped talking. Two men approached where we were sitting. We both were startled.

"Oh, sorry, we didn't know anyone was here. Sorry," the one said. They were young businessmen. They left.

"Washington's diaries vanished? And they noted this—why? It was a flag book after all," I observed.

"Exactly," she said. "The implication was clear. The diaries spoke of the flag."

Pepper then explained that George Washington kept meticulous diaries throughout his career, from 1754 to his death in 1799.

"Washington didn't just keep a diary; he also kept journals of his activities, observations, and expenses," Pepper continued. "In fact, according to the University of Virginia, which studies his diaries, Washington kept diaries for every month of those years."

"Think about that, Hackworth," she said. "When he fought the French in 1754, he kept his diaries. Throughout the Revolution, he kept his diaries. When the British were shooting at him, he kept those diaries. At Valley Forge, he kept those diaries. When he was inaugurated, he kept his diaries.

"And letters. Lots of letters to friends, allies, Martha, and the Continental Congress. You name it, and George Washington wrote about it or to someone and kept a copy!"

And then she paused and fixed her eyes right on mine.

"According to the university, these diaries, journals, and letters were maintained through thick and thin for 45 years by George Washington. And out of those 45 years, only four months are missing," she said.

"And what months are missing?"

"The four months beginning April 1789 through July 1789. The critical months when he was sworn in as the first president and went about setting up the government."

"Wait a minute, Pepper," I interrupted. "How can this be possible? This is perhaps the most important time for the nation."

"Republic," she replied.

"The start of the Republic, not the nation," she continued. "But we will get into that later. The point is that these flag experts noted that the diaries were missing in their book about the flag! And that notation was removed from the second printing."

"By whom?" I asked.

"Beats me," she said. "When I realized the difference between the two printings, I knew something was up. But then, when my boss asked me to send back the first printing to the Smithsonian, I really got suspicious. I told my boss I needed it for the project, but within a couple of days he gets a phone call that all but demands the return of it."

"And then, out of the blue, my boss tells me the project is on ice. The Smithsonian decided not to go forward with the project."

We stood up and started walking to the Westin Hotel and the waterside walkway adjacent to it. We didn't speak as people walked by us. Finally, we were alone again.

"Let me guess, Pepper, you didn't let this go," I said.

"No way," she said. "And that's when I remembered that Professor Redmand was a vexillologist. So I went to Providence and had dinner at his house."

"What did he say?" I asked.

"Not much, at first. It seemed like he already knew all of this. He kept looking down at the floor and shaking his head up and down. And then, out of the blue, he interjects something very odd."

Pepper stopped walking. We watched as a small yacht went by a larger one, making no sound.

"Isn't it obvious, Hack? Professor Redmand was a highly regarded expert in American history, teaching in the Ivy League to the alleged best and the brightest."

"Yes, I know. And I think he had a crush on you."

She smiled. "He obviously was complicit in telling the lies. And I think it bothered him."

The sun started setting; the yacht was now just a dot on the shimmering water.

Pepper continued.

"I asked him if this was true and if he was complicit in telling the lies. It struck a nerve with him. You should have seen his face."

"He said it was the only way to advance in academia, and it has always been that way. Tell the official story, maintain the status quo, perpetuate the orthodoxy, attack those who question it, and write papers that apologize for it."

"Then he did something unbelievable. He stood up and led me into his library. He placed his hand on a book in the case and tilted it. I realized it was a lever of some sort, because then the bookcase cracked open about a foot."

"Follow me, Pepper," he said.

"I squeezed through the thin opening and stepped onto dimly lit stairs. There was a cool draft of cellar air that hit my face and then whooshed back against my neck. I followed him down the stairs into a little foyer with a table in the center, on which was a bust of Benjamin Franklin. The stairs continued downward, but he motioned for me to stay on that level," she continued.

"He said he was going to show me something. He said, 'They already know about us, and this is not safe here. These rooms and their treasures will soon be buried. But I can't let this be buried,' Professor Mac told me."

"You wait here, he said, and then walked down the stairs and disappeared. Seconds passed. Then a minute. I look more closely at the winding stairs. They were very dark, very old, and made with great craftsmanship.

"Then Professor Mac reappeared, holding a small wooden box. He opened it, took out two items, and placed them on the table. One was a piece of parchment.

"The other was the 12-star flag."

Chapter Nine

"-- for the quarantine flag of the mother country was a yellow flag with a dark spot, a representation of the plague-spot in the middle -- those colors were, doubtless, chosen for the rattlesnake flag, to indicate the deadly character of the venom of the rattlesnake, and the danger of treading on it."

–The National Flag of the United States, by Schuyler Hamilton, Lippincot, Philadelphia, 1853

Her weapons "she conceals in the roof of her mouth, so that, to those who are unacquainted with her, she appears to be a most defenseless animal; and even when those weapons are shewn and extended for her defence, they appear weak and contemptible; but their wounds however small, are decisive and fatal. Conscious of this, she never wounds till she has generously given notice, even to her enemy, and cautioned him against the danger of treading on her."

– Benjamin Franklin in the December 27, 1775 edition of The Pennsylvania Journal on why the rattlesnake was the perfect mascot for the Americans.

We didn't say a word to each other. Pepper grabbed my hand, and we turned back on the walkway, hand in hand. She had the softest hand.

We were both quiet, remembering Professor Redmand.

"Do you remember what we wrote on his whiteboard that day in his office that got us in trouble?" she asked.

I didn't answer. All of this information was too much. But I needed to know more.

"Pepper, did he explain what the 12-star flag meant?"

"Funny, you ask," she said. "You know Professor Mac had that annoying way of making you discover the truth. Of leading you to the water and making you drink."

She let go of my hand and pulled her long black hair back behind her ears.

"He gave me a little flag history. He told me that stars on flags were ancient symbols of sovereignty. It all started with the star, which the Three Wise Men followed to Bethlehem. This all-powerful star, issued by all-powerful God, would become a symbol of power and authority—the very definition of sovereignty," she said.

"From those ancient times, more than 2000 years ago, to the present, the star was used by nations to symbolize their power and authority. And so a star became the symbol for the sovereign state in America and was used to express this fact on the flag.

"That's why, in 1777, the Continental Congress stated that the flag of the thirteen united States was to be of 13 stars. The flag was to symbolize the sovereign power of each state, united together to oppose the British."

"Did he say anything else when he gave you the flag, Pepper?"

"Yes," she said. "A warning. He said forces in the government would go to great lengths to get it, as well as other organizations. But he would not say their names. He wanted me to write a true history of the flag, beginning with this flag."

"I saw a great opportunity and so commenced with my research. I took a leave from Worthman and set out on this project. Someone became tipped off of my work, and, well, here we are."

"They are spying on us, Pepper," I said, telling her about my encounter with the Homeland Security agents.

"On us and everybody," she said. "It used to be that the government spied on individuals. But now it spies on everybody all the time—or at least has the capability. It's really easy to spy when people post their pictures and ideas online. In the past, the only public place that had pictures of people was the WANTED posters at the Post Office—when the government would post your picture!"

She paused and looked around.

"I am convinced that they came upon my work by mining internet search data, emails, or library research."

"Why do you say that?" I asked.

"It's just a feeling, but I swear all of my problems began when I started using search engines."

Now we both stopped and paused. We both knew Google and other search engines actively cooperated with the government. In fact, the government has the capability to intercept all inquiries typed in the search bar in real-time and bypass the search engines.

"Then I get thinking," Pepper said. "Google and the search engines probably mine all of our searches for their own products. Did you think their ideas of a driverless car, of smart glasses, of taking pictures of every house, of Google Earth, and a hundred other projects originated with them?"

"No way. They steal other people's ideas and content and profit from them. Just like the forces in the government monitor what we say, what we write, and what we are researching. It sounds paranoid, but ..."

I broke her off.

"Paranoia and I have become fast friends. It is not paranoia. The agents said they have been monitoring my email, internet searches, social media posts, text messages, and phone calls. Even my mail!"

I stopped, grabbed her hand, and turned her to me.

"Pepper, why did you give me the stinkin flag?"

She smiled that smile, and I instantly forgave her. Truth be told, even though all of this was dangerous, it felt so exciting to be with her at this moment. I didn't want to be anywhere else.

"I had no intention of involving you in this, Hackworth. But it got too hot. I was visited by those agents as well, who asked me all sorts of questions about my research. They knew I had the 12-star flag, but how?"

She then relayed that after the agents left her, another man knocked at her door.

A very sincere-looking man.

"His name is Vaughn Clark. He said he knew I had the 12-star flag and that he was sent to retrieve it. Obviously, I didn't give it to him."

"Sent by whom?"

"SOL."

"What?"

"SOL"

"S*** Out of Luck?"

We both laughed. Then we stopped. Then we started again. We were laughing together like we used to. Like on the very first day of kindergarten, we just had a way of connecting like no other person I knew.

"We are SOL, Hackworth, but that's not what he meant."

"What is SOL? Is it short for something, or is that the name of the group?"

"Beats me. The best I can figure out is that it means 'sun' from the Latin 'sol.'"

"Maybe it has something to do with the fact the sun is a star?"

"I don't know what it means, but he was very sincere. Honest. I trusted him."

She started laughing. "And it didn't hurt that he was an athletic, good-looking blonde."

"Oh, no, same old story. Headline: Pepper Stillwater Falls for College Athlete."

We both laughed. A nervous, uncomfortable laugh. Pepper and I broke up because she fell for a college athlete.

"He told me to trust him with the flag, that he wanted to preserve the truth."

"And he said he was sworn to fight the government for it."

We were quiet for a moment. I was trying to think about what she just said and not about her affair with the athlete.

"He's the guy who got into it with the government agents at the coffee house, right?"

She nodded.

"He's also the guy who tried to steal the flag from me," I said, relaying the incident in the cab.

We kept walking but didn't say much more. It was all too much. And we didn't want to start talking about what happened to Professor Redmand.

"Where are you staying?" Pepper asked.

"Don't know. How about you?"

"I came to Boston after leaving you in Philly. My cousin has a small yacht at the Charlestown Marina, where I can stay. She is in San Diego for a while."

"How did you get to James Hook so fast?"

"I know you, Hackworth, and when I got the message, I headed down to James Hook, and wallah, you were there!"

"This is all such a coincidence," I said.

"There are no coincidences, Hack. This was all meant to be. You are coming and staying on the boat. It's actually really nice."

She got no argument from me. Where else was there to go? Some flea-bag motel where the wall paper moves, like in Providence?

"OK, let's go then; I am exhausted."

We didn't say a word until we almost got there.

"Pepper," I whispered. "What are we going to do?"

"I don't know Hack," she said. "I don't know."

The marina was a private community of boats, big and small, located in Charlestown, MA, the oldest neighborhood in Boston. Yacht is a fancy word for a houseboat, and as we walked along the deck separating the slips, there were many different boats, some really nice, others not so much.

The marina was like a large RV park except it was on the water, with electrical, internet, water, and sewer connections provided for each boat.

"We're here," Pepper said, pointing to a boat smaller than its neighbors.

As we climbed the steps to go aboard, my eyes caught a strange sight: a much larger, sleeker, black boat moored about 20 feet away.

It was unlike any other at the marina. It was solid black and looked like it could be a submarine. Thin window slits gave it an odd appearance—almost like it was a miniature warship. And an array of radar, sonar, and boom instruments atop the roof proved it was sophisticated inside.

I have been around boats my whole life and have never seen anything like it.

A figure—a man—turned and leaned into the ship's black frame. Then he disappeared.

The way he moved reminded me of someone.

"Come on, we have to go to bed," Pepper said as we walked down into the dark central cabin. "I'll take the front, and you have the back."

She stumbled around, looking for a light switch. There before us was a comfortable seating area with books and a small table in the center. Bedrooms were in the front and back of the ship.

"Oh, Hack. I almost forgot to tell you," Pepper said, grabbing a piece of paper off the table and holding it above her head.

"I kept the map," she said, waving it. "Professor Mac gave me the flag and this parchment, and I kept it!"

"I just gave you the flag."

Her arm came forward, and she handed me the old map. It had burnt edges, like someone tried to destroy it.

It was stiff—three words larger than the others.

"JOIN OR DIE."

The Death of General Warren at the Battle of Bunker Hill, 1775 — by John Trumball

WEDNESDAY

Chapter Ten

"By the rude bridge that arched the flood,
Their flag to April's breeze unfurled,
Here once the embattled farmers stood,
And fired the shot heard round the world."

– From Concord Hymn, by Ralph Waldo Emerson,
commemorating the Battle of Lexington and Concord, April 19,
1775. The flag unfurled was the Bedford, MA township flag.

I awoke from my sleep to the sound of Pepper humming a song and the smell of good coffee. On my night stand was the parchment she handed me last night, the one Professor Redmand gave her with the 12-star flag.

It was an antique map of the 13 states showing lands reserved for the Indians. There was a group of odd flags on top above a snake and the words "JOIN OR DIE." On the bottom right was an illustration of some sort.

Another flag with a star in the middle appeared on the right side above the illustration. It looked like the flag Pepper gave me, but the number of stars was impossible to calculate because of the way it was folded.

I rolled out of bed and walked into the galley.

"Ah, yes," I said. "Good to see that a woman's place is still in the kitchen."

"Well, good morning to you. And cut that woman's place crap."

She smiled and walked to the table with two plates of scrambled eggs, home fries, and sausages. I looked at the table, and there was juice and toast.

Finally, a good breakfast.

We both ate voraciously. Dangerous living has a way of making you hungry. And you never know when you will get your next good meal.

On the galley table was a built-in computer, which was turned on.

"Have you checked for his obituary?" I asked.

Pepper shrugged her shoulders. It wasn't up yet.

The news headline on the computer screamed: AUTHORITIES INVESTIGATING POWER OUTAGES; SUSPECT FOUL PLAY BY TERRORISTS.

"Isn't it weird that the electricity keeps going out?" she said, her freshly washed black hair shimmering in the light that poured in from the boat's kitchen window. "Not just in Philadelphia, but Boston, too?"

"It must be the same power grid," I responded. "And don't forget Providence. Lights went out there, too."

We both nodded and continued eating.

"Oh, of the tribulations of modern man," she said."What a joke! Think about the real trials and tribulations of our ancestors. Months at sea. No food in the winter. Resentful natives are burning down your village, followed by resentful settlers attacking the natives. Rampant disease. Early death. War on your doorstep."

"And no internet, phones, or texts," I said. "Life was absolutely miserable!"

We laughed. Then we got on to the problem at hand.

"Pepper, you said you were in Boston to do research on the flag. The funny thing is, I came here to do research as well."

"Professor Mac told me to visit the State Capitol in Boston and..."

I interrupted her. "And Albany, Philadelphia, Washington, and Raleigh"

She looked up. "He told you the same thing?"

"Obviously," I said. "But I have a question, Ms. History Expert. Why Philadelphia and not Harrisburg, which is where the State Capitol is?"

"Don't know, Hack," she said. "Except that Independence Hall—the place where the Declaration of Independence and Constitution were written—was actually the State Capitol of the Commonwealth of Pennsylvania!"

"Well, look at that," I joked. "I have a real expert as my tour guide."

"So is that our plan, Hackworth? We just go and get this done and get to the bottom of this right now?"

"What choice do we have?" I said. "I don't want to go back to Philly just yet, what with Homeland Security agents and my boring job waiting for me."

"I'm always up for a road trip," she said. "I have the keys to my cousin's car."

We finished breakfast and headed to the Statehouse. It was a cold morning, but sunny. As we walked out, I noticed the sleek, black yacht was gone.

And then it hit me.

"The strange man! That's who was going into the black ship last night."

"What strange man?" Pepper asked.

"The guy who wanted the first edition of the flag book—I told you about him and Tory!"

"Why would he be here?" Pepper asked. "That's absurd, Hack. Anyway, he's gone, and we better be, too."

The Commonwealth of Massachusetts State House was only a couple miles away, but it still took half an hour to get there because of traffic—we could have walked and been there quicker. We parked nearby.

A plaque in front of the magnificent structure said it was completed in 1798 at a cost of $133,333.33. Masonic Grand Master Paul Revere oversaw the laying of the cornerstone, the "Dome of the Rock" of American liberty.

There was no problem entering the building. We immediately headed to the Senate chamber. It was to be in session in two hours, and security at first refused to let us go inside.

But Pepper flashed her smile and asked in a somewhat patronizing tone. The security officer melted and let us in. If I had tried to sweet talk him, he would have had us thrown out.

We entered the ornate chamber, which was originally for the state's House of Representatives. It was this room that was crowned with the magnificent gold dome. Federalist in style, the chamber arranged the senators desks and chairs in a broken circle.

"Have a seat, Senator," I said to Pepper.

She chuckled as we both sat down and looked to the front of the room.

We stopped laughing.

Our eyes immediately went to the large golden eagle on the wall behind the central podium. The eagle had an American shield of red and white stripes and a blue canton of stars. But that is not what arrested our conversation.

In the eagle's mouth was a ribbon banner that stretched across the entire wall. Its words were large enough to be seen even from the back seats that we occupied.

The banner read, "God Save The Commonwealth of Massachusetts."

We were dumbstruck.

We had heard the English saying, "God Save The Queen" or "God Save The King".

But "God Save The Commonwealth of Massachusetts"?

The security officer entered the room. "No sitting in the seats. Come now; it is time to go," he said.

No charm from Pepper would change his mind. He was visibly irritated that we would enter the Senate floor and casually take a seat.

"Let's go," I said to Pepper, and in a flash, we were outside and walking through the Commons.

"What do you think this clue means?" she asked.

"Easy," I said. "In Providence, the professor said it would be written in marble. In Boston, it would be as the Senators would see it. The answer is simple: he wanted us to see firsthand the sovereignty of the state."

"The star is an ancient symbol that represents sovereignty, he told me," Pepper said.

"You are right," she added.

I liked hearing her say that.

"But isn't it strange, this idea of God saving a state? What about saving the United States?" I said. "That is our country."

"Exactly the point, Hackworth. To us, raised on lies and conditioned to think a certain way, just to see something like 'God Save The Commonwealth of Massachusetts' is an oddity."

She continued: "The people of that age apparently didn't think like we did, or else they would have something like 'God Save The United States.' Come to think of it, for the people of Massachusetts, this was their country."

"The word Commonwealth strikes me as funny too," I said. "Commonwealth is a national term denoting sovereign parts. The British Commonwealth today includes Canada, Australia, and England. Yet Massachusetts is suggesting its parts—primarily its towns—are sovereign, just like them."

I recalled my tour of the statehouse years ago and seeing the Hall of Flags. The flags of each town were hung, a dignity afforded to nations had it been at the United Nations building.

"Pepper, you're exactly correct. Massachusetts considered herself a nation and her towns, states."

"That's what a commonwealth is," she said. "The parts have sovereignty, and in Massachusetts, the townships were the parts."

She stopped walking and pointed to a bench we could sit on.

"Hackworth, did you notice that the eagle that held the banner had an American shield over its breast?"

"So?"

"Well, it would be one thing if the shield had been a Massachusetts symbol. It would have been more in keeping with the sentiments of the banner. But it didn't. Instead, it was the United States on the shield."

"I don't know what you are getting at," I said.

"Well, the two should not go together," she said.

"Unless they should," I quickly responded.

We were on the same wave length.

"The shield and the banner only seem odd to us; we are misled about the origin and structure of our country," I continued. "But to those people of that day, this was the way of the world. They joined a union to protect themselves, like a neighborhood watch."

Just then, a large "bang" broke through the air. As one, Pepper and I dove down in reflex. We looked around.

BANG. The sound pierced the air again. I pointed to Pepper. In the street, workmen were dropping steel sheets to cover a construction hole on the road. But the look in Pepper's eyes was pure terror.

"What are we doing just sitting here like this, reacting to every bump as if it were our death knell?" I said, grabbing her arm. "We need to get out of here and get to Albany and then wherever and settle this once and for all."

BANG. The next steel plate was dropped.

We hustled through the Commons and left Boston within the hour. Pepper borrowed her cousin's Mustang convertible for the trip to Albany, and even so, we avoided the EZ Pass Lane and paid the tolls of the Mass Turnpike the old-fashioned way. Not that it mattered. Every car and truck was photographed, coming and going.

The loud noises in Boston woke us up and reminded us of the danger we were in.

But somehow, together, we both felt less afraid. In all of our conversations, Pepper and I avoided talking personal. And given what had been happening, it was good that we didn't talk about what happened to us.

Obviously, she wasn't married or serious with anyone. Nor was I. And we both knew it without saying as much.

I was glad she was not married.

The ten years since college have done nothing to dim her good looks. She was as vibrant and beautiful as the first day I met her with my mom. When we put the top down on the car and sped westward, her hair blew backward, exposing her flawless face.

With the big sunglasses she was wearing, she looked like a movie star.

"Welcome to New York, the Empire State," the sign declared. And just as we passed it, the potholes in the road offered their own welcome. We slowed down as we entered a work zone.

"The empire is crumbling," Pepper snarked.

The cars and trucks ahead of us slowed down as well until we were all at a crawl, one slow lane with concrete walls and orange cones on each side of us.

Then the traffic stopped.

I leaned my head around the car in front, and there, about a mile up the road, it looked like an accident scene. There were lots of State Trooper cars on the banks with their lights on.

The traffic was stop-and-go. The car in front would go about ten feet. Then stop. Then move again.

Pepper pointed to the sign.

"Cameras," she said.

Sure enough, the traffic sign running across the road had a series of cameras pointed in a whole bunch of directions.

"Did you notice the cameras on the Commons?" she asked.

I didn't.

"They are everywhere. They were in the Statehouse. They were even on the wharf. Now, they are on the interstate! They can watch every step you take in public."

It was true. Ever since the terrorist attacks of September 11, 2001, surveillance cameras have been popping up all over. On city streets. Toll bridges. On police cars. And on the police themselves. Cameras in our pockets, on our phones, at our door, and on our computers.

"Big Brother is truly watching us," Pepper said, referencing George Orwell's 1984, about a totalitarian state.

The car jerked forward ten feet, then stopped. As we got closer to the flashing police cars, I could make out four or five State Troopers, a couple on each side of the single-lane road.

They were stopping each car!

Pepper and I realized this at the same time and turned and looked at each other.

I knew she felt the same as me: let's turn around, cut across the median, and get out of here.

It seemed too strange that there was a roadblock on the very road we were on.

"If you turn around, they will come get you," I said. "Only people who have something to hide flee in the other direction."

The car jerked forward. We were about ten vehicles away from the State Troopers.

"We have done nothing wrong," Pepper stammered.

"No, nothing. Just lied to Homeland Security, have information about a murder, and possess stolen federal property."

"These are New York State Police, not Homeland Security," she said. "Last I knew, they were separate from each other."

The last she knew, perhaps. But over the last ten years, the federal intelligence agencies have integrated the various state and local police forces as part of the War on Terror.

The car jerked forward. We were now three cars away from the checkpoint.

"They are probably looking for a child abductor or something," I said. "No way is the State Police the Gestapo."

Pepper pulled the car up, and a trooper, standing in the middle of the road, placed his hand up to stop.

We were both nervous.

On each side of the car, a trooper gestured to open the windows. Simultaneously, Pepper and I lowered the windows.

"Good afternoon, Officer," Pepper said, smiling. She took off her sunglasses. And smiled again. The trooper returned the smile.

"Officer," I said to the trooper on my side. I took off my glasses and smiled. He didn't smile back.

"Where are you headed?" they both asked at the same time.

"Albany," Pepper said.

"New York City," I said.

"Well, which is it?" my trooper asked.

We were both silent. Then I answered, "We are headed to New York City by way of Albany." I could lie on the fly.

"What's going on?" Pepper asked the trooper on her side.

He ignored her question. We then noticed a tall, third trooper heading towards the car.

We had both seen this guy before.

And he had seen us.

Pepper stiffened up like a dead body.

"Hack, Hack," she said urgently.

"It's him!"

I looked closer, and then I realized what she was saying.

He walked up to the car on Pepper's side, and the officer standing there quickly moved out of the way. You could tell this guy was the supervisor of the other troopers.

He took off his trooper hat, bent down, and put his head into the car.

He had a sincere, happy face.

"Hi guys," he said casually.

He looked right at me and nodded, making a reassuring motion with his head. I was disarmed by his sincerity. It felt like he was protecting us in some way.

He looked at Pepper and smiled.

He again nodded his head up and down and whispered to us, "It's OK."

Then, as quickly, he pulled back and yelled an order.

"They're OK. Next car!"

The trooper in the road got out of the way and motioned for us to proceed.

Pepper slowly drove by the State Police, and within a half-mile, the road construction ended and the Mustang was back at 70 miles per hour.

We both exclaimed at the same time:

"Vaughn Clark is a State Trooper!"

Chapter Eleven

"Why stand we here idle? What is it that the gentlemen wish? What would they have? Is life so dear or peace so sweet as to be purchased at the price of chains and slavery? Forbid it, Almighty God. I know not what course others may take, but as for me, give me liberty or give me death!"

– Sketches of the Life and Character of Patrick Henry, by William Wirt, Philadelphia, 1817 from a speech to the Second Virginia Convention on March 23, 1775

"The first thing I have at heart is American liberty; the second thing is American union."

– Patrick Henry, 1788

Pepper hit the gas and didn't care about the ruts in the road. In between bumps, I could feel my burner phone vibrating madly. Tory was filing his first report.

With Tory helping solve the flag mystery, I was sure we would be successful. He was a natural historian and lover of American history, probably because it was in his blood. He didn't have some fancy college degree. He was self-taught and constantly learning, reading every book that came through the bookstore that interested him.

Growing up reading rare books and learning from his elders made him a fount of insight. The bookstore itself was a veritable storehouse of knowledge. But that he grew up with such a background in Philadelphia, one of the most historic cities in America, meant learning from more than just books. Tory saw every exhibit in every nook and cranny of the extensive Independence National Park, where the Declaration of Independence and U.S. Constitution were written.

The burner phone in my pocket vibrated again. I opened messages, and a torrential stream of text bubbles popped up on the screen:

Hi Hack! So I did what you asked and researched the flag. But where do you start? Obviously, the peopling of America. And where does that start?

Ultimately, it all started in Africa!

All humans are nearly identical to each other—99.9 percent of the DNA in you is the same in everyone else. But because of that 0.1% difference, we can know with certainty human origins and migrations.

Humans originated in Africa. Our DNA lineage begins with the first female in Africa, 200,000 years ago.

"Is Tory texting you?" Pepper asked, not taking her eyes off the road.

"Yes, about the flag."

"Well, read it to me," she said.

I continued reading out loud:

Africa, Europe, and Asia aren't really separate; instead, they are one contiguous landmass. We'll call it Afro-Eurasia. People migrated every which way out of Africa. Over time, certain physical adaptations were made to people depending on their environment and their proximity to the equator (sunlight). That's why we look different from each other.

The Americas are separated from all this by two oceans, an island formed by the limits of Afro-Eurasia.

The first immigrants to America were people from Afro-Eurasia who crossed the Bering Land Bridge near Alaska and spread out to the southern and eastern parts of the Americas.

The later immigrants were also from Afro-Eurasia, but they came by boat. They mastered the oceans and, thus, the world.

These were the English, Spanish, French, and Dutch.

"And the Portuguese, don't forget them," Pepper said.

When explorers land, they usually plant their flag. Norse explorer Leif Ericsson carried the Raven flag but never planted it. We planted the American flag on the moon! A flag is a medium of information, a symbol of what it represents. Used in battle to identify a side, a symbol worth dying for.

In murals and paintings, flags become iconography—a pictorial illustration of a subject.

"That's very true," Pepper said. "Think of the picture of the flag being raised on Iwo Jima in World War II."

The Roman Empire fell in 1453 when Muslim Turks conquered and took over Constantinople. That means the Americas were visited by Europeans less than fifty years after the fall of the Roman Empire!

I stopped reading. "Wow, Pepper," I said. "That means the world was just coming out of the medieval period when the first explorers landed here."

And they brought elements of that empire to the western shore, including the use of flags. Each British colony was created separately and was independent of the others. Rhode Island was created for freedom of religion, and Maryland as a safe harbor for Catholics. The Pilgrims came to the western shores to create a new society, which they named after the Massachusett Indian tribe.

From 1619 to 1755, the colonies were created by a charter and each colony was given self-governance with its own legislature and a royal governor.

Over time, the Americans conceived a new kind of freedom. They already knew British legal liberty. But they learned natural liberty from the natives. They also saw firsthand the opposite of liberty: grotesque slavery! Combining the three experiences together, Americans gave the world a new idea—liberty and the pursuit of happiness.

Tensions were high between the French and the British on the western frontier (present-day Ohio Valley), the lands west of the Appalachian mountains.

In 1754, George Washington, a young Virginia militiaman with the rank of Lt. Colonel, went on a mission to western Pennsylvania when he confronted the French Ambassador Jumonville. The parties clashed, Jumonville was killed, and the French and British went to war for the prize of North America.

At the very same moment, Benjamin Franklin introduced a plan of union at a colonial congress in Albany, NY. The plan was influenced by the Iroquois Confederacy and *would create a united defense against enemies in the west. Franklin's sketch of a disconnected rattlesnake with the words "Join or Die" became a symbol for the cause of union.*

Ultimately, the colonies rejected the plan of union as an encroachment on their right to self-government.

After winning the war, the British issued the Proclamation of 1763, which reserved the western lands for the Indians. This staggering turn of events meant that the colonies could not grow westward, even though their charters said otherwise. They may have won the war against the French, but the Americans lost the thing they wanted most—the western lands!

"Ah, it's starting to make sense," Pepper said. "Wasn't Washington a land surveyor by trade? And wasn't he the largest landowner in America at the time of his death? I think he was."

I kept reading Tory's text.

Worse, the British imposed the Stamp Tax in 1765 to pay war debts. But this was unheard of—up to that point, only each colony itself could tax through its own legislature.

Now arises a shadowy group of patriots known as the "Sons of Liberty" to defend their rights. Liberty means to be free from arbitrary rule, and that is exactly what they opposed. Their protests get the Stamp Act repealed and later, they would lead the Boston Tea Party. It was their guns and powder that the British attempted to seize in Lexington and Concord that would start the war!

And the Sons of Liberty had their own flag.

They took the solid red Meteor Flag of England and then broke it up with white stripes to show they were no longer one.

It was a flag of disunion!

"Rebellious stripes," the British called them.

Here's the cool thing: That flag lives to this day. Take the stars and blue off the American flag, and you have the Sons of Liberty flag—the rebellious stripes!

More later ... T

Chapter Twelve

"Half a truth is often a great lie."
– Benjamin Franklin

Pepper raced down the interstate, gaining speed to pass another car. "Slow down!" I shouted at Pepper. The wind was blowing so hard in the convertible that it felt like we were doing 100 miles per hour.

It was like Pepper thought she could run away from her life in that Mustang.

She was fixated on the road and wouldn't look at me.

"Slow down, Pepper!"

She heard me, glanced at me, and then slowed the Mustang down and pulled off to the side of the road.

"It just sunk in—Vaughn Clark is a State Trooper!" she said.

I could tell she was feeling paranoid, like I felt on the train. It seemed no matter where we went, something followed us.

For my whole life, I never felt like this. It was like we were rats in a maze, and a giant head with two eyes was watching every move.

"This makes no sense," she said. "He never identified himself as law enforcement when we met. There is no way he is a cop."

"Way," I said. "There is a way because he is a cop. And judging by how the other officers reacted to his command, I suspect a ranking one."

"What would a State Trooper be doing in Philadelphia two days ago, trying to rob you?" she asked.

"Beats me. But tell me how Homeland Security could have a picture of him and not know who he is if, in fact, he is a State Trooper? They have to know."

"It doesn't make any sense," she said.

"Hack, he knows where we are going. I am certain of that."

"You mean he knows we are headed to the capitol in Albany?"

"Then maybe we shouldn't go," I said. "Maybe we should just keep driving to Buffalo."

For a moment, I thought about Pepper and me driving to Buffalo, going incognito, changing our identity, and living a simpler life. We could get married. I could work at the Buffalo Evening News; she could become a teacher.

Pepper sensed my mind was wandering.

"Here's a better idea," she said. "Why don't we trap him?"

"Huh?"

"That's right, why don't we lay a trap for him at the capitol and get to the bottom of this?"

"Yeah, right, Pepper," I said. "We are going to trap a man who could throw us in jail."

"If he wanted to do that, why didn't he grab us at the roadblock?" she asked. "Or arrest you in Philadelphia?"

"New York State Troopers have no jurisdiction in New York City, let alone Philadelphia. They have no power there," I replied.

"Hack, don't you see? He let us go!"

This was true. This guy could have had us arrested on the spot. It was almost like he wanted us to know he was a State Trooper. He wanted us to know he was letting us go.

"It could all be a trap," I said. "He may want us to think he is on our side so he can lure us to a private place and kill us."

"Vaughn Clark could be the murderer of Professor Redmand."

Pepper would have nothing of it. For a second, it sounded like I was trying to convince her not to date the basketball player at Brown and stay with me.

"I am a good reader of people. Vaughn Clark is sincere. He's honest. There is something about him, something I trust."

It was silent. She started the car and pulled out. A sign said "Albany, Left Lane" and "New York City, Right Lane."

Another sign said, "Buffalo, stay left."

Pepper swerved left.

I knew we weren't going to Buffalo.

If the Massachusetts Statehouse was a glowing symbol of 1700's America, the New York State Capitol was a gray symbol of the Gilded Age and Robber Baron. It looked like the Shawshank Redemption prison. Or the summer home of a railroad magnate.

Designed in the Moorish-Gothic style, it could be mistaken for a European castle.

We pulled up, got out, and walked in. We both wanted to see what Albany offered before Vaughn Clark caught up with us.

Professor Redmand said, "Albany is next, and the 12-star flag will appear." Our eyes scanned every possible flag, banner, or patch as we walked in and towards the security screening area.

Cut into a long hallway with high ceilings were a series of built-in desks. To the left were a metal detector and a conveyor belt scanner, the kind you see in airports.

Three police officers stood guard, one with a German Shepherd at his side.

"Look at you," Pepper cooed, approaching the shepherd.

"Stay away," the policeman holding the leash barked.

"Empty your pockets and place the contents in the tray," the policeman closest to us ordered.

Pepper walked through the detector, smiled at the officer, retrieved her small purse, and waited for me.

I walked through, triggered the alarm, and the third officer moved closer.

"Take off your hat and put it through the scanner," he said.

I had been wearing my wide-brimmed fedora since leaving Philadelphia. With it, no umbrella is needed.

I walked back through the detector. No sound.

Retrieving my articles on the conveyor, I joked to the officer.

"It's my Indiana Jones hat."

He didn't say anything. Didn't smile. No expression whatsoever.

Walking away, I turned to Pepper.

"Why do they have to be so nasty in New York?"

But she, born in New York, now did the same thing as the officer. She ignored me and focused on every possible nook and cranny in the castle for signs of the 12-star flag.

We went into the Assembly Chamber. One flag above the speaker's chair was in the room. It had fifty stars.

We went into the Senate Chamber. It looked like the Grand Banquet Hall of King Henry VIII. The flag here had fifty stars.

Pepper saw a person at the tour desk.

"Excuse me, ma'am," she said. "Where do you keep the flags?"

It was a great question. Many of the state capitols and the nation's capitol have a special place where historic flags are kept. Often times, these include Civil War banners or a flag that was brought to the moon.

"Down the hall and then hang a right," the woman said. She wasn't really friendly either.

"Bingo," Pepper said. "Let's find it, take a picture, and then get something to eat. I am starving."

So was I.

We entered the East Lobby. Gothic columns filled the room, with flags coming off each one. Pepper meticulously examined every flag. Flags of New York. Flags of the United States. Flags from every war up to Vietnam.

All kinds of flags.

But none with 12 stars.

I was growing fatigued. I had counted so many stars on so many flags, I could count no more.

But Pepper kept going.

A tour through the flag collection was taking place, so we casually joined it and listened. A tall, thin woman was giving the tour. She had wire glasses and a tight bun of gray hair.

"The truth is, until the Civil War, the American flag was not so common," she was saying.

"The American flag was not present at any battle of the Revolutionary War. Snake and State flags were the standard."

That seemed like an odd thing to say, I thought. Every battle scene painting I ever saw had the Stars and Stripes.

Someone on the tour asked a question.

"But what about the painting of George Washington crossing the Delaware at Valley Forge? There is a Stars and Stripes on that ship!"

The person asking was a veteran—a former Marine, judging by the insignia tattooed on his arm.

"We all know the painting well," the tour guide said. "It was called "Washington Crossing the Delaware" by Emanuel Leutze in 1851. Let's just say the artist took license with the scene."

"How so?" the veteran demanded.

"Well, he crossed the Delaware on December 25, 1776, to attack the Hessians—six months before June 14, 1777, when the flag resolution was passed."

The veteran listened intently.

"He could not have flown a flag that wasn't made yet. He probably used the Pine Tree flag, given that was the flag his earlier ships flew."

"She's describing the pine tree flag with the words 'APPEAL TO HEAVEN' in bold type," Pepper said, leaning over my shoulder.

The tour guide continued:

"In fact, every painting you see of Washington and the flag, whether it be that one or Rembrandt Peale's portrait at Brandywine or Trumbull's at Yorktown, is not accurate. After the Constitution began, the early leaders were trying to promote the idea that the Union was the reason for the revolution, when it was not!"

"And the great painters, including Trumbull, Peale, and West—they all took great licenses—because that fit the narrative of the paying customer, Uncle Sam."

The veteran was getting a little perturbed.

"You can't be right," he said. "In the Rotunda in the Capitol in Washington, DC, there is a very famous painting of Washington in battle with an American flag."

The tour guide tried to maintain her composure.

"All of these paintings were attempts to invoke the patriotic spirit," she said. "The federal government commissioned many of them, decades after the actual battles. But we know for a fact, beyond dispute, that the Stars and Stripes we love so much did not come into widespread use and adoration until the years leading up to the Civil War."

I took my hat off and leaned into the tour. There were nine people on the tour: the veteran, his wife, a senior citizen couple, and a mom with her teenage children, probably homeschoolers.

The homeschool mom raised her hand. The tour guide nodded for her to speak.

"Betsy Ross designed the flag at the direction of George Washington in 1776," she said. "See, here's the picture."

The mom handed the guide a school book entitled "Old Glory." The book was opened to a painting of Betsy Ross sitting and knitting the flag while Washington and others gazed on in approval.

The tour guide didn't blink. "Most probably, the Betsy Ross story is a fable, created during the centennial celebration of the Declaration of Independence in 1876. Most historians do not believe the story to be true. She is said to have made the flag in 1776, when the Stars and Stripes were not even created until 1777."

"How we view the flag today is the result of the many trials and tribulations our nation has endured," the guide continued. "American love and pride for the flag really took off when the southern confederacy fired on the flag at Fort Sumter in 1861."

I had to ask the question. "So are you saying we have been lied to about our flag?"

The tour guide seemed agitated. The veteran seemed even more agitated.

"Lie is a strong word," she said. "No, I am not saying we have been lied to. I am saying we've been taught a narrative."

The veteran had enough. "Come on, honey, let's leave! This is all nonsense."

With that, the veteran and his wife stormed off.

The tour guide looked at me disapprovingly. Her look seemed to blame me for the veteran's departure.

"Are you part of this tour?" she asked sternly.

I turned and followed the veteran out of the East Lobby. Pepper had caught the very last part of this scene.

"Good old Hack, screwing up the party," she said. "I can't find anything here. We may be on a wild goose chase."

The tour was now directly in front of us. I hid behind a column, so the tour guide couldn't see me and listened to her.

"I will let you walk around for a few minutes here, and then we will go to the Governor's Reception Room," she said. "There you can see the Dodge mural that was intended to be in the rotunda of the flag room. Unfortunately, the rotunda was never built, and the mural was separated from the Flag Room."

Pepper and I looked at each other.

"That's it! Come on," she said, racing out of the lobby and heading to the Governor's Reception Room.

In a matter of minutes, we were there.

Pepper and I walked into the room. It was eerily quiet, with a small desk off to the side and an attendant sitting behind it. The reception room was actually used by the governor, for his office was adjacent to where we were standing.

A literature desk had a book titled *State Capitols: Temples of Sovereignty* opened to the page describing the room we were in.

"William deLeftwich Dodge was commissioned to create a series of murals to complement a Flag Room that would honor New York State citizens who served in the military," the book stated. "Dodge began work in 1920. It would take him five years to finish. In 1929, the murals were installed."

"Dodge made the murals under the assumption that they would be forty feet from the ground floor, as plans at that time included a tower capped by a dome that eliminated the current floor. These never came off. But so good was Dodge; the paintings do not suffer for want of distance," the book continued.

"In the center is the Spirit of New York (also titled the Goddess of Harmony), holding a sword in one hand and a shield in her left. The New York Seal dominates the shield. Behind her are the flags of various nations she has been a part of."

Pepper studied the room. Indeed, it was designed to be opened up from the floor below. The floor that was built under the murals had the effect of putting the viewer very close to the murals.

In other words, the murals were meant to be viewed from forty feet below, not the ten feet of height of this room.

Why didn't they build the room as originally planned? Pepper wondered.

She stepped into the center of the room and looked up at the murals. There was an impressive goddess, the symbol of New York, in the center. And four flags on each corner surrounded her.

Pepper looked closely. An American flag was above her left shoulder.

A star was in the middle, the same size as the other stars.

Pepper counted the stars that encircled it. The artist Dodge made the flag as though it were flying in the breeze.

Some of the stars were not visible.

I joined her in the center of the room. And I looked up.

We tried to count the stars but had to estimate how many because of the flow of the flag.

Pepper looked at me.

"There are 11 stars circling the 12th," she said. And she counted them out.

She was right. It was a 12-star flag.

I went back to the literature desk and asked the attendant how many stars were encircling the star in the middle. Pepper joined me.

The lady said there were 12, "because it represents the original 13 colonies."

"What?" I thought. "That doesn't make any sense."

Pepper pulled me aside. "Let's go; we've seen everything we need here."

Just then, the tour guide was coming with the remaining part of her tour. The veteran and his wife had dropped out. So did the senior citizens. All that remained was the homeschooling family.

I squeezed past them on the way out.

The tour guide shot me a dirty look.

Chapter Thirteen

"The yellow flag, with the rattlesnake in the middle, and the words underneath, "Don't tread on me," the standard for the Commander-in-chief of the American Navy, was probably the flag referred to by Paul Jones, in his journal."

– The National Flag of the United States, by Schuyler Hamilton, Lippincot, Philadelphia, 1853

We found a little diner some miles away from the Albany Capitol. Pepper was running all of the details through her head out loud.

"None of this adds up," she said. "If the 12-star flag is such a big secret, why is it right there in plain view?"

"The other thing I just can't figure out is the number 12," she continued. "There were 13 states that signed the Declaration of Independence and 13 states that formed the United States."

"Are we sure about that?" I asked.

I then repeated Professor Mac's lying quote.

"That which is taken for the truth is often a lie;

And that, believed a lie, is often the truth."

The waitress came to the table. Pepper and I ordered the same thing we always did at diners: a cheese, lettuce, and tomato sandwich with french fries and a milkshake. It felt like we were back at Brown.

"Did he tell you any of the lies?" she inquired.

I had to go to the bathroom, but I wanted to finish the point.

"Professor Mac said our history was changed by the establishment. That lies were necessary to cover up truths. And that these lies became the norm in our schools so the people would think like the establishment wanted them to."

I recounted what the Professor said.

"The history of the birth of the United States of America is not true. He said 1776 is not the birthday of the USA and that the Declaration of Independence and the Revolution were not a war for our nation's independence."

She was staring at me intently.

I tried to remember the other lie. From Great Britain?

"Oh, and the Constitution did not come from 'We The People,' nor did it create the nation we have today."

She didn't say anything and kept staring at me, her finger on her lips. Then she spoke.

"Hackworth, all that's nonsense. Of course, there was a Declaration. Why do we celebrate July 4 then? And there most definitely was a Revolution against Great Britain; my relatives fought in it! And I have seen the actual Constitution in Washington, DC, and it most definitely starts with the words "We The People."

"That's basically what I said to him," I replied.

"But that is exactly what he taught us at Brown," she said.

"I know."

The waitress came to the table with our milkshakes. We both loved black and whites made with vanilla ice cream and chocolate syrup.

"What if our history is like this milkshake?" she said.

"Huh," I said, still working the straw.

"What are you drinking?" she asked.

"A black and white milkshake."

"And what is it made of?"

"Vanilla ice cream and chocolate syrup."

"Well, Hackworth, what if our true history is the vanilla ice cream and the lies Professor Mac refers to are the chocolate syrup?"

"What?" I didn't follow her reasoning.

"In other words, what Professor Mac is saying is that our true history has been flavored differently, so that it becomes something different altogether."

"That's it," she said, without waiting for my reply. "That is what he means when he calls it a lie. Our history has been twisted. It has been changed and tweaked, but the essence is the same."

The sandwiches and fries came. I asked for extra mayo on the side, but the waitress didn't bring it.

"And maybe the Constitution is like the cheese, and the Declaration is the tomato," I said sarcastically. "You may be on to something, Pepper. We could have a History Channel show on the Food Network!"

I laughed at my own joke. She didn't.

"You are exactly right, you idiot," she said.

"Huh?" I said, taking a bite.

"All history is written so that you come away with a certain taste, a certain understanding of the past, *and not another*."

I finished my sandwich and excused myself to the bathroom. Pepper went to work on her meal.

The diner was a roadside establishment, serving good homestyle food at reasonable prices—a reminder of what travel dining was like before national hamburger chains dominated the new interstates and killed regional ethnic cuisine.

That is what I thought when I passed the other customers on the way into the bathroom. On the way out, an old cloth dryer was used to dry my washed hands, the kind with the towel in a white box that you kept pulling around a circle to find a clean spot.

There was no clean spot. The towel didn't look like it had been changed in years.

I walked back into the dining room and was stunned.

Someone was sitting in my seat!

I couldn't make out who, just a pair of hunched shoulders.

I could see Pepper was nervous.

I froze. This wasn't right. I sensed a great danger.

Pepper looked up at me. She was about six tables away. The man with the hunched shoulders reacted and turned.

I felt like leaving, but what about Pepper?

"Stay strong, Hackworth," the voice said in my head. "Stay strong."

I took a deep breath and walked with purpose to the table.

"Come on, Pepper, we're getting out of here."

"No, no," she said. "Sit down, Hack; Mr. Clark wants to speak with us."

"I don't think that is a good idea."

"Just sit," she said, sliding in on the booth bench seat. I hesitated and looked at him, then sat down.

"Tell him what you just told me," Pepper said.

Vaughn Clark slowly picked up a french fry—one of my french fries—and placed it in his mouth.

He slowly chewed it.

"You can cut the tough trooper crap," I said. "Tell me how you found us here. Did you slap a tracking device on the car at the roadblock?"

He looked up at me. His light blue eyes were not like those of a trooper at all. They had warmth and sincerity in them.

There was something about this guy that you trusted. You did not feel ill at ease.

"Maybe," he replied and paused. "Look, I am not your enemy. I am your friend. We have the same cause."

"And what cause is that?" I said.

"The truth," he said. "The American truth."

"Then start telling us the truth," I said. "Did you kill Professor Redmand?"

"No, of course not."

"Who did?"

"I don't know," he replied.

The waitress came over and interrupted us. She asked him what he wanted.

"Water," he replied, grabbing another fry in a deliberate way. The waitress left.

"Who do you think killed Professor Redmand?"

"Who do I suspect?" he said. "Probably the Feds or someone associated with them."

"Are you with the Feds or associated with them?" I responded.

He laughed. He had a great smile. Nice white teeth.

"That's funny," he said. "No, no, I am not."

"Then why are you here?"

"Because we have the same cause."

The conversation wasn't going anywhere.

Pepper broke in.

"Mr. Clark, you told me before that you were with SOL. What exactly is SOL?"

He again grabbed a fry and deliberately placed it in his mouth. You could tell he did not want, or could not tell us.

"SOL is an ancient group of Americans who seek after and defend freedom and liberty."

"Ancient group? Like the Freemasons?"

"Sort of," he said.

Pepper asked again. "What is SOL? What do the letters stand for?"

He was looking at the fries. I almost told him if he took another one off my pile, he could pay the bill.

He looked up from the table.

"Before I answer that, I need to know something," he said.

"What's that?" Pepper said. The way she said it told me she was suspicious.

"I need to know if you still have the, um, flag."

"Flag, what flag?" I said in a mocking tone.

"The flag I tried to take from you in the cab."

There was silence at the table.

"The flag Professor Redmand gave you."

He looked straight at Pepper.

"Our flag."

Pepper and I glanced at each other.

"Whose flag?" Pepper said.

"Our flag," he replied. "Do you have our flag?"

"Are you saying the SOL owned this flag?"

He was becoming annoyed. His voice turned a little firmer.

"Yes, it is our flag. Do you have it?"

Pepper nodded in the affirmative.

"We want it back," he said.

Pepper answered him. "I was given that flag by someone who owned it. Now I own it."

"That person did not have a right to give it to you," he said. "That was a *mistake*."

The way he said the word mistake suddenly made him sound more sinister. I was getting nervous.

"How do you know who gave it to me?" Pepper asked.

"Because Professor Redmand was a long-time SOL member."

"I think this meeting is over," I said. "I can guarantee you, Professor Mac was not involved with the likes of you."

"Hold on," Pepper said. "I need to know. What is the SOL? What does SOL mean?"

Vaughn Clark knew he could not evade the question again. If we were going to get anywhere, he had to answer her.

He took a deep breath, then breathed out.

"Sons of Liberty."

Chapter Fourteen

"Don't fire, until you see the white's of their eyes."

– Massachusetts Colonel William Prescott's order to his soldiers holding Bunker (Breeds) Hill, at the Battle of Bunker Hill June 17, 1775. The British won the battle, but at a great cost of soldiers. It was just two months after the first shots were fired at Lexington and Concord and like those battles, it told the British and the world that America wasn't going down easy.

The waitress came to the table and asked if we needed anything more. I ordered another shake. Pepper got nothing, and Vaughn Clark just asked for a refill of his water.

Tory had texted me that the Sons of Liberty were founded in protest of the Stamp Act of 1765. I recalled that the British Parliament passed the tax to help pay the enormous debts incurred defending the colonies in the French and Indian War, but it violated colonial charters. The war ended in 1763. With their founding, the Sons of Liberty began organizing up and down the coast, laying the groundwork for the Revolution they would help lead ten years later.

"I know about the Sons of Liberty," Pepper said, "but that was 250 years ago. I never heard they were around today."

"We have always been around," Vaughn Clark said. "And we trace ourselves back to the settlement of America."

The waitress refilled his water glass.

He continued.

"There are periods in history, units of time, in which society is stable and the economic conditions are suitable for the people to thrive. Likewise, there are periods of upheaval, war, revolution, famine, and social change.

"Think of a see-saw. One end is stability, acceptance, and prosperity. Where the people are free to live and express themselves as they see fit and make their own decisions. Be protected by their government.

"The other end is authoritarianism, bondage, and little prosperity except for the powerful and well connected. Where people are taught what to think and are slaves to their circumstances, where decisions about education, take-home pay, mortgage rates, food prices, taxes, social policy, and etiquette are determined by others that they must obey."

He took a sip of water and continued speaking.

"These periods have a halfway point, where the see-saw is not all one way or the other. Tipping points. And when the seesaw tips toward total control, there is a natural resistance to push to the other side and restore freedom and liberty.

"Such points in history are easily seen from today's vantage point. The Stamp Tax protests in the 1760's would be the start of the Revolution of 1776. The unrest of the 1850's would be the start of the Civil War in 1861. The rigid, conformist society of the 1940's and 50's would lead to the counterculture of the 1960's."

"Are we at a tipping point now?" Pepper asked.

"You know the answer to that question."

Pepper nodded her head as if she understood.

"But you are a State Trooper," I said. "It doesn't make any sense that you would be involved with such a group."

"Name every hero from our revolutionary past. They were all involved in such a group."

He paused and looked at me. "And you are involved, too."

"How so?"

"Are you not sitting here now with me? Aren't government agents looking for you? Watching you?"

"Well, then I don't want to be involved."

"Good, then give me the flag," he replied.

The meeting had come to a standstill. Vaughn Clark rose from the table.

"Here is how you can get in touch with me," he said, handing Pepper a card.

"But I warn you: as long as you have our flag, you are in danger. They will stop at nothing to get their hands on it."

We just looked at him.

He left the diner.

Pepper got up and went to the other side of the booth. She then leaned in and started talking. It was like she thought the diner had ears; she was so close and whispering.

"Look what it says on this card," she said.

There wasn't a name, phone number, or address.

Just this:

Friday

Franklin Institute

Midnight

"I think Vaughn Clark is asking you out on a date this Friday," I joked.

"Hackworth, I think he's inviting us to one of their SOL meetings."

We figured out the note must be referencing the Franklin Institute in Philadelphia.

The meeting was in two days.

"We're going," Pepper said. "We need to know more about these people."

"The odd thing is, Pepper, this was the next location on Professor Mac's instructions. He said, 'Philadelphia's truth is right before your eyes.' How could he have known to tell me this if he didn't know about the meeting?"

Pepper tapped her finger against her lips.

"Professor Mac was obviously a member of the Sons of Liberty. I think we need to go somewhere before Philadelphia."

"Where?"

"Back to Providence and the professor's secret room."

"Are you nuts?"

"Yes, I think I am," she said. "I have been letting Professor Mac lead me as if this is a school project. I am not in school anymore, and I want to get to the bottom of this now."

"But that's the place he was murdered."

"I know," she said.

Pepper's idea to go back to Boston and Providence instead of Philadelphia had one upside: less time driving. From Albany, Boston was half as far as Philly.

She was right. Professor Redmand was probably a member of the Sons of Liberty. And the answers to our problems very well lay in his secret chamber.

That was the kind of educator he was: he would dangle the carrot, make you want it, and then use your curiosity as a force to keep you moving forward. He was the best teacher.

We got into the Mustang and headed towards the Mass Pike. We were going back to Boston to prepare for the visit to Professor Mac's house in Providence.

"I am not making the same mistake twice," Pepper said. "These interstates are a way to control and monitor us."

"In a way, that's why they were built," I said. "The federal law that created the interstate was called the National Interstate and Defense Highways Act. Its roots go back to 1922, when the feds asked General Pershing to create a map of roads necessary for defense. After General Eisenhower saw the Germans' Reichsautobahn during World War II, he realized the great value of a national road system for defense purposes."

"Great," Pepper laughed. "Another innovation brought to you by the Nazis!"

"Are you kidding me?" I said. "Interstates are awesome. And the fact is, the superhighways originally began in the States. The Pennsylvania Turnpike was the oldest expressway in America, built by Pennsylvania starting in 1940. Same with the Mass Pike, started in 1957."

"Then why do I see that Interstate symbol?" Pepper said.

"Because the states were enticed to make their expressways part of the national system."

"You mean they were bought off?" Pepper said.

"Exactly," I replied.

"Doesn't that seem to be the way of our world?" Pepper said. "We trade our freedom for convenience. The interstates provide us great convenience to move about fast, while at the same time giving the government the power to quickly deploy soldiers to quell rebellion."

"Or, more likely, to fight off invaders," I said. "What you said is almost a metaphor for the internet. Except we trade our privacy for convenience. The internet provides us great convenience to get information, while at the same time giving corporations and the government the power to monitor what we are thinking and doing."

Pepper pulled over and consulted an old, paper map to find the best route to Boston via the back roads.

"Ah, old school," I joked. She smiled.

"The thing that scares me," she said as the car pulled back onto the road, "is how everybody is ensnared, whether on the interstate or on the internet. The government has gained power to monitor and control us."

"Or so they want you to think! They can monitor us, but control us? Not if we don't let them." I said.

As if on cue with our conversation, Pepper stopped the car at a stop sign. A long series of traffic lights could be seen down the main village street we were passing through.

"But everybody is ensnared," she repeated. "Let me give you an example. I am convinced all of this problem began because the government was able to monitor my internet searches. It wasn't that they were targeting me because they thought I was a criminal; they FOUND ME because of what I was thinking."

She continued: "And they probably found out about the Sons of Liberty and others this way."

"I remember my father used to keep a picture of me as a little girl in his wallet, and he would take it out on his travels and show it, then put it back into his pocket," she said. "If he were alive today, he would show not only pictures but videos, stored in the cloud or on a phone where anyone can view them."

"You know what is really creepy, Pepper? It's that the people watching us, spying on us, reading our emails, posts, and searches are the military, or at least, have military weapons and tactics."

"I guess we got that idea from the Nazis as well," I added.

We were both quiet. We knew at least some of this was true, but it had not stopped us all of these years. The conveniences—the better way of living—were more important than our freedom and privacy.

The subject died, and we remained quiet. The truth was the truth, and there was nothing we could do about it.

Finally, I broke the silence.

"I wanted to ask you about something said back in Albany. The tour guide said that the American flag did not mean to the Revolutionary generation what it means to us today. Is that true?"

"Yes, it is true," she said. "That's probably because the Revolutionary generation lived under a monarchy. And at that time the King's flag belonged to the King and national government, not the people."

"But the tour guide said during the Revolution that state flags were the norm," I said.

"Yes, but there were other flags, like the rattlesnake 'Don't Tread On Me' flag. There was also the Rhode Island flag with the anchor symbol of the state with 13 stars," she said. "My favorite Revolutionary War flag was the Beaver Flag used by the New Yorkers. It was based on the Dutch Beaver Flag that was used when New York was New Netherlands."

"A beaver? Our forefathers fought under a beaver flag?"

"Well, some New Yorkers did anyway," she said. "Different states fought under their own state banner."

We talked about the Marine veteran and how he became upset hearing the tour guide talk about the flag.

"Do you blame him?" she said. "Imagine fighting in Iraq, Vietnam, or Korea and watching your buddies get killed defending that flag. You wouldn't like someone telling you it wasn't there at the beginning."

"Especially if you were taught it was," I interjected.

"The American Flag is the one symbol that is above politics," Pepper said. "It is something we all can rally around. Think about what happened the day after September 11. Everyone flew their flag. I remember seeing a flag on every building, people wearing pins of the flag, and newspapers printing full pages of the flag to be hung as well."

"It's been that way since the Civil War," she continued, pressing down on the gas pedal. "When the Confederates fired upon Fort Sumter in Charleston Harbor, what do you think the northern newspapers reported?"

She paused and looked at me. I was hanging on every word.

"They reported THE FLAG WAS FIRED UPON," she said. "And with all of the veterans in the north who had fought in the Mexican War or in the Indian Wars, this was tantamount to treason."

"In fact, the first recorded mass display of the American flag was during the Civil War," she said.

It made sense. The flag rose above all politics; it unified the nation. It was a symbol that brought people together.

And the government understood this very well.

Suddenly, the facts were starting to make sense. If the American flag was the great unifier and the government knew this and used it to their advantage, then the government would go to great lengths to preserve and promote the flag's power.

"Pepper, I think I've got it. The 12-star flag must contradict the government in some powerful way for it to go to such lengths to conceal it."

"I know that," she said. "Remember, I said that what was in the box would cause an earthquake? I said that not because I knew why, but because I knew the lengths being taken against me."

"The flag must contradict them. But how?"

"I think it goes to the lies Professor Redmand talked about," she said. "The flag becomes a propaganda tool; a story is built around it that makes people associate the flag with the government. So, the flag and government become synonymous. One becomes the other."

"But what if, in truth, the flag and the government are not one?" she said. "What if they stole the flag and its meaning to increase their power?"

"That sounds like a great defense when they arrest you," I joked. "Your honor, I did not steal the flag—the government did!"

"Funny," Pepper said.

And then she burst into laughter.

Our conversation had eaten up a lot of road time quickly. We didn't mind driving the local roads while we were so engaged. We drove through a small, rural village, and Main Street was lined with American flags.

"Americans sure love the Red, White and Blue," she said.

Chapter Fifteen

"We have it in our power to begin the world over again."

– Thomas Paine, Common Sense

We arrived in Boston and headed to the Charlestown Marina. My phone started vibrating, and I knew it was Tory—he was the only one who had the number.

Hey Hack! Sorry for the delay. I've been researching the American Revolution, and the more I read, the more stuff is unearthed that I think you'll want to know. Our history has been reduced to a collection of cliches that don't even scratch the surface. Dad's working on Saturday, so we don't have to...T

Yikes, work! I needed to check in with the office.

I called the office secretaries unlisted phone line, even though it was late. It was installed by the senior executives, who were annoyed when they were put on hold. Rosemary and Naomi were the office secretaries, and they both loved me.

Rosemary answered.

"Hack, where are you?" she asked. "Don't you look at your phone? We have texted you, called you, and emailed you."

"You're in big trouble," she said.

"I've been in bed and just been able to get the strength up now," I said in my classic fake-sick voice.

"Oh, really," she responded.

"And why doesn't your number come up on the board? Are you in trouble?" she continued.

Busted.

"Are you OK?" she asked with concern in her voice. She could sense that I was holding back.

"No, no, I ..."

But she interrupted, "Because two federal agents have come by looking for you."

She paused.

"Brian Trowbridge and Neuman Church," she said. "What have you done?"

"What did they say I did?" I asked. My fake-sick voice was morphing into my nervous voice.

"They didn't say anything. They did say you would know what it was all about. And they told me to call them the minute you made contact with the office."

"Don't do that, Rosemary," I said.

"Of course not," she replied. Rosemary and Naomi were both Puerto Ricans. They knew how to look after each other and thankfully looked out for me.

"Are you in trouble?" she asked again.

"I can't talk right now, but I need you to cover for me," I begged.

"I will as long as I can, but editorial is looking for your interview with the ink product manager, and the deadline is Friday," she said. "Just saying..."

Ugh! Rosemary instantly put my mind into the boring life I had been living before this all began. Before there were flags, secret rooms, and murder. Before there was Pepper back in my life.

Whatever danger the present situation posed, at least I got to be with Pepper. And the way my heart beat these last few days, it would be hard to go back to the drone-worker life of water coolers and secretaries.

"Cover for me, please, Rosemary. I will check in again soon."

Pepper was tapping the clock on the dashboard. The call was coming on one minute, after which it could be traced—or so we thought based on TV reruns.

"Stay safe, Hack," she said.

Pepper parked several blocks from the marina, and we took the back way to get there. We passed the spot where the black yacht was; it had left.

We made our way onto the boat, expecting to find it ransacked by the spies looking for the flag. But it was just as we left it.

We had picked up some Chinese food on the way and set about eating it in the galley. Pepper was lost in thought eating General Tso's chicken as I ate beef and broccoli.

"We have to be prepared to stay a while in the professor's secret room," she said. "I was only there for a second, and only halfway down the stairs. But I sensed there were lots of books, papers, and other things. And other rooms."

"What are we looking for?"

"The answers to all of this," she said. "I know, or should I say my intuition is telling me, that the answers are in that room."

It seemed logical. Professor Redmand had gone to great lengths to conceal his studies, and he must have devoted a large portion of his life to maintaining such a collection.

"We will need to bring food, maybe even sleeping bags and pillows," she said.

"Sleeping bags? We are going to stay overnight there?"

"Yes, maybe several nights," she said. "I am not leaving Providence without answers. And I am sick and tired of driving around looking for clues."

Pepper went to the refrigerator and returned with two bottles of Mexican Coca-Cola (the kind with real sugar, unlike the cheaper corn syrup version sold in the states).

"We eat Chinese and drink Mexican," I said. "God Bless America."

We settled in the living room and picked up on our conversations. Pepper had said yesterday that this whole thing started as a result of working on the book *So Proudly We Hail*. She said that the Commodore and Admiral had made reference to the fact that George Washington's diaries from April 1789 to July 1789 were missing.

"Let's talk about what happened in April 1789," I said.

Her eyes lit up.

"That month is when George Washington, the first president, was inaugurated in New York," she said.

"But why is that significant?"

"I am not sure," she said. "But if we stay on the surface without knowing the facts, we could say it was the beginning of the country we know today. The Constitution went into full effect with his inauguration, and the federal government began."

"Began. That is an interesting word."

"How so?" she said.

"Well, if something begins, that means it is implemented. Washington implemented the federal government for the first time."

She interrupted. "And wrote down his thoughts, feelings, and plans about the start of the government. And it is those thoughts, feelings, and plans that no longer are known!"

"That's it," I said. "Washington obviously wrote something that doesn't wash with the official history. Those diaries are missing because the Father of Our Country expressed ideas that contradict what became the government's narrative."

Pepper nodded in agreement. "Precisely right. And those diaries mention the flag, or else the Commodore and Admiral would not have mentioned them in the first place."

Pepper had said earlier that it had taken the two Navy men fourteen years for the book to be published, and it became available only after both of them were dead.

"Tell me again, why were men from the Navy involved in writing a book about the flag?" I asked.

"Because the Navy was the primary user of flags during the Revolution," she said. "Think about it. The states are all maritime-based. The oceans were the first superhighways connecting them to each other and the world. And when you're at sea and fighting the enemy, you need to know from a distance who is a friend and who is a foe."

"John Paul Jones, the Father of the U.S. Navy, was the first to actually fly flags on December 3, 1775, on the *Alfred*," she said.

"Flags?"

"Navy flag ships fly three flags: the ensign, the jack, and the flag of the commanding officer," she said.

Pepper explained that the ensign is flown at the stern (rear) of the ship, the jack from the bow (front), and the commanding officer flag from the main mast.

"Well, what flags did John Paul Jones fly?" I said, sensing we were finally getting somewhere.

Pepper wasn't going to answer me just yet. She shared what she learned from reading the book authored by the Commodore and Admiral.

She explained that the Continental Congress instructed Washington to borrow from the Council of Massachusetts Bay two armed ships, and, together with vessels from Rhode Island and Connecticut, the Continental Navy was born.

Washington also purchased and outfitted his own two ships and called them the *Franklin* and the *Lynch*. They were joined by four others: *Lee, Harrison, Lady Washington,* and *Warren*.

It was the *Lee* that captured the British supply ship *Nancy*, loaded with muskets, shot, and gun powder. Capturing these war supplies was the whole purpose of outfitting the ships.

"Would you get to the flags, please?" I said as she walked into the galley to get two more Cokes.

"I am, but you needed to hear all of that to understand," she said. "Of these ships, the *Lady Washington* was captured by the British, and her flag was taken."

"One flag or three flags?" I asked.

"Just one," she said. "And that flag is still on display in London's Admiralty Office."

"And it was..."

I made a gesture with my hand as if to lead her.

"You won't believe it," she said.

"A 12-star flag?" I said.

"No, silly," she said, purposely dragging it out.

"I give up," I said, putting my hands up in a mock surrender.

"The flag was white with a pine tree in the center and words in all capitals above it. The words said, 'AN APPEAL TO HEAVEN.'"

Silence. We didn't speak for several minutes.

"The first flag was a pine tree and an appeal to heaven?" I asked in disbelief. "Wow!"

"Yes, this flag was flown on all of the ships under Washington's command, according to Commodore McCandless," she said.

"Is that the flag John Paul Jones flew?" I asked.

"No," she said. "All the while Washington's fleet was at sea, the Continental Congress named Esek Hopkins commander-in-chief of a squadron it had assembled. He sailed from Newport aboard the Rhode Island warship *Katy* to the Delaware River to take command of the new ships. He met John Paul Jones there, who was in command of the squadron's flag ship, the *Alfred.*"

"What flag did John Paul Jones fly?" I asked again, growing exasperated.

She smiled. She liked being in control.

"The Gadsen flag," she said.

"The what?"

"The rattlesnake on the yellow silk flag," she said.

"You mean..." I stammered. "The 'Don't Tread on Me Flag'?"

"The commander's flag that went up the mainmast was the rattlesnake flag!" she said again.

"And what about the other two?"

"The jack was a flag of 13 red and white stripes with a rattlesnake crawling and the words 'Don't Tread On Me.'"

"And the ensign?"

"That was the Grand Union Flag, which had 13 stripes and a small Union Jack in the canton."

"So where the stars go today, there was a British Union Jack?"
I asked.

"Yes," Pepper said. "And it was this style of flag that Washington raised in Cambridge on the first day the Continental Army came into existence."

When the British saw the flag, they figured it was a sign of loyalty to the King to have the Union Jack present on it. Washington did not get the reaction he expected.

"Commodore McCandless records this fact and then notes that the Grand Union Flag and Stars and Stripes were never carried in the field by the land forces during the Revolution," she said.

"They only carried their state flags, right?" I said. "And the rattlesnake? That's what the tour guide said."

We stared at each other, burned out.

Even under this stress, she was beautiful with little make-up, flat hair, an unflattering shirt, and her hair scrungee now a wrist band.

We stared at each other, nervous.

There was so much to take in, both with the flag business and the Pepper and Me business.

Simultaneously, we stood up and brought our empty bottles to the galley.

And without saying a word, we went to our separate cabins.

LIBERTY

Signing of the Declaration of Independence, 1776 — by John Trumball

THURSDAY

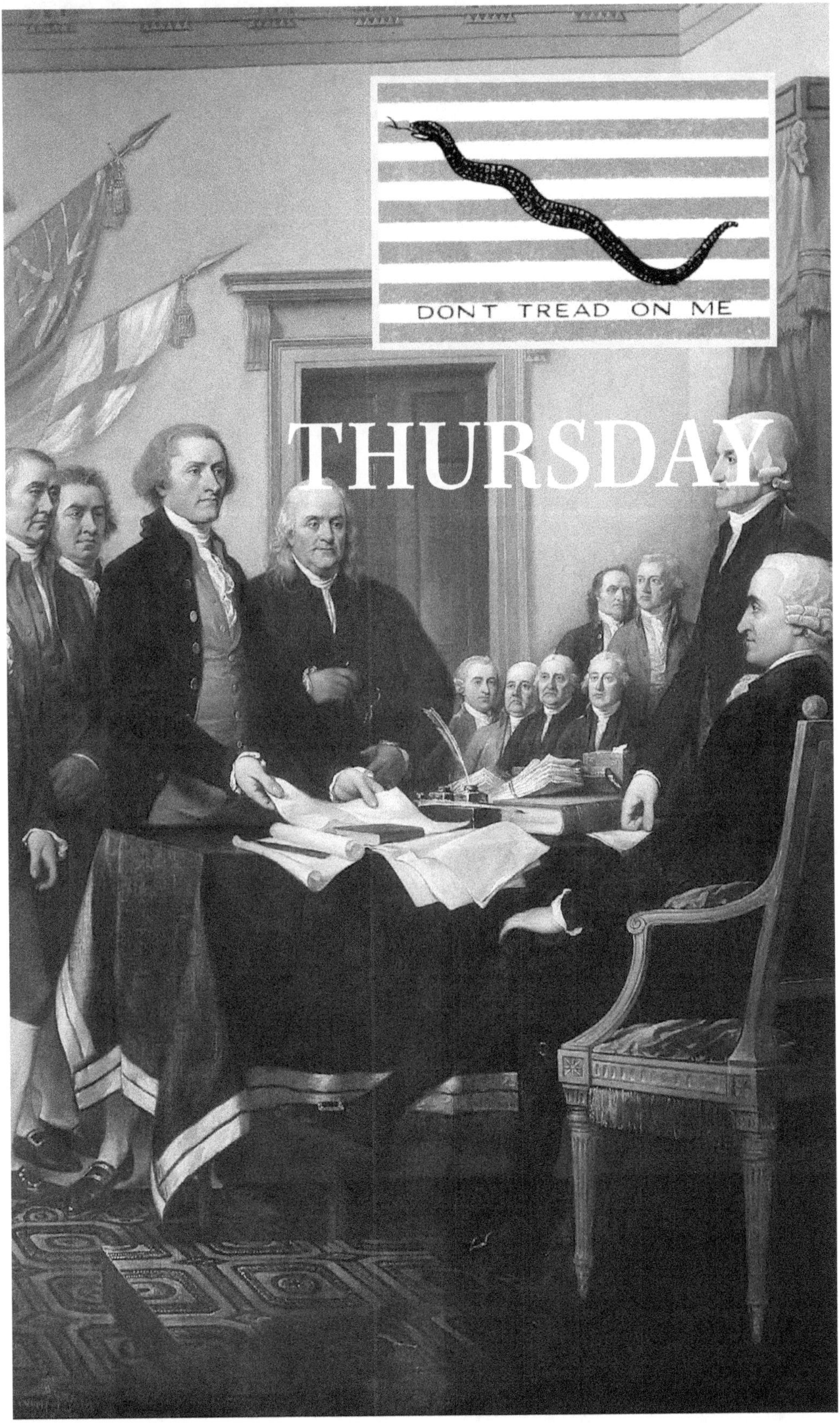

Chapter Sixteen

"The Constitution only guarantees you the right to
pursue happiness. You have to catch it yourself."

– Benjamin Franklin speaking of the Pennsylvania Constitution of 1776

The sound of the coffee machine bubbling its last bubbles woke me. My arm was over my head, covering the right eye. My cabin was so cozy, like a soft bed in a closet. Back and forth, back and forth—the boat gently rocking throughout the night—meant the best sleep in years.

I was having a very lucid dream where everything was vibrant, important, and remembered. I was dreaming about Pepper, or more precisely, I was dreaming about Pepper and me.

The smell of coffee filled the boat.

Not wanting the dream to stop, I tried to focus my mind and stay in that place of bliss. We weren't talking at this moment; we were just staring at the geese in the little pond. It was a place we could be alone and one we visited often while at Brown.

The last gurgle of the machine forced my left eye open. Through the barely cracked cabin door, I could see Pepper was in the kitchen.

The dream was over. And what I saw awake was better than a dream—to see Pepper moving about without making a sound, stuffing a backpack with food and supplies. She was very organized and meticulously planned things out.

She was so focused on the task at hand, she didn't notice me watching her.

Pepper glowed. I guess that's the only way to say it. She didn't need makeup to make her skin glow. The fire was inside her and shot out of every pore. She didn't need to put on an air of a determined, honest, and sincere soul. It radiated from her. She didn't need colored contact lenses to make her eyes blue.

She didn't have to do any of those things because she was those things. There was nothing fake about her.

Her black hair could go from flat to poof with just a change of the weather. It was flat at the moment, scrunchied into a ponytail.

Pepper looked up to the highest shelf of the cupboard, then bit gently on her lip and squinted her eyes slightly. She made that look, which indicated she was concentrating on the difficult task at hand.

That look meant she was not going to give up.

I quickly shut my eyes to feign sleep, wanting a few more minutes of watching her. Of remembering her when we were closer, back in college and elementary school.

Her eyes squinting, and the bite of her lower lip—that was the look she gave me when I told her our relationship was over.

She said that would mean she would date other guys. I played it cool, like it didn't bother me.

It's true; it didn't bother me. It absolutely killed me. Pepper was the first girl I was completely in love with—mind, body, and soul.

Just the thought of her with another guy was more than I could take. The feeling inside was like that of a demon. A demon awoke when I thought of the two of them together. A demon that could only be exorcized by putting Pepper out of my mind. By forgetting about Pepper.

She dated a basketball player. A guy who didn't really love her but loved the idea of getting her. Every time I saw them together, the demon would awaken in me.

Every time I saw her in Professor Mac's class, the demon was there.

What was the feeling? I guess it was wounded pride because she rejected me.

But it was something more than that. Pepper had thrown away everything we had by cheating with the basketball player while we were still together. It was like I didn't matter anymore. She was not only rejecting me; she was rejecting "us" and all that we had built since we were little kids.

One day we were having a sandwich in the campus cafe when a friend of mine came up to our table with the basketball player. It was the first time she met him. The animated, lively Pepper I knew became the super-animated, super-lively Pepper I didn't know.

You know when someone's energy is totally focused on another person, so much so that there isn't enough to sustain the energy with anyone else. Well, the four of us could feel that.

Pepper and this guy had a magnetic attraction, and the energy between them locked in to the exclusion of everyone else.

She was laughing at something he said, then slapped him on the shoulder.

Super-lively Pepper was really attracted to this guy.

Over the next several weeks, we went on like nothing happened. Pepper was the same fun girl, and our relationship was the same as it had been.

But whenever the basketball player appeared, and it was increasingly often, Super-Lively and Super-Animated Pepper appeared. It was like he was able to make the genie come out of the bottle.

Her smile would get bigger. Her laugh was louder. She would end up jokingly hitting him on the shoulder.

Soon they would hug when they met, like they were long-lost friends.

I hated the basketball player. He already dated ten of the hottest girls, and now it was Pepper's turn to be taken away by Prince Charming.

A loud noise came from the galley. Pepper was stuffing the backpack, and a can of tuna fish fell from it. She looked up. I gave her a quick shrug and turned to my side, no longer able to watch her.

You see, just thinking about the basketball player even now disturbed me so much that I didn't want to look at her anymore. I turned and looked at the wood ceiling and thought about how it all ended up.

After one more encounter of Pepper and the basketball player meeting, hugging, joking, and laughing, I had it out with her.

Or should I say, the demon jumped out of me and had it out with her. At that moment, I knew the demon's name.

It was Jealousy. "How can you take on like this with him when I am standing right next to you?" I asked her.

She denied there was any chemistry between them.

She denied and denied. And every time they met thereafter, and every time the Super-Animated Pepper broke forth for him, jealousy raged inside.

Until the day I caught them.

Professor Mac was taking the class to the original state capitol in Newport for a special study. For some reason, the basketball player was in the building that day. I don't know why, because he was not in our class.

I think he was stalking her.

Pepper and him hugged when they met, and I could tell she knew I was watching them. So she was very careful to feign no interest because she had told me—or told the demon Jealousy—that there were no feelings between them.

She hugged him the way a girl hugs her brother—you know, the arms extended and the hips back so no body parts came into contact.

The basketball player would have nothing of it. He pulled her close to him and started making soft circles on her back.

This guy was a pro. He was like a farmer who knows how to stroke his animals to get them through the gate.

Their faces were inches apart.

She pulled away and forced him to let go.

Did she do that for my benefit? I would find out 15 minutes later. The class had now started a little tour of the building's second-floor library when I had to excuse myself and go to the bathroom in the basement.

When I went back upstairs, the class was not there. Professor Mac must have taken them somewhere else. Looking for the class, I walked into the old library and turned around a book shelf, and there, right before me, were Pepper and the basketball player, tightly embracing and kissing with her arms around his neck.

She wasn't fighting him off, like she did a little while ago.

And their bodies were close.

Just as they paused in their kissing, Pepper turned and saw me, and as she tried to pull back once again, the basketball player took his left hand and turned her face to his. The way his huge hand held her head, he might as well have been palming a ball.

She didn't resist.

And me? My face dropped, my shoulders sagged, and my back hunched over.

I walked away.

On the bus back to campus, she sat with me. The basketball player wasn't there. He had disappeared. Pepper looked all concerned and upset. I couldn't figure out if she was upset about hurting me—or hurting us—or if she was upset because she was caught.

When we finally had a chance to talk, the demon Jealousy came out, and I lost it. I was crying. She was crying.

And then, in one swoop, I killed "us."

We agreed to break up and see whomever you wanted to see. And except for Tory's Christmas party, we never really saw each other again for years.

Until now.

I stuffed the demon back deep inside and let him come out every now and then to haunt me whenever I thought about Pepper. The demon knew just how to do it—how to get me thinking about her, about everything, right up to them together in the old library.

The demon never aged and never got tired. It was always ready to come out whenever my mind summoned her.

Pepper and the basketball player broke up two weeks later. Surprise, surprise! He was on to the next conquest.

But Jealousy's twin demon, Pride, would have nothing to do with her.

She tried to get back together. And not just once.

She tried to get closer. I wouldn't let her.

She tried to have fun together like we used to. Pride said no.

And anytime I thought, "Well, maybe, because I do love her," Pride would join his twin demon Jealousy, and the two would not let me believe.

They convinced me that it was over.

And it was.

Until Pepper texted me three days ago, we had not spoken to each other since the break-up (not including a "Hi" at Tory's party).

And I planned on never seeing her again.

I turned again on the bed and looked through my squinting eyes. Pepper was peering out the galley window as the boat gently rocked.

Pride and jealousy were settling back into their home deep inside of me. Their brief appearance right now made me realize their teeth were gone. They no longer bit my soul. They had lost control over me. And I had contempt for them.

If anything, strangely, their reawakening had actually stirred something inside of me.

They made me want her more than ever.

"Get up!" she yelled from the galley. "Come on. I know you aren't sleeping."

"Ahhh," I groaned.

"Don't fake it," she said. "Saw you watching me."

I kept on faking just waking up and did not acknowledge her charge.

"Come on, we have a busy day."

We sat and ate; the only sound I made was the fork hitting the plate to get more of the scrambled eggs.

Pepper, though, was chattering a mile a minute. Flags this, constitution that. I didn't hear a word.

I just pretended to listen to her so I could look at her.

She glowed.

Then she said something that brought me right back to the reality of the moment.

"Professor Mac's full obituary is online," she said. "Read it."

There on the screen was a picture of the now deceased professor, a picture of him from like 1950. Why is it they run these pictures of the person you never knew? Those "just out of college" pictures.

"He was a good-looking man," I said, remembering that Professor Mac was infatuated with Pepper's charms, which she poured on any professor to bump up her grades.

The obituary provided the standard facts. He had been married for 30 years before his wife passed away. He attended Columbia University, where he received his doctorate in American history. His entire career was at Brown. He was a congregationalist and a member of the United Ministry in Providence.

Come to think of it, Professor Redmand looked like a Presbyterian minister. Tall, thin, and formal.

There was the part of him being a vexillologist and a past president of some society of vexillologists.

"Professor Redmand worked for one year at Yale University, helping establish the Avalon Project, which collected and catalogued early American documents. His work included a six-month stint at the University of Virginia studying George Washington's extensive writings," the obituary stated.

I looked up at Pepper.

"Interesting, huh?" she said. "Now I know why he gave me the flag. He must have known about the missing diaries."

There was nothing else to be gleaned from the obituary.

I looked at the picture of Professor Mac one more time. He was my favorite teacher.

"Come on, we're packed and ready to go," Pepper said. "I have flashlights, sleeping bags, and some food. And this."

She held up a small silver object.

"It is a digital spy camera I got a couple of years ago. We will need to record important documents quickly while we are there."

"And what about this?" she asked, pointing to a small pistol kept behind the captain's wheel. A note card said it was a Ladysmith from Smith and Wesson, 5-shot, .38 Special.

"Should we take it?"

Something said we were going to need it. I grew up in the country and was no stranger to pistols, rifles, and shotguns. I carefully picked it up by the handle only, pushed the latch with my thumb, and flicked it open. It was not loaded. Next to the gun was an envelope with five bullets, which I slowly placed in each chamber, then clicked it shut. I double-checked that the safety was on.

Pepper held her hand out flat to take the gun.

"I'll keep it in here. Tell me when you need it."

She put it in the front zippered area of the backpack.

"OK," I said. Both of us knew everything was going to change.

And maybe not for the better.

"Let's go."

Chapter Seventeen

"These are the times that try men's souls. The summer soldier and the sunshine patriot will, in this crisis, shrink from the service of their country; but he that stands for it now, deserves the love and thanks of man and woman."

– *Thomas Paine, December 19, 1776*

For Pepper and me to get to Providence, the drive is about an hour south of Boston. But for Roger Williams, who founded the city, it must have taken days. Fleeing from the crazy Puritans in Salem, MA, Williams founded Providence Plantations, and religious liberty in America was born.

"He was the first in the New World to argue that an individual's conscience could not be controlled by the state," Pepper said. "And the first to secure the right as a fundamental law. He lived his faith, learning native languages and trading fairly with the area's tribes."

"All of this happened around 1643!" she said.

Pepper expertly drove the Mustang into "Little Rhody," the smallest state in the USA. It is the size of a county in other states. Rhode Islanders were and remain fiercely independent. "It seems the very largest and very smallest states have the most state pride," she said.

"A sea-faring people, Rhode Islanders moved cargo between Europe, Africa, the Caribbean, and America. Cargo, including human beings imported as slaves," Pepper said. "The Brown family and namesake of our alma mater were sea-faring entrepreneurs who profited from the slave trade."

Hearing her talk about this reminded me of one of Tory's rants a while ago at the bookstore. I think he actually changed their minds on the matter.

"Slavery wasn't invented in America," Tory once lectured several friendly protestors who had just walked in. "It's been a part of human existence since the beginning of human beings. In fact, it still exists in Africa! And most surprising of all, slavery was banned in America almost a century before the Civil War."

The protestors intently listened to his argument, as did I.

"Vermont banned it in 1777, and the newly independent states did as well, with Pennsylvania in 1780, Massachusetts in 1783, Connecticut in 1784, and Rhode Island in 1784. And in 1787, Congress forbade it in the states that would become Ohio, Indiana, Michigan, Illinois, Wisconsin, and Minnesota!"

To their credit, the protestors gave Tory an honest hearing. We all agreed that when you speak of America and Americans, you should be particular. You must be specific. Which Americans? When? Where? Why?

Pepper raced past the State Capitol, the headlights of the Mustang cutting through an ocean fog drifting in. I looked for The Independent Man statue but couldn't see him. The fog made it appear he was gone.

I turned my head to look where I last saw Professor Redmand, but the fog obfuscated the lawns as well.

Pepper and I were silent on the trip. There was a lot to talk about, but she was intent on driving and getting there.

The time for speculation was over. Pepper was convinced that answers were to be found under Professor Redmand's home.

He lived in College Hill, near the original colonial settlement and Roger Williams' home. We began the incline when the State Capitol appeared again, but this time off in the distance. What an incredible sight, but The Independent Man was still invisible in a dense cloud of fog.

Professor Mac lived in an old, distinctive home built by a seaman in the 1700's in the Federal style. I had never been there, but Pepper was a guest several times when Mrs. Redmand was alive, and they entertained students and professors.

"Where's the police crime-scene tape?" Pepper asked.

There was none. There was something stuck to the front door, but we couldn't make it out. The newspaper said he was murdered in the foyer of the house when burglars forced their way in. The police said there was a struggle and insinuated that the good professor tried to fight off the invaders.

Providence has its share of bad characters, so it seemed as likely he was murdered by criminals as secret agents.

"What are we going to do? Just walk into his house?"

"Exactly," Pepper said. "There is a small patio in the back that is relatively private. We can get in through the back, then get our gear from the car."

The streets were not busy. It was mid-morning on Thursday, and people were at work or in class. Some students were nearby, with earphones in their heads, in their own world, and oblivious to what was happening around them.

Pepper got out of the Mustang and walked to the back of the house like she owned it. I followed.

A small pathway, maybe four feet wide, separated the Redmand house from the neighboring house, which appeared as if no one was in it and had curtains closed.

The people in that house must be at work. So far, so good.

We came around the back. Professor Mac's patio had sliding glass doors into the house. Pepper went to the doors and tried to open them.

They were locked tight.

Off to the side, there were green cellar doors, the kind that lay at an angle, covering steps that go down into the basement. Pepper opened these doors and walked down a couple of steps into a vestibule to reach the cellar door. This door was padlocked shut.

She emerged from the vestibule.

"We will have to break the padlock," she said.

She grabbed her backpack and walked back down the cellar stairs.

I just watched her and the properties in the backyard. Pepper was taking command of this break and entry, and I was happy to let her.

She went to the car and came back with a hammer and chisel.

And then, resting the chisel on the padlock, she took one whack.

WHACK. The noise vibrated out to the top of the vestibule.

"People can hear that," I said, looking left and right.

WHACK. She hit it again. The lock didn't budge.

WHACK. A third time, nothing.

She came up the vestibule steps, walked over to the patio, and sat down on a rusty metal chair. Then she got up and tried one more time.

WHACK. A fourth time, nothing.

"It's not going to be easy," she said.

I looked around, walking over to a concrete wall. The house behind us had a large yard separating the two properties. The house on the other side of the Redmand's looked like student housing.

No one was around.

"Let me give it a try," I said, stepping into the vestibule and placing the chisel on top of the lock.

I hit the chisel as hard as I could.

WHHAACCK.

The padlock gave way and fell to the ground. I looked up, and Pepper was already there.

"I will get the supplies," she said, and in a moment, she returned and threw the sleeping bags down into the vestibule.

She took out a flashlight from the backpack, and then I carefully pulled the slanted cellar doors shut.

It was pitch black. She turned on the flashlight and led the way into the dark basement.

We were in!

Pepper flashed the light around in the basement. The floors were made of concrete and were dirty. An old washing machine was next to an old furnace. A new washing machine and dryer, bright white and clean, were on the other side of the furnace.

Pepper pointed the light at a set of stairs.

"This way," she said.

We ascended the wooden stairs and came to the top. Pepper slowly opened the door, and we were on the first floor.

"This way," she said, leading me into a central hallway. She walked as if she lived there, heading towards the front door.

Suddenly, she stopped. Without saying a word, she pointed to the rug next to the front door.

I looked down and knew immediately what it was.

Two dark red stains were on the carpet.

It was dried blood.

Professor Mac's blood.

She looked right at me. The house was pretty well lit from the sun coming into the front windows. I could see her tremble.

It was right on this spot that Professor Mac died.

We didn't move for a moment, each saying a silent prayer.

We slowly stepped into the parlor off the front door, and I realized this was the library. Old bookcases lined the room—the kind that are built right into the wall. There had to be a couple thousand books, all neatly standing in the cases.

All of them are old. Very old.

Tory could make a mint selling these books.

On one wall was a collection of American history books going back to the first settlements.

In the middle of the room were two club chairs, the kind of small-backed leather loungers you would find at an old-fashioned gentlemen's club in London. Next to each chair was a side table. Nothing was on them except the stains from past beverages that were placed without a coaster.

The room smelled of stale pipe tobacco. I didn't know the professor smoked a pipe, but then I saw on the second table a small box with a pipe on top of it. With his bushy eyebrows and pipe, Professor Mac could pass as Santa Claus, but for his weight.

Pepper went to the bookcase on the right. I went to the window and broke the sheer curtain that covered it.

No one was outside.

And then Pepper stopped.

"I don't know how he did it," she said nervously. "I don't know how he opened this bookcase."

"Try to remember what you saw that night."

She went back to the parlor entrance and, in a hushed tone, said, "He walked over here."

She walked to the bookcase.

"And then he reached in and did something, and the bookcase moved."

A piercing car horn ended her sentence.

Then came the quick, brief sound of a police siren.

"Whirrr. Whirrrrrr. Whir."

We froze. I went back to the window and looked out.

Wouldn't it be our luck that a Providence City Police car was right next to the neighbor's house and had pulled someone over. The policeman got out and walked to the other car.

Pepper's eyes flashed towards me.

I shook my head, put my palms out, and nodded, "It's OK."

The flash of the police car lights made the room glow red, then nothing, then red. A stripe of red light, and then nothing.

For about ten minutes, we did not move and waited. Finally, the pulsating red ended, and the policeman gave the ticket and went on his way.

I walked to the bookcase. "Is this where he put his hand?"

"I'm not sure," she replied.

I looked at the books at this location. At first glance, they seemed to be a multi-volume encyclopedia set. All the books were of the same tan color, with jagged edges of pages sticking out around the tops of them. There were about 30 of them that looked like this.

I read the spine of one of the books. It read:

Volume XXII

1782

The books were a complete set of the records of the Continental Congress, from 1774 to 1789! The Congress was meticulous in recording reports and debates (or maybe some things were left out).

"Pepper, what did he do to open the case? Did he move a book? Did he pull it or push it?"

"I didn't see," she said. "Couldn't see. His back was to me when I came in."

"But did his hand pull or push?"

"I didn't see, but maybe his hand went in. There must be a lever or something."

I took Volume XXII off the shelf, half expecting this bookcase to magically open.

I studied the shelf. It was just an old mahogany piece of wood with one brass-faced anchor bolt. I tapped the back wall of the case. It was solid mahogany as well.

I put the book back.

And then I repeated this with the volumes surrounding it, carefully taking each book out and examining the shelf.

We were feeling frustrated. And scared. There was an eerie quiet in the house.

My phone vibrated with an incoming message.

"Hey Hack -- FYI -- remember that strange guy looking for the flag book? He just left. He came in and asked how to

get in touch with you. He left his name and #. Still working on the other stuff. -- T"

I read the message to Pepper, then sat down in Professor Redmand's chair.

She was too focused on the bookcase and wasn't listening.

"He was standing right about here, and his body was turned towards me," she said, replaying the scene.

"Where did the case open?" I asked. "Maybe we can pry it loose."

"We walked in here," she said, pointing to a spot on the bookcase. "Right here."

I pulled the books off the shelf, looking for a seam, a latch, or a hinge—anything that would indicate a break in the bookcase.

Nothing happened. It was solid mahogany, except for a brass anchor bolt.

It had been about an hour since we arrived at the house, and we were growing exasperated.

I returned to the leather chair and put my hand on my chin.

"Are you sure you weren't dreaming all of this, Pepper?" I said.

She looked at me, tilted her head, and frowned.

"No, really," I said. "This is all too Harry Potter for me."

"Then leave," she said nastily, turning her back and resuming her search. It was then that I noticed something odd, and a thought came into my head.

What I discovered was that the *Journals of the Continental Congress* were in the middle of the case, surrounded by individual books.

All of Professor Redmand's other book sets were located on the opposite wall, neatly placed together.

I intently studied the other book sets. the *Encyclopedia Britannica* volumes were next to the *Encyclopedia of the English Language* volumes, which were next to the *Yale University History of the World* volumes. The *Catholic Encyclopedia* volumes were next to the massive set of *Messages and Papers of the Presidents*.

Above, the *Harvard Classics* volumes, which were next to the *Colonial Charters and State Constitutions* volumes, which were next to a set of *Elliot's Debates on the Federal Constitution*.

If it had been the Franklin Antiques Bookstore, we would have put the *Journals of the Continental Congress* with these other sets and not with a bunch of individual titles.

"Wait a minute, Pepper."

She was crouching, meticulously looking behind books that could not possibly be the key.

"Professor Redmand would not do something randomly; everything had a purpose. He would have used one of the Journals as a code," I said. "He would have picked a book that had meaning to him, to history, or to something."

She looked puzzled.

"Can't you see him entertaining someone in this library and then saying, 'Where do you think we keep the secret key to my secret room?'"

"OK, I understand," she said. "You mean, he picked a book of special meaning to hide the access point?"

"Exactly. And it is one of those," I said, pointing to the *Journals of the Continental Congress*.

"But we have gone through each one," she said.

I rose from the chair and walked over to her. I scanned the Journal volumes.

My eyes settled on one.

Journals of the Continental Congress

Volume IV

1776

The year 1776 was when the Declaration of Independence was signed.

"It's that one," I said.

Pepper looked at the book and then at me. There was hope in her eyes. She took the book off the shelf.

"Get your flashlight," I said.

Taking it, I carefully examined the bottom, sides, and back of the space.

The light reflected off the brass anchor bolt. But this bolt was different from the others. It was an anchor bolt shaped like a ship's anchor, the symbol of Rhode Island.

I felt around the bolt. Nothing.

Then, for some reason I cannot tell why, I pushed the brass anchor bolt inward as if it were a button.

And in it went, making a clicking sound.

"Pepper!"

The case moved just a little. What had seemed like a solid wall of book-laden mahogany now had a seam in it.

Pepper rushed to the spot and put her hand in the seam.

She pulled on the edge, and the case opened effortlessly, as if it were weightless.

Cool air poured out of the dark void, blowing our hair back and rushing onto our faces.

We both looked at each other with our mouths open, like we had just run a marathon.

I looked down at the bottom of the case and saw wheels upon which it moved. It was amazing how easy it was to move, given the great weight of the books.

I pulled the bookcase open a little more.

Eeeeecccckkkkk. it squealed.

Now, we were really in!

Chapter Eighteen

The cool air pouring through the cracked opening slowly came to a halt. Then it reversed direction. Pepper and I looked at each other as a flowing breeze now came from behind us and into the blackness that lay below.

It felt like we were being drawn down into this chamber. It was a second, separate basement, only much bigger than the one we had first entered.

The faint sound of clicking could be heard, and as our eyes darted to each other, we could make out lights turning on below.

And with those lights, the faint sound of music.

"What the..." Pepper whispered.

We pulled the door open a little more. It glided along the floor with ease, despite being over a foot thick and heavy with books.

The clicking we heard now stopped with the last light being turned on, the one for the circular stairway going down. The staircase was made of the same mahogany as the bookcases—real mahogany, not stained oak like at the bookstore. Ornate spindles held up a thick, dark railing on both sides. It might have come from an old ship that used to access the decks below. It was very old.

"No way did our dear Professor build this," Pepper said as she led the way down to a landing with a small table in the center. The landing was like a mezzanine level just before you entered the theater.

But it wasn't a theater. More like a museum.

"This is where I waited for the Professor!" Pepper exclaimed as we stood on the landing. Exquisite mahogany paneling covered the walls, and now I was certain that this wood came off a seafaring vessel. And judging its age, it probably brought the first settlers to the western shore, for that's what it was in the 1600's: people from the east crossing the ocean and settling on the western shore. It was their west coast.

The music was becoming clearer—a vibrato sound—as we continued downward. The same mahogany that was valuable in ship construction because of its water resistance was also used to make fine musical instruments like violins and cellos.

The music was from the walls themselves, made when the cool air passed through its notches and activated when the book-case door was opened and the air flowed through.

It was an odd tone, a binaural sound—two tones with varied frequencies that the brain converts into one tone.

"Aaa-uuummm," it sang in a steady wave. It wasn't too loud and actually felt like it helped you focus your mind.

I finished the stairs, passing Pepper, who stopped to carefully examine the walls.

"These walls are the same as upstairs," she said.

"Meaning what?"

"Meaning all of this below was probably built at the same time as the house. And the house was built to cover this up."

We came to the bottom floor, stood in the foyer, and took in the elaborate, underground chamber.

A wooden archway served as the entrance. The arch keystone was a carving of the All-Seeing Eye topping the pyramid. Pepper poked my shoulder and pointed at it.

"That's the Eye of Providence. It's like an early version of what is on the $1 bill," Pepper said. "It was first created in 1776 as a symbol of God watching over the American cause."

Below the keystone were four words burned into the mahogany wood.

The words read, "Live Free or Die."

We slowly walked through the archway.

It was like entering a church. It was certainly as dead quiet as an empty church and almost as grand as a cathedral. Yes, it was like a church museum. But looking around, it could also be a meeting chamber, a classroom, or a command center.

It wasn't dirty. It was old, but not dirty. And not moldy in the slightest, either, though a bit chilly.

And like in a church, there was a center aisle (nave) that led to an elevated platform, behind which was a giant illustration of a colonial scene.

And then we saw them and let out a gasp at the same time.

"RATTLESNAKES!"

On each side of the illustration were rattlesnakes—giant tan and gray vipers climbing 20 feet, with 13 rattles on the tail and piercing fangs at the head.

The lighting in this part of the grand chamber made them so real-looking, so lifelike, that we thought for a moment they were actually slithering up the wall.

"I hate snakes," Pepper said.

But the snakes didn't move. The snakes were carved pillars, sort of like Bernini's twisted column in Saint Peter's in Rome. They both faced a flag in the illustration, whose details we could not yet see.

We walked down the center aisle to better take in the scene. The object the snakes were looking at was a flag being raised.

We walked closer, and both started to count the stars on the flag.

"Four, five, six."

"Seven, eight, nine."

"Ten, eleven."

"There are 11 stars in the circle, plus a slightly larger one in the center."

"The snakes are guarding a 12-star flag!" I exclaimed.

We now slowly turned to take in the whole chamber. It was bigger than the house, and how could this be? We did not know. It looked like it was carved out into the street and road in front of the house.

And unlike the basement we first entered, which had a ceiling so low we had to stoop as we walked through it, this rectangular room had at least 20-foot ceilings in various areas.

On each side of the room, going down the length, were white marble busts of heads sitting atop mahogany pedestals. The walls were finished in the same mahogany as the house, and in various places there were more bookcases, though not as many as we had seen.

"The professor did not build this," Pepper whispered, as if not to disturb the ghostly heads that haunted it.

Along the center aisle were a series of tables with meticulously laid-out stacks of paper. Each stack had a tent card with a title on it, identifying the subject of each pile.

We walked down the elevated platform and turned around, looking back from where we came.

There, directly above the Keystone archway, was a large statue of gold.

Pepper and I recognized it immediately.

It was a model of The Independent Man holding his spear atop the State Capitol.

We walked up to it. Our heads were at its feet, as it was resting on a large mahogany base.

It seemed like more than just a replica. It seemed like the artist's model. The detail with its gold coating was breathtaking.

"What is this place?" I asked Pepper.

"I don't know. But I can guess. It seems like a church, but not to worship God. Perhaps it worships liberty," she said. "Could it be that the Sons of Liberty ceremonial meeting hall was meant to instruct people—to pass down through the generations the cause of liberty?"

Behind the golden statue was a row of flags.

"Those are the flags on the top of the map!" Pepper said, leaning down and opening the backpack.

"See, it is," she said, holding the map up to the flags.

I walked closer and saw a plaque that read:

Flags of the American Revolution:

the Rattlesnake Flag,

the Taunton Flag,

the New England Flag,

the Rattlesnake Naval Flag,

the Rhode Island Flag,

the Grand Union Flag,

the Crescent Moon Liberty Flag,

the Appeal To Heaven Flag.

We studied them, looking at the map and then at them.

"What flag is missing in this display?" Pepper asked.

"There's no stars and stripes," I replied. "That's what the tour guide in Albany said: The stars and stripes were never carried during the Revolutionary War."

"Exactly."

We turned and looked around. Pepper gestured left and right, pointing to various wall displays filled with paintings in gold frames. One display was half of a liberty bell, sticking out of the wall. I walked closer to read the plaque under it:

"The Old Statehouse Bell named Liberty

"Proclaim LIBERTY Throughout all the Land

unto all the Inhabitants Thereof," it says

Cracked Tolling For Marshall's Death, 1835

He was Liberty's enemy."

Above the busts were signs in the same style as the entrance.

On one side, it said "Hero." The words were burned into the mahogany wood and finished in a gold metallic paint.

On the other side, it said "Rogue."

We recognized most of the faces on the busts.

Each pedestal had a nameplate, and under the nameplate was a small card with words.

There had to be at least 20 pedestals on each side of the chamber. Or more.

When we had returned to the entrance foyer, we now walked to the Rogue side.

We went to a bust.

It was Alexander Hamilton.

We read the card under his name.

"Father of Wall Street,

Made from 13 Wall Streets

Who Almost Killed the Mother, States

And raised the child for

His friends' profit."

"This is bizarre," I said to Pepper. "Maybe Professor Redmand was nuts?"

"What did he say?" Pepper began. "That which is thought to be the truth is a lie, and the lie is the truth."

I looked at her.

"Hackworth, if you were taught a lie for your whole life, then I can see where this would seem bizarre."

"How did Hamilton almost kill the States?" I asked.

"Beats me," Pepper said. "I do know that Wall Street began when state war debts were assumed by the federal government and Hamilton was in charge of the Treasury. The states used to have their own money, their own custom houses, and their own Wall Street. But now it was consolidated."

We walked to the bust next to Hamilton in the "Rogue's Gallery." It was John Marshall, the famous Supreme Court Chief Justice, who is called the great expounder of the Constitution.

His card read:

"Thief of Washington's Diaries,

Concealer of Madison's Journal,

Perverter of the Constitution
Robber of the Truth, Whose
Cloak He Claims A Right To Wear."

"Your missing diaries, Pepper. John Marshall stole them!"

Her face was expressionless.

"Fascinating," she said. "The provenance of the diaries shows that George Washington left them in his will to his nephew, Bushrod Washington. Bushrod was approached by John Marshall, who took possession of them to write a biography of Washington. As a side note, Bushrod was appointed to the Supreme Court and served while Marshall was Chief Justice."

"Yes, yes," she continued. "That makes sense. I remember reading that Marshall did not take great care of the diaries and that he returned some here and there over the years after having given some of them back."

She was on a role. "But if Washington had written entries that contradicted Marshall, especially about the flag of the Republic, you can see why he would want them destroyed."

"What does Concealer of Madison's Journal mean?" I asked.

"That's easy," she said. "James Madison kept a detailed journal of the debates in the Constitutional Convention. It has come down to us and helps us explain all that went on in Philadelphia in 1787."

"But this journal was kept secret for many years and didn't become known until after John Marshall had expounded the Constitution," she said.

"So?" I replied.

"So, John Marshall substituted his views of the Constitution with those of the actual people who debated and voted it into existence!" she said.

"Hack, there were two kinds of people in the convention. Those who wanted to destroy the states and have a national government. And those who wanted to preserve and protect the states and have a federal government. Guess who won?"

"The national government people?"

"Haha. You really are a 'C' student," she mocked. "No, silly. It was the side responsible for preserving and protecting the states. They voted down a national government not once, but twice. Instead, they created a republic."

She paused.

"Yes, yes," she said. "Yes, Hackworth. This is all making sense now! I think I'm starting to understand."

She was excited. Super-animated Pepper was here now, except her love interest was a historical mystery and not a basketball player.

"Don't you see?" she said. "John Marshall is held up as a hero outside this chamber, just like all of these others in the Rogue's Gallery. That's the lie! He wasn't a hero; he was a scoundrel."

"Marshall ruled that the Supreme Court has the power to say what is constitutional and what is not. He ruled that the Supreme Court has the power to void state laws," she said.

"But the Constitution did not give that power to the Supreme Court or the Congress," she said. "In fact, the convention rejected any council of revision or veto over state laws!"

I was beginning to understand. "So Marshall purposely conceals the debates and votes of the convention because he was on the side of those that lost there."

"By Jove, I think you are beginning to understand," Pepper said. "He knew the nationalists lost in writing the constitution, so what does he do? He impresses the nationalist argument onto it, with most of the country not knowing what was happening and not even knowing Madison kept a journal on what was agreed to."

"OK, we know some of Washington's diaries are missing. But what happened to Madison's journal?" I asked.

"It was purchased by the federal government... in the late 1830's!" she said.

"So the real record of the debates—of what was voted on and approved and what was rejected in the constitutional convention—was kept secret for 50 years?" I inquired. "And in the meantime, John Marshall never references it in his rulings?"

"Exactly," she said.

"And the law that gives federal courts the power to void state laws is still used today?"

"Apparently."

"A power they were never to have?"

"Perhaps."

"I feel like we are Alice in Wonderland, and nothing is what it should be."

Pepper didn't reply. Her eyes were on the walls behind the busts of the rogues, and she then looked across the room to the wall behind the busts of the heroes. She didn't speak; she just pointed.

Behind the Rogue's gallery was a giant-size framed poster of the Constitution with its "We The People" easily visible from where we were standing. Pepper pointed to it and then gestured for me to follow.

Next to it was a similar-sized blow-up of a document I didn't recognize. It said, "We The People Of The States of..." and then listed the states.

In between the two framed documents was this note:
"The Same Constitution,

In Words and Meaning

One Preamble, Legal

The Other, Poetry"

"Yes, I know this is true," Pepper said. "At the Philadelphia Convention, the delegates voted and approved the final constitution. That is the one that lists the people of the states individually. Then it was sent to the style committee to be prepared for public release. They changed the very first words of the preamble because they didn't know which states would actually approve it."

"You mean our constitution is "We The People of the States of New Hampshire, Massachusetts, etc.?"

It was starting to dawn on me that everything taught is a narrative—a version of facts twisted to make people think a certain way. To control them.

I remembered my conversation with Professor Redmand in the park. "If those things are lies, what is the truth?" I asked him.

"If only it were that easy, Hackworth. You need to feel the reality. You need to see it. Then you will understand."

I was just starting to see it now, and beginning to understand.

It didn't feel very good.

Chapter Nineteen

"We hold these truths to be self-evident, that all men are
created equal, that they are endowed by their Creator with
certain unalienable Rights, that among these are
Life, Liberty and the pursuit of Happiness ..."

*– The unanimous Declaration of the thirteen united
States of America, Philadelphia, 1776*

Our fascination with this strange place was interrupted by nagging pangs of hunger. Without realizing it, we had spent over three hours here, which meant six hours since our last meal.

Plus, this place was a little chilly, and I couldn't wait to get outside and get some fresh air. Years ago, I read that Ben Franklin's number one health tip was to leave your bedroom window open at night so you could inhale fresh air.

Pepper decided to stay in the hall while I went out to retrieve sandwiches and coffee.

It was agreed that we would spend the night. So I also picked up some bagels and cream cheese for the morning, not sure what she had in her backpack.

The second I got outside, my burner phone went crazy, vibrating that new messages were received. Tory was busy sending me information; the problem is that none of it came through. Of a dozen messages, each only had "Message cannot be downloaded" where the message should be.

I waited to see if it would update and download. It didn't. Then, a couple of texts appeared:

CTO -- When the British marched through Mount Vernon, they freed George Washington's slaves on the condition that they join the British and fight against Washington. Many left and joined the British, who lost in the Battle of Yorktown, VA, that ended the war.

BTW -- Flag Symbols information:

The Red and White Striped Flag—"the"rebellious stripes"—is the Sons of Liberty flag. The Sons gather when their liberty is threatened.

The Canton—this is the blue corner on the flag. By placing it there, it symbolizes that the rebellious stripes are subject to the authority shown in the canton.

The first canton to be placed on the Stripes was the Union Jack. It was replaced by the 13 stars on a blue field, one for each state that declared independence and confederated.

LOL—Conneciticut's Dansey Flag used in the revolution had the Rebellious Stripes on a solid field of green.

When I returned, Pepper was over at the center tables, looking at what seemed to be maps. They weren't maps, but woodcuts of historical images.

"Hack, this is incredible," she said. "The Professor has a collection of 12-star flag images from the past. Check this out."

She then held up an odd print.

"This is called 'L'Hommage de l'Amerique a la France' from a fabric design," she said. "It says the original is in the Smithsonian Institution."

It was a picture of a Native American holding a 12-star flag with 11 stars encircling a center star. It was dated 1790.

"He looks like you," I joked. "He could be your great-grandpa."

Indeed, Pepper was part Lenape, though an almost indiscernible one, as she was also part Irish, Italian, French, and Dutch. The Lenape descended from people who lived along the Delaware River and hung out at the Jersey shore long before the Europeans showed up.

"Ha, ha," she laughed, then held up an almost identical print. This one had the same Native American holding a flag, but this time it had 13 stars with none in the middle. This one was dated 1786.

"The French must have given this as a gift to the United States on two separate occasions," she said. "The 13-star flag is the U.S. under the Articles of Confederation. It's proof that something happened to the flag after the Constitution went into effect. Thirteen stars before it; 12 stars after it. Very interesting."

I handed her the sandwich. She was too much into her work to even unwrap it.

Not so much me; I gobbled into the roast beef and provalone and swallowed it with coffee.

"Look at this," she said, moving around the table.

"It is a woodcut of Washington's inauguration by Henry Alexander Ogden. Note the flags," she said, pointing to the giant rattlesnakes. "It's where the big illustration on the wall comes from."

Various flags were shown flying, each with one star in the middle and eleven circling it. There were 13 stripes.

She then held up another copy of what seemed to be the same print.

"This one says INTENTIONALLY ALTERED on the back," she said. It had 13 stars, with one in the middle.

Pepper paused. I could tell she was becoming enlightened.

"Could that star in the middle represent the new federal government created by the Constitution?" she asked.

"But that doesn't explain why there are just eleven states," I replied.

She kept working at the table. She held up a modern photograph of a 12-star flag. It had a big center star with a circle of six stars and four other stars, one in each corner.

"It says SOLD AT AUCTION," she remarked.

The flag was beautiful with its stars and stripes. It looked very old but was well preserved.

Pepper was still looking at the artifacts on the table.

A photograph of a 12-star flag with a written caption taped to the picture read: *"One of the 12-star flags at the start of the Republic in 1789 was acquired by antique flag collector and Revolutionary War veteran Nathaniel Fillmore, who also possessed the Bennington Flag. The 12-star flag hung in his son Millard Fillmore's home office. Mrs. Fred Meatyard donated it to Aurora, NY Historical Society."*

Next to that photograph was another, with a 14-star flag with a caption that read: *"First Republic Flag after all states joined the union, 1791. Location unknown."*

"Hack, I think I am onto something," she said. "Look!"

The expression in her voice was uplifting. Even though I was tired, she had a way of sparking curiosity in me.

She held up an old piece of skin-like paper.

In big type across the top was the headline, "Constitution of the Sons of Liberty of Albany." The date was 1765.

She read the beginning: *"As in our present distressed condition, while under the greatest apprehensions of yet threatening Slavery, our surest refuges seem the mercies of God, and our own fixed and unanimous resolution to persevere to the last in the vindication of our dear bought Rights and Privileges, the very Essentials of our peerless Constitution, These, in the awful presence of the Righteous Jehovah, serve to bind us, the Subscribes and public Assentors hereto in the Articles following ..."*

"Yes!" she said. "My thinking is correct. This is the headquarters and meeting place for the Sons of Liberty! Yes, they met in taverns and hatched their plans, but they also had a secret headquarters to conduct business and train the newbies. That's what we are in."

"Then Professor Redmand was a member of the SOL."

"And a most special one, to be entrusted with all of this," Pepper said. "Some of this stuff is more than 250 years old!"

She pointed to a stripes-only flag on the wall titled "Our Flag" and started reading the plaque next to it:

"Rally around our flag
Sons & Daughters
And know them by theirs
Ours is stripes of red and white
White for purity of purpose, Liberty
Red, the blood shed for her"

We were quiet. You could hear the subtle binaural tone emanating from the walls as the cool air flowed. The sound seemed to help me understand—it put my mind in a different place.

While I was contemplating all that was happening, Pepper walked over to the "Heroes" side of the room.

She was standing next to a bust of George Washington.
The card under it said:

"Father of His Country
Defender of The Mothers
Protector of The Daughters
The Republic's First Hero
Betrayed By Political Parties"

Pepper was studying the card.

"Washington was opposed to political parties," she said. "He did not consider himself a Democrat-Republican or Federalist. He spoke out against what he called 'the party spirit.' He was against alliances, foreign and domestic. He wanted Americans to be friendly and trade with everyone around the world."

"The constitution does not mention political parties in any way," she said. "During the Revolutionary period, there were no parties. It was us against them. Friend or foe. And the leaders spoke out against factions. Not only Washington, but Hamilton spoke out against them."

"But wasn't his vice president a Federalist?" I asked.

"Yes, John Adams was a Federalist, just like Jefferson was a Democrat-Republican. That must be what is meant," she said. "The parties spawned from the constitutional convention. Those who wanted a national government vs. those who wanted a federal system that retained power in the states and people. After losing the fight over crafting the constitution, the nationalists went to work within the government itself," she said.

"That's who the Federalists were," she continued. "They were really nationalists but disguised their intentions with the name Federalists, which implies the old confederation."

"And who were the Democrat-Republicans?" I asked.

"They were led by Thomas Jefferson and believed each state was its own republic with its own parts—towns, counties, and cities. This group won the day in the constitutional convention, even though Jefferson was not there. The Constitution created a republic with its parts, states.

"And here's the killer fact: When the nationalists led by President John Adams started imprisoning newspaper editors under the Alien & Sedition Acts, the people revolted up and down the coast. They put the Democrat-Republicans into power, where they dominated for nearly 50 years," she said.

Pepper was studying a document on the table about George Washington.

"This is unbelievable Hack," she began. "Without the French, we would be British today!"

She read from the paper:

"On September 5, 1781, the President of Pennsylvania welcomed French General Count de Rochambeau and General George Washington as their armies marched through Philadelphia on their way to Yorktown, VA, where the British ultimately surrendered. The Americans had no money to pay their Continental soldiers and must borrow $20,000 in gold coin from Count de Rochambeau. Between paying for the American troops, sending twice as many French soldiers to Yorktown as there were Americans, and deploying the formidable French Navy, the French forced the British out of North America. In doing so, King Louis bankrupted France and ultimately lost his head in the French version of the American Revolution."

"I still don't like them," I said.

"Like who?"

"The French."

"Hack, come on," she laughed. "Why? Because of one bad experience in Paris?"

She was referring to our trip from Paris to Rome during junior year. We were buying tickets in Paris, and I asked for them in English, but the man at the counter was insulted because I didn't at least try speaking French. "What do you think?" he yelled, slapping his forehead and closing the ticket door. "You think I can go to JFK airport and speak French?" He was very rude, and it was very embarrassing.

We laughed and found ourselves drowning in this esoteric knowledge of the past. We continued looking at busts and reading cards. It was getting late, so we began preparations for the night.

"Pepper, we are going to have to figure out how to shut the bookcase," I said. "If anybody comes here, they will find this place, and we cannot let that happen."

She agreed, and we returned to the upstairs parlor. The problem was that we could figure out how to open and close the bookcase, but not from inside the room.

We carefully inspected the walls at the top of the stairs, even the stairs themselves. The landing at the bottom also bore no sign of an opening or closing device.

The best we could do was almost shut the bookcase without fully closing it. If it closed, we would be trapped in the subterranean chamber.

Pepper set up the sleeping bags on the floor near the Independent Man. It was then that I took notice of the floors. They were made of the same mahogany as stairs, walls, and ceilings, with planks two feet wide.

I got into my sleeping bag, and Pepper into hers. In between us was the backpack. We had to leave the lights on because there were no visible switches to be found.

"This is like a dream," she said. "That we're here now."

"A dream or a nightmare? The truth shall set you free, it is said. I fear the truth will entomb us."

"What do you mean?" Pepper said, trailing off.

"The people who built this went to great lengths to conceal it, lest others find it. Obviously, something has happened to have us now here and in possession of the 12-star flag. But why does all this matter?"

"We'll find out," she whispered, then turned to sleep.

I continued to stare up at the Independent Man.

And wished I was him.

Surrender of Lord Cornwallis at Yorktown, 1781 (Detail) — by John Trumball

FRIDAY

Chapter Twenty

"And it is a very general opinion that if we succeed in establishing our liberties, we shall ... receive an immense addition of ... families who will come over to participate in our privileges ... Tyranny is so generally established in the rest of the world that the prospect of an asylum in America for those who love liberty gives general joy, and our Cause is esteem'd the Cause of all Mankind."

– Benjamin Franklin report to the Continental Congress, April 9, 1777

I hate camping. I hate lying on the ground and having hard rocks stick in my back or behind, waking up to sore muscles and smelling like bacon from the campfire wood smoke. Take away the bacon smell, sticks, and rocks; that's how I felt as I came awake. Lying on that hard, cold stone floor all night made my body ache, just as if I were in a tent in the Adirondacks.

The bright light of the room kept my eyes half shut. I sat up and looked for Pepper.

She wasn't in her sleeping bag.

In fact, her sleeping bag didn't look like she had been in it at all. Just a few feet away, she was sitting in an ornate chair with lion's feet at the middle of the center table, reading through a large stack of papers.

"Huh," she mumbled to herself. "Washington's Continental Army did not fight in the north. The major victory at Saratoga was fought with the New England militia. And after June 28, 1778,

Washington's army does not fight another battle until Yorktown, three years later."

I wasn't really listening to her. Instead, my attention was drawn to the North Carolina flag right behind her. The date "May 31, 1775" was printed on it.

"Good morning," Pepper said, getting up from her seat and standing over me. She looked like she had been up all night.

"Morning."

"Wondering about the date?" she said, pointing to it.

"Because I know what it means," she smiled, then paused. "And I'm close to knowing everything."

Though exhausted, she had the twinkle in her eye of someone who had found the treasure they were searching for.

"That day, May 31, 1775, was when a *county* in North Carolina declared its independence from the King," she said.

"A county?"

"That's right, a county declared independence more than a year before the Declaration."

She walked to the table and brought back a piece of paper.

She read it. "Free and Independent People are, and of right ought to be, a Sovereign and self-governing Association."

Something clicked inside of me upon hearing her words.

"Wait, so the county in North Carolina is sovereign like the townships in Massachusetts?"

"And they declared their independence a year before July 4?"

"A year, a month, and four days," Pepper said.

Next to the North Carolina flag was the stranger "The Bucks of America" flag. That's what it said on the tan flag with a buck deer, a pine tree, and 13 stars in a blue canton (upper left square).

Walking to that flag, Pepper continued:

"This is the flag of the Bucks of America," Pepper said. "The Bucks were a militia of free black men in Massachusetts. The initials J.G.W.A. indicate the Bucks were sanctioned by both John Hancock and George Washington."

"Newly freed slaves?" I asked.

"No," Pepper said. "Just free men who joined together and offered their services to fight for liberty and freedom against the British. Not every black person was a slave or a former slave!"

"OK. OK," I said. "So?"

"So the Bucks of America, a force of 100 men, fought at Bunker Hill, and some died. They fought under the New England Flag and, with other militia, inflicted 50% casualties on the British side."

"And one of the first Bucks was Crispus Attucks, an American whaler and sailor who was the first American killed in the Revolution. He was shot during the protests at the Boston Massacre in 1770."

"Do you understand?" Pepper continued. "The American Revolution was a bottom-up revolution. The real deal. The war was on a local level, and militias fought when the British encroached on their state. They fought for their liberty and their freedom in local and regional militias.

"But not everyone. John Adams said 1/3 of the people were for the revolution, 1/3 of the people were against it, and 1/3 didn't care," Pepper continued.

"Well, I bet there were no Bucks of America in the South," I said, interrupting her discourse.

Pepper shook her finger at me.

"First, it was a local war fought with 13 capitols and 13 independent states—each state different, with differing parts, some rural and some urban. It's wrong to lump people into groups. Didn't Tory tell you that?"

"Maybe you have a point, but what does this have to do with the 12-star flag?" I asked.

"Hold on, you need to see something," she replied, leading me to where the two constitutions hung on the wall. Next to them were two other documents, blown up so they were easy to read.

They were two copies of the Declaration of Independence.

She pointed to the one on the left.

"That's the original," she said.

And then, pointing to the other one, she said, "And this is the one they put in the school books."

The original was written in hand, and the other one was printed on a large sheet of paper called a "Broadside," which essentially was a poster of news nailed to a wall.

"What do you notice about the printed one?" she asked.

"I don't know, what?"

"Notice the big words in all capital letters."

It said, "UNITED STATES OF AMERICA."

"Now let's go to the original," she continued. "The one on display at the National Archives in Washington, DC."

Her fingers pointed to a spot on top, and it read, "... of the *thirteen united* States of America."

"I see it," I said. "The words 'States of America' are bigger than the other words."

"Hack, for goodness sake. Don't you get it? The word "united" is in smaller case, and it is used as a modifier with the word thirteen."

"I get it," I said. "The original Declaration did not use the phrase "United States of America" as a proper noun. The word 'united' is an adjective. Don't forget, Pepper, I am a writer."

"The one with all of the capital letters is a broadside, printed by a nationalist at the time," she said. "But it is a lie! No such entity existed in 1776, and it wouldn't exist until Maryland joined the Articles of Confederation in 1781. Until that year, there was no legal United States of America."

She gestured me back to the table and opened her knapsack. She took out some fruit, and we ate in silence. There was so much information being thrown at me. I felt bewildered.

"The states declared their independence from Great Britain," she said, "but they were always independent of each other."

"Tory was right about American liberty," she added.

Pepper then detailed how liberty took root in the early days, quoting an article written by Professor Mac. Dissenters, rebels, and castaways were the first settlers, fleeing persecution in Europe. They came to America to practice their religion and to live their lives as they saw fit. And the American wilderness took them in and helped them prosper.

Into that wilderness, they brought their English notions of liberty—legalistic liberty, what the King can and cannot do to the people—built on contracts, charters, and constitutions.

But after living in that wilderness and in subsequent generations, the Americans witnessed the liberty of the Indians. Their natural liberty of being able to live as they wanted day after day, answering to no higher authority beyond their tribe.

Against this backdrop was the intimate knowledge of indentured servitude and slavery, where you were not able to live as you wanted and had an ever-present authority who believed it "owned" you.

"Soon enough, the people in the colonies started acting like the people back home," she said. "When the extremists in Salem, MA, persecuted so-called heretics like Roger Williams, he fled from them and started Rhode Island, where people were allowed to practice any religion or none at all. The first synagogue in America was built in 1763."

This was possible because charters from the King gave the people local legislative control over their lives, she explained. Virginia's General Assembly was the first, beginning in 1619. The people of the colonies swore allegiance to the King but not to the British legislature—the Parliament. They had their own legislature to make laws and lay taxes.

In fact, there could be no tax other than that established by their colony's legislature.

When Parliament began to tax them to pay for their defense, the colonists resisted because they had no say in the matter. No one represented them in London because they had their own Parliament in their colonial legislature.

"And the Sons of Liberty were born," Pepper said. "The year was 1765, and the Sons organized around the principle of local control. Of the right to live their lives and make their own laws. To be free. To be independent."

We walked back to the North Carolina flag.

"This liberty movement was not directed by a central authority," she said. "It happened throughout the colonies. What were called Sons of Liberty in some places were called Regulators in North Carolina and other names elsewhere."

"The people rose up and fought the revolution, not to create a central authority like the nationalists have taught us," she said, "but to escape a central authority—*the King!*"

Pepper went on to explain that in the treaty ending the revolution, the King named each state and recognized them as "free, sovereign, and independent states," the same words used in the Articles of Confederation that created the United States of America.

"So the states fought the war together for their individual independence," I said. "That is not what we are taught."

"But how could we be taught such a thing when everyone knows our nation was born in 1776?"

We both laughed.

I walked back over and sat in the chair. Pepper remained in front of The Independent Man. She was radiant. She didn't look like she was up all night anymore.

"Hack," she said, turning away from the statue and looking directly into my eyes. "I have solved the mystery."

She stared ahead with her finger tapping her lip.

"Or should I say, this place was built to educate so there would be no mystery in the first place."

Chapter Twenty-One

"At least one thousand Men are barefooted and have
performed the late marches in that condition ..."

– George Washington to Continental Congress, September 23, 1777

"Soon I came in sight of the camp (at Valley Forge). My
imagination had pictured an army with uniforms, the
glitter of arms, standards, etc., in short, military pomp of
all sorts. Instead ... I saw, grouped together or standing
alone, a few militiamen, poorly clad, and for the most
part without shoes ... such were the colonists—unskilled
warriors who learned in a few years how to conquer the
finest troops that England could send against them."

*– A French Volunteer of the War of Independence, by the Chevalier de
Pontgibaud, edited by Robert B. Douglas, NY, Appleton-Century, 1898*

Pepper walked to the Hero's side of the hall and stopped at the
Benjamin Franklin bust.

"He's one of the most recognizable people in the world," she
said, "and that was before he became the face on the $100 bill."

She read aloud the card under it.

"Mighty Franklin, Brilliant & Striking
Like The Lightning He Tamed
And the Rattler he charmed
Father of Revolution and Union
A President Betrayed Spoke the Truth
'A Republic, If You Can Keep It'
And We Did"

Of all the pedestals with busts, Franklin's was the tallest.

Pepper repeated the words.

"What does this mean?" she said rhetorically. "Well, you know the lightning part, where Franklin discovered it was electricity. But did you know he invented the lightning rod, which saved people from losing their home and their reputation? For before his discovery, people thought lightning was God striking the guilty!"

"Can you imagine losing your house to a bolt from the sky, but all your neighbors are wondering what you did to deserve God's wrath?"

"Did you know Franklin was President of Pennsylvania when the Constitutional Convention met in Philadelphia?" she asked.

"Did you know he was one of the American representatives when the treaty with the King was negotiated, the treaty that recognized the independence of each state?"

"What's the point, Pepper?"

"None of it would have been possible without Benjamin Franklin," she said. "That's the point."

"Franklin's the one who invented the rattlesnake "Join or Die" motto. He tried to get the colonies to unite in 1754 to fight the French. They met in Albany and made a plan of union, then sent it to the colonial legislatures for their approval."

"And did they approve?"

"No, not one," she said. "Each colony had separate charters and separate rights, and guarded them jealously. They refused to give up any control."

"Twenty-one years later, the rattesnake was reborn on the 'Don't Tread on Me' flag and became the principle Americans organized around. Franklin sold the French on the idea of supporting the American cause, and they rushed weapons and gunpowder to the states in time to guarantee victory in the Battle of Saratoga in 1777. That victory set the stage for deeper French assistance that ultimately would see the Americans win, all because of Franklin."

Pepper opened the backpack, grabbed a bottle of water, took a sip, and handed it to me.

"By the time the war ended, the states agreed to a league of friendship, a confederation for defensive purposes, with each state having an equal vote."

"They were like their own countries," I said.

"Yes, they were. And the new constitutions each state created were all the rage in Europe. The American States were showing the European States how to organize government, respect freedom and liberty, and do so without a king or religious leader."

She paused and took another sip of water. "These were all firsts for human beings in the modern age: to throw off royal and religious control and establish constitutions that put law over men. And with the new printing presses, the whole world would come to understand what the Americans had done."

"Then some powerful people got an idea. Seeing the success of the state constitutions, they fancied a federal constitution, and in 1787 they met at what was known as the Philadelphia Convention, but we call today the Constitutional Convention."

"After much debate and discussion, the constitution was approved," she said. "But instead of requiring each state to ratify it, the convention said it would go into effect if only nine states did. The problem was that the current constitution, the Articles of

Confederation, specifically said it was to remain in effect until EVERY STATE LEGISLATURE approved the changes."

"So they didn't follow the legal amendment procedures?"

"Haha. No! And it gets better," she continued. "The states were asked to ratify not by their legislatures, which would mean sure defeat, but instead by conventions called in each state. The reason was that these conventions could be more easily manipulated than state legislatures."

"Manipulated?"

"Yes," she said. "The nationalists had a clandestine network in each state to push it through. And when that didn't work, they used bribery and deceit to get the vote."

"Are you saying the Constitution's ratification was a fraud?"

"Not any more than politics are a fraud."

"Follow me," she said, rising from the table and leading me to the Rogue's Gallery.

We stopped at Edmund Randolph's bust. He was governor of Virginia and a member of the state's ratification convention.

The card under his bust read:

"For State Rights, But Poor

Sells His Principles, Now Rich

Tricked His Friends In The Deal

What Better Man to be first U.S. Attorney General?"

"What does all that mean?" I asked.

Pepper explained. Randolph was publicly opposed to the Constitution. But he was experiencing money problems. Suddenly he came into money, and at the exact same time he switched his vote! More importantly, he betrayed his allies and fed the nationalists secret details of the opposition's strategy.

"His ultimate reward? He was the first Attorney General of the United States," Pepper said.

Such things happened up and down the coast. In New Hampshire, the vote could have gone either way. So, the nationalists found a group of opponents and took them out to lunch. A liquid lunch. They all got drunked up. Meanwhile, the vote is called while they are away, and the Constitution is approved by a handful of votes.

Massachusetts was like Virginia in that the governor, the great John Hancock, was not a fan of the Constitution. But that changed when it was whispered in his ear that Washington would need a vice president from New England. Hancock took the bait but didn't get the job. That went to his personal attorney, John Adams. But the nationalists got his vote.

"And on it went throughout the states," Pepper said. "But there was one state that did not play the game. Rhode Island."

She walked to the front of the hall and now pointed at the Rhode Island flag. I stared at the word "Hope", which is taken from the motto "Hope In The Divine."

"Rhode Island refused to send delegates to the Philadelphia Convention," she said.

"And they were the only state to allow the people themselves to vote on the new Constitution."

Her voice boomed in the hall as she said the words.

"Every other state had conventions where the dirtiest politics were played out, but not Rhode Island. They wanted the people to vote directly on whether to join the Constitution."

"And what happened?"

She paused for effect.

"What do you think, Hack? Over 90% of the Rhode Islanders voted NO!"

"So Rhode Island did not join the United States?"

"No, the people declined the offer," she said.

I laughed. "So the only state that even got close to "We The People" deciding to join, those people said no?"

"Exactly," she said. "But one other state that had a convention did decline as well. They said they would not join unless there was a bill of rights guaranteeing the people's liberty and state rights."

"North Carolina?" I said, half questioning.

"Right again," she said. "And that is the key to the 12-star flag!"

I took a sip off the water bottle.

"When the U.S. Constitution went into effect, there were only eleven states," she said. "Rhode Island and North Carolina were not part of the United States. It would not be proper to have the old 13-star flag at Washington's inauguration."

"So, a new flag had to be created for the new Republic," I said. "But that is 11 stars. What does the 12th star represent?"

"Ah," she said. "The new star, the slightly bigger star in the center..."

She paused for effect.

"That star is for the United States itself!"

"What?" I didn't follow.

Pepper now walked back to Franklin's bust.

"Franklin was asked what the Constitution created. He replied, 'A Republic, If You Can Keep It.' This was what George Washington called it as well. A national government had been rejected; a federal one was created instead.

"Well, that Republic made by the Constitution needed a symbol of sovereignty itself. The states each had a star of sovereignty. The United States needed one now, too," she said.

It was true that the first flag—the flag of the Articles of Confederation for 13 independent states—was 13 stars and 13 stripes, recognizing the sovereignty of each state. But that would not be appropriate for the new Republic with only 11 states.

"And George Washington is the one who had it placed on the flag," Pepper said. "He called the United States a republic, just like Franklin. A confederated republic. Unfortunately, Franklin and later Washington were betrayed."

"How was Benjamin betrayed?" I asked.

Pepper detailed that within a year of the new Republic, Franklin died. And Pennsylvania, under the direction of Supreme Court Justice James Wilson, revised its state constitution. It abolished the powerful, single-chamber legislature. It replaced the President with a Governor. And it weakened the state's bill of rights.

"Franklin's body wasn't even cold before the nationalists took apart his Commonwealth of Pennsylvania," Pepper said. "And went to work on the rest of the country."

"Don't you see, Hack?" Pepper said. "The nationalists lost in the Philadelphia Convention. They did not get their nation. Instead, a Republic was born."

"But that hasn't stopped them from consolidating power in the federal government," she said. "Not then, not now."

I stood up and walked to the Independent Man and studied the flags of North Carolina and Rhode Island.

"When did the two holdouts join?" I asked.

"Forget that for a moment," she pleaded. "Think about this: The flag is a symbol of our country, and so what does the 12-star flag symbolize? And what does it not symbolize?"

Pepper raised her closed fist in the air and then counted off with her fingers, saying it symbolizes:

1. States existed outside the Union.

2. States rejected the Union.

3. States were independent of the Union.

4. The Republic of 1789 did not exist in 1776; there were only 13 independent states.

5. The Republic is sovereign because of the states.

"And there you have it," she said. "None of this is taught as our history. In fact, the exact opposite is taught. And anything that contradicts their false narrative is destroyed."

"But why?"

Chapter Twenty-Two

"This Quaker wears the full costume of his sect. He has
an agreeable physiognomy, spectacles always on his eyes
but little hair, a fur cap always on his head. He wears no
powder but neat and linen very white, a brown coat
makes his dress. His only defence is a stick in his hand."

*– French Police intelligence report on Benjamin Franklin, the newly
arrived American Commissioner, January 15, 1777*

And as I said, "But why?" the lights started to flicker. At first, it
was just a blink or two. We looked at each other. The lights
flickered again.

And then went out completely.

We froze.

The hours spent here were a respite from our trials. Hidden in
the underground chamber, wrapped in old and arcane history, we
gave little thought to the dangers that awaited us up above.

The lights going out turned on that fear.

It was absolutely dark; there was not even a blinking smoke
detector light to pierce the blackness.

"Hack, look!" Pepper exclaimed, pointing at the rattlesnakes.

Pulsating with a twilight blue luminescence, the snakes became sinister and appeared to wriggle.

Their heads pointed towards each other, and their fangs were
clearly visible. The illustration behind the snakes now had a yellowish hue.

Pepper went to the table, looking for her backpack, where she kept the flashlight. Finally, a beam of light pierced the dark. She shined it around the room.

"There must be a power outage," I said.

"Noo," she said sarcastically, carefully moving the light around the room. It was a strange sight, with shadows falling off the busts and highlighting the frames around the documents that hung on the wall.

Her beam of light stopped on The Independent Man, and she turned off the flashlight.

It glowed. A yellowish, golden glow. How it was illuminated, we did not know.

We followed the glow from The Independent Man, which reflected on the illustration that the slithering snakes framed. The combination of pulsating twilight blue and golden yellow was breathtaking.

This was somehow being done without electricity. There was a purpose in turning off the lights, maybe as part of some initiation held here.

"Hey, there's a date above the illustration," Pepper said, pointing to cursive writing above the heads of the snakes.

In cursive writing, "April 30, 1789" glowed white. We did not notice it when the lights were on.

"Pepper, what happened on that date?"

She turned the flashlight on, walked back to the table, and started going through a small pile of papers.

"I saw that date here, and... oh, yes. There it is. It is the date George Washington was inaugurated in New York City."

She read from the paper:

"Washington was inaugurated at the newly designated Federal State House, which was taken from the British in 1775 by the Sons of Liberty. The building was the former City Hall and would serve as the new Republic's capitol building."

"So that must be what the illustration depicts," I blurted out.

"Yes indeed, Hack. The inauguration of Washington began the United States under the Constitution, and the flag that flew on top of the building was the 12-star flag," Pepper said.

"So the flag that is in my apartment..."

Pepper interrupted me.

"Is the first flag of the United States of America," she said. "And that's why they want it."

Silence as we thought about what was just said.

"And Hack, you know what else is unbelievable? They called that building the 'Federal State House.' They saw the federal government becoming like a state, with a constitution and a state house."

On her words, the power came on and the room was fully illuminated. Gone were the twilight blue snakes, the glowing Independent Man, the yellow illustration, and the date in white letters.

"We have to get out of here," she said. "But first, we have to take pictures of as much as we can."

She handed me the digital spy camera, and I started at one end of the long table, which had numerous stacks of paper. They were short stacks, each with a title page.

"Just take a picture of the tops, right?" I asked.

"Yes, we don't have the time for each page," she replied.

I looked at the title page of one stack. It read, "The Educational-Industrial Complex: Control, Tactics, and Methods."

The next pile had a top page that read, "Judicial Control: Harvard, Yale, and Nationalist Orthodoxy."

This table was obviously dedicated to the ways the lies were perpetuated.

"Goals 2000, No Child Left Behind, Common Core: The Takeover of History Education from Local Control."

There were half a dozen other piles with similar top title pages. I photographed each one.

Pepper pointed to the back wall. "Make sure you get pictures of that."

I walked back and saw various poster-sized pictures. One was the famous Spirit of '76, where the old man and young boy carry the flag and beat on the drums with an American flag behind them. The card under the picture read: *"Made in 1875 by a Union Veteran who didn't know better."*

Another picture was titled, "Betsy Ross makes the first flag of the United States of America, 1789."

I stopped at that picture and exclaimed, "Betsy Ross is sewing a 12-star flag!"

Pepper waived me off.

"Just take a picture of it... of everything!" she said.

And so I did. The pilgrims landing, the Indian treaty signed, Bunker Hill, Philadelphia Independence, the Treaty of Paris.

"And these," Pepper said, pointing to a group of photographs of flags on the wall.

One was thirteen stars encircling a larger 14th star in the middle. It had 11 stripes. Another had 12 stars in four rows of three, with the title "Daughters of 1812 Flag."

I took a picture of each.

"And these," Pepper said, standing in front of a group of framed images. One was a music score from the vice presidential inauguration of 1840. It showed flags with stars in the center. Another was a Washington Memorial invitation. It had only nine stars on it.

Pepper called me back to the table.

"Did you get pictures of these stacks?" she said.

"Hold on, cut it out! I can just go so fast."

I walked over to her. This part of the table was full of paper stacks with titles like:

"Public Health As A Basis For Central Control."

"FBI Blackmails Corrupt Politicians To Maintain Power."

"Nazi Tactics In Intelligence Services."

"National Security Agency: Total Information Awareness."

"Franklin Starts Post Office To Stop Royal Mail Spying; 200 Years Of Mail Spying Programs."

I held up a report from the U.S. Information Awareness Agency. Its logo features the Eye of Providence as a satellite spying on the globe. "An actual federal spying agency uses the All-Seeing-Eye," I said, "to show us it has God-like powers. That's creepy."

Other titles of stacks included:

"How To Live Off The Grid And Enjoy Eating Dandelions."

"The Secrets Seymour Hersh Exposed."

"Using Wikipedia To Redefine The Past."

"Trilateral Commission: Mission Accomplished."

"NASA, Nazis, and UFOs."

"The Censorship Industrial Complex: Big Tech Backdoor To Canceling The First Amendment."

"The Legal-Industrial Complex."

"Pharmaceutical Ads Market Medical-Industrial Complex."

Snap. Snap. Snap. I was taking the pictures, but what value would they be if I didn't copy the actual pages under the title?

"Googlification of Knowledge Serves National Government Control: China Case Study."

"Centralization, Mass Media, and Disinformation."

I was tired. I put the camera down and sat in the chair. Pepper joined me. We realized it was foolhardy to try and photograph everything in this room.

It was quiet. Then I broke the silence.

"When did North Carolina and Rhode Island finally join the United States?"

"North Carolina joined once the Bill of Rights had cleared Congress," she said. "They were adamant that a statement reserving all undelegated powers to the states and people was in there. That became the 9th and 10th Amendments."

"Rhode Island, however, didn't come in so easy," she said. "There was a second vote to approve the Constitution, and once again, the people voted overwhelmingly to reject it—with or without a Bill of Rights."

"But then it got interesting. Come over here," she said, walking to the other side of the table and pointing to some stacks.

"Rhode Island Resolutions: How the USA Bullied Little Rhody" said one, among others like it.

"What happened? I asked.

"Oh, there was lots of pressure. Attacks in the press. Threats to make Rhode Island part of Connecticut or Massachusetts. But the biggest threat were the Rhode Island Resolutions, which passed the Senate in 1790. These basically made Rhode Island a foreign nation, and not a favored one at that.

Rhode Island pleaded that she be left alone, but the U.S. would not relent."

"Why?" I asked.

"Because of money," Pepper answered. "The only way for the federal government to fund itself under the Constitution at the time was through import duties and excise taxes. They needed a uniform custom house system to impose taxes."

She continued:

"The federal government needed to raise revenue to pay the interest on the debt—its debt and the debt it was assuming from the states. Debt holders on Wall Street needed to be paid. To not have a rock-solid income source would have meant disaster. No one would have bought the bonds otherwise."

"If Rhode Island was outside that system, shippers would avoid paying the taxes and bring goods in through Rhode Island. And remember, Rhode Island's reputation as a seafaring state involved buccaneers and piracy," she continued. "They were not above evading the law."

"Another explanation is that the United States did not want Rhode Island to remind the other states what could have been for them. Imagine if the other states fared poorly under the new government while Rhode Island thrived.

"Finally, on the third try, and without letting the people vote, Rhode Island was coerced into saying Yes," she said. "Let that sink in: *it only passed because the people did not directly vote.*"

We were feeling pressure to leave. Why? I can't say, but there was a sudden realization that we needed to leave.

"What else should I take pictures of?"

Pepper pointed to the busts.

I began on the Heroes side: James Otis, Isaac Barré, Samuel Adams, and Sarah Fulton.

"Hey, Pepper. Here's a woman!"

I read Sarah Fulton's card:

"Daughter of Liberty

Mother of the Boston Tea Party

Doctor to Bunker Hill's Wounded

Washington's Letter Courier"

"Yeah, I saw that," Pepper said. "If you keep reading, you'll see that Sarah Fulton was instrumental in the tea party. It was her idea that the rebels dress up as Indians."

"Was she a doctor?" I asked.

"No, hardly," Pepper said. "She set up and worked at the field hospital for the Americans wounded at the Battle of Bunker Hill. There were no doctors available. They were all loyal to the King."

"And Hack, there's another woman a little farther down. Make sure you don't miss her," she continued. "Mary Katherine Goddard printed the copies of the Declaration of Independence and her name appears on the bottom."

I kept working on the Heroes side and photographed George Washington, Benjamin Franklin, Thomas Jefferson, George Mason, Patrick Henry, Elbridge Gerry, and Roger Sherman. There were more to see, but I stopped at the name Abel Upshur.

Under his bust, it read:

"Deliverer of Texas, Murdered

Defender of Liberty & Rights

Whose Pen Revealed

Harvard's False Story"

"What the?" I asked. "Harvard's story?"

Pepper explained that Abel Upshur was a Virginian who served as Secretary of the Navy and Secretary of State in the 1840's. He helped bring Texas into the Union.

Upshur wrote a blistering retort to Joseph Story's book on the U.S. Constitution, challenging Story's assertion that sovereignty existed in the federal government and not the states. Story was Harvard educated, and his legal arguments would become orthodox at the school.

"Go look at Story's bust on the Rogue side," she said. "He was one of Marshall's boys who enlarged the Supreme Court beyond what the Constitution intended. Story asserted that the power Congress gave to the Court over the States was constitutional, even though it was contrary to what was decided in the convention."

"Abel Upshur was murdered?"

Pepper looked at me. "How do I know? The papers I read say Upshur, then Secretary of State, President John Tyler, and the new Secretary of Navy were aboard the brand new USS Princeton. During a demonstration of its firepower, one of the guns exploded and killed Upshur, the Navy Secretary, and almost Tyler. The paper implies it was an assassination attempt to try and stop Texas from joining the Union."

I walked over to the Rogue's side to see Joseph Story's bust. It read:

"Boy, Betrayer of a Son
Is He Wise Enough
To Judge Himself?
And for Marshall's Land?"

"This is fun," I said. "But I don't have a clue what it means."

Pepper laughed and related what she read last night. Judge Joseph Story's father was a Son of Liberty and one of the leaders of the Boston Tea Party. Judge Story was also only 32 years old when he was appointed to the Supreme Court and quickly became a fervent nationalist.

"That is what is meant by 'Boy, Betrayer of a Son,'" she said.

"A case came up called *Martin vs. Hunter's Lessee.* Judge Story wrote the decision. Marshall recused himself from the case because he had a financial arrangement with Martin, the plaintiff. When the Virginia Court ruled against Martin, the Supreme Court reversed the decision and... surprise, surprise," she said.

"Let me guess," I interrupted. "They ruled for Martin."

"Yes, and Marshall profited. But in doing so, Story argued the Supreme Court had power over prior State Court decisions," Pepper said. "This sparked outrage, especially from the highest Virginia Court, which asserted the Constitution did not give this power to any federal court."

"But Pepper, of course the Supreme Court has that power, or else it wouldn't be supreme, right?"

"Ah, that gets right to the heart of the matter," she said. "Voiding state laws and decisions was debated and rejected in the Constitutional Convention. There were attempts to have a powerful council of revision. These were rejected."

"If you read the Constitution, you will see various places where the federal government can intrude upon state rights, but because this particular power is not expressly given to the Feds, many argued that they did not have it."

"So when the California people pass a constitutional amendment for their state, the federal court has no say in the matter?"

"Exactly," Pepper responded. "And think about it. It is the highest form of tyranny for one judge to overrule the legal determinations of millions of citizens. It is a dictatorship when that happens. And it happens all the time."

"What is meant by 'wise enough to judge himself'?" I asked.

"Well, think about it, Hack. Justice can only be done when an impartial and independent judge sits in judgment of two parties. What Marshall and Story asserted is that even when an issue involves the powers of their own court, they have the right to judge."

"So they can judge themselves? That sounds quite perverse," I said.

"Not just that, Hack," she said. "But in any case in which federal and state sovereignty collide, the Supreme Court is biased because it is part of the federal government. It is difficult for it to be impartial, as it must serve its masters in the other branches."

"But Pepper, doesn't the Constitution say the Supreme Court is over everything else?"

"Absolutely not," she replied. "It says *the Constitution* is over everything else and that the judges in the states are to keep it that way!"

Chapter Twenty-Three

"The idea of being taken prisoner was foreign to all of our men. In the event of capture they looked forward to being tortured by the savages. Our fate was now to be determined, probably within the next few hours, and we knew that nothing but the boldest conduct would insure success."

– Virginia General George Rogers Clark just before winning Illinois for his state in 1778, later to be made a county of Virginia and eventually becoming a state. From the Sketch of His Campaign in Illinois, from The Capture of Old Vincennes, edited by Milo M. Quaife, Indianapolis, 1927

Being with Pepper, learning new things together, letting our curiosity get the best of us—this was real living and sparked my imagination. At this moment, I vowed not to return to my mediocre life when this was over.

Looking at the stacks of documents—of little-known knowledge—it dawned on me just how much the internet, social media, and the smartphone have changed us. These documents are very old, some several hundred years. They are preserved, to be studied.

Today, in the digital world, they could easily be deleted. Or made impossible to find. Internet search engines deliver approved information from expert sources instead of all the information available, including contrary information or what is called "misinformation."

And when you read it here in this chamber, it is secret. It is private. It's none of anyone's business, not a company nor a government. No cameras, no IDs, no cookies—no one looking over your shoulder.

It's the individual, subject to no one.

So far in the 2000's, it's all different than it was in the 1900's. Everything you read, want, or buy can be tracked, monitored, or recorded. And you don't have to go to a faraway city to live recklessly. Now, it's beamed into your home and pocket.

And who cares? Because it is, after all, a BETTER AND FASTER way to live.

Or so I had thought.

My mind raced...

This old chamber, made before electricity was harnessed, continues in its mission for individual liberty. And has for centuries. Perhaps the digital age is not superior to the old ways.

The Age of Internet has ushered in the dictatorship of the Master Computer over people who, separately and independently, send to it their thoughts, questions, ideas, urges, biases, wisdom, language, selections, etc., all recorded and used by corporations selling products, governments policing thought, or others trying to socially engineer what we think on a global scale.

And the answers the "search engine" gives are the "correct answers," as determined by a faceless elite in charge of the official narrative—who manipulate your search for knowledge—and you don't even know it.

All this data is collected and combined with all other human expressions into a giant archetypical machine that grows in power with every successive entry, until it reaches the point where it knows what we are thinking before we think it. Then it will be time for artificial intelligence to ensure enslavement.

I looked at Pepper. She was speed-reading the novel *Johnny Tremain,* a story about a young man in Boston who ultimately fights in the Revolution.

I turned and looked at the rattlesnakes, then at The Independent Man statue.

Just being here felt so liberating. Seeing the past, you understand that freedom and liberty have always been a struggle. By every generation. In every age. Liberty—she is pursued and never completely attained.

It was a struggle then. It is a struggle now.

It will always be a struggle.

I started to understand something about myself, my country, and Pepper. I couldn't put into words what I felt about the first two. But I knew right then, looking at her engrossed in that book, that I loved Pepper and wanted to be with her when this was over. And that I would pursue her even if she couldn't be completely attained.

And I was getting hungry. "I could go for some cheese sandwiches and a milkshake right about now," I said.

Pepper shut the book and then looked up at me.

"You talking about diner food made me think of Vaughn and what he said."

She tried to remember. "Something about tipping points."

I answered. "Yes, he said the see-saw tips toward centralization and control; there is a natural resistance to push to the other side and restore freedom and liberty."

"Hackworth, there is some truth to what he said. And it is the story of our history. The first people who came to America were escaping persecution from the government and religious authorities. They sought freedom and liberty. But soon, centralization and control took hold."

"That's what happened to the founder of Rhode Island, Roger Williams," I said. "The community of Salem tried to control him, and he fled."

"And that's what happened in the Revolution, when the people of the states rose up against the tyrant King," Pepper said.

She paused for a moment and said a word that I had never heard before.

"Obscurantism."

She held up a piece of paper that read:

Obscurantism = hiding the truth.

As in the story of our flag.

"That's what some one or group did and is now doing—hiding the truth about our flag," she said. "They obscure the truth. They teach narrative for history and leave little room for questioning what really happened."

A slight breeze began to blow behind us, and Pepper stopped talking. Her back straightened up. She didn't move.

First it started faint, and then the music got louder, and we realized the bookcase door above had been opened! The vibrating mahogany told us, in wonderful tones, *we have a visitor!*

Slowly, Pepper turned to me and put her finger to her lips.

"Shhh," she softly said.

Her finger then pointed straight up.

"Someone's coming down the stairs," she whispered.

I froze. And listened. Then, ever so faintly, we could hear a sound over the music.

It was footsteps.

We didn't move. A familiar feeling started in my toes, worked its way up my spine, and tingled the back of my neck. Fear slowly gripped my body.

Without saying a word, Pepper pointed to the backpack. She unzipped the front pocket and handed me the gun.

I took it, turned off the safety, and put it in my coat pocket.

When I looked up, Pepper was heading to the entrance and staircase.

I grabbed her arm and shook my head back and forth.

"Nooo," I said silently, shaking my head.

She was firm, strong, and confident. She jerked her arm to throw off my grip and pointed to the entrance again.

She resumed walking, and I followed.

We got to the archway and turned our ears toward the top of the steps.

Thump. The sound of a thick book dropping on a table blended like a drumbeat with the mahogany music.

Someone was upstairs. But who? And how many?

Pepper pointed again. She started going up the stairs.

I grabbed her arm again and shook my head.

"Nooo," this time a little harder.

She took her right hand and raised it, palm up, as if to say, "It's all right; let's go slow."

I loosened my grip, and we slowly went up the stairs, careful not to make a sound.

When we got to the top of the stairs, I moved in front of Pepper. I don't know why, but I knew inside I had to be in front. My eyes peered through the crack in the bookcase and into the library.

My breath was knocked right out.

There, not ten feet away, was the Homeland Security agent who had come to my apartment.

Brian Trowbridge.

"Their car has been there a while," a voice said, walking into the parlor.

It was the other agent at the apartment.

Neuman Church.

I turned and looked at Pepper.

She had an expression I will never forget.

The look of someone who has been caught robbing a store. Or caught telling a lie.

She was terrified.

And I was, too.

"Providence Police said they saw it parked yesterday mid-morning, which would coincide with when the drone lost her," Church said.

"Drone?" I thought. "They were following us with a drone?"

"The drone got her going over the bridge at about 10:30, so that seems about right," Trowbridge replied.

"But where is she now?" he said. "She hasn't used her phone in days."

Pepper grabbed my arm and pointed back downstairs.

We slowly made our way back to the chamber, walked to the other side of the room, and crouched behind one of the rattle-snakes.

"Oh my..." Pepper gushed in a hushed tone.

We were silent. I could see in Pepper's face that she was running scenarios through her mind. She then spoke.

"We have to split up," she said.

"How?" I asked. "There is only one way out."

We were silent again.

"Hackworth, they can't catch both of us, or else we lose."

She looked right into my eyes.

"You have to get out."

"Me?" I said. "Me? No, Pepper, you're the one they wanted from the start. You're the one who knows about all of this, much better than I do."

I returned the look, directly into her eyes.

"You are too valuable to lose," I said. "Me, not so much."

We were silent again. Then Pepper gestured back towards the staircase.

"I can't hear anything," she said. "Maybe they left."

We made our way back up the stairs. It was wishful thinking on her part.

"She's here," Church said. "I can feel it."

The other agent spoke. "The emails we intercepted from the Sons of Liberty spoke about this place in a special way. What did the Professor say to us that night?"

"He said we would never find 'it'," Trowbridge said.

"It," he said again.

They both snickered. I could see Agent Church's face. His square jaw and pudgy cheeks dominated his appearance, along with cold, black, steely eyes.

He looked absolutely sinister.

"Let's take this place apart until we find 'it' because I bet then we will find HER."

Pepper started creeping down the stairs. This time she didn't point out or tell me what she was doing.

I quickly followed her back to the archway. She was breathing heavily, trying desperately to slow her breath.

The agents wanted Pepper!

"Brian, I did want to show you this. This part of the bookcase moves."

Suddenly, we heard the bookcase door being rolled open.

Pepper looked towards the stairs. Then back at me.

"Hackworth, listen. We don't have much time. Do you have the camera?"

I nodded yes. I was speechless.

Terrified speechless.

"Here are the keys to the Mustang," she said.

"No, no," I replied. "We do this together."

"Hackworth," she said, taking command of the situation.

"You listen to me. You have the flag now, not me! Both of us cannot go down. You need to get out, go to the meeting in Philadelphia, and contact SOL," she said rapidly. "You can save us and the flag if *you* can get out."

She grabbed both my hands and looked up at me. "What can they do to me? Arrest me? Put me in jail? It'll be OK. You need to keep that flag away from them."

I just stared at her. There was no changing her mind.

"Stay behind the rattlesnake," she said pointing to the one on the left side.

I grabbed the backpack and started walking to the snake, but stopped.

We looked at each other, then reached out at the same time and hugged, nearly squeezing the breath out of each other. I assumed my position behind the snake, holding the gun handle in my coat pocket. Pepper went immediately to a large table just off the center of the room on the main aisle. She sat down, put on reading glasses, and started flipping through papers.

I heard the agents coming.

"Brian, what the hell is this?" Church exclaimed.

"Hold it right there," Church screamed as he entered.

He was talking to Pepper.

"Don't you move, DON'T YOU MOVE!" he yelled.

"What the hell?" Trowbridge said, looking at the rattlesnakes.

"Don't move," Church said.

I peered around the snake.

Church was holding a gun at Pepper.

Trowbridge also had a gun drawn.

"Now slowly stand up and don't try anything stupid," he said.

"What the hell is this?" Trowbridge asked again.

Pepper slowly rose from the chair. She didn't say a word.

The two agents lunged at her, pushing her over the table. Church grabbed her right arm, twisted it behind her back, and then her left.

I heard the handcuffs click.

Then I heard several clicks of the handcuffs.

Pepper let out a squeal as the cuffs were tightened.

"Oh, I am going to do a lot more than make your wrists hurt," Church snarled.

He flipped her around. Raising his hand, he violently slapped her face.

Saliva from her mouth went flying towards me. I couldn't look and pulled my head back.

Whhaacck. Church slapped her again.

"Start talking, Pepper," Trowbridge said. "What is this place? Where's Hack Lancaster? And where's our flag?"

Pepper wouldn't say a word. It was quiet as the agents gave her a chance to speak.

Nothing.

"Where's our flag?" he demanded again. "That is government property that you have stolen."

I looked around the base. Church still had his gun out, pointing it at her head.

I pulled the Ladysmith from my pocket. It was a bit of a distance, but I could probably hit him.

"I... don't... know," she said.

"Oh, look, the pretty girl talks," he said, putting his gun away.

"That's enough, Church," Trowbridge said, reaching down to help Pepper up. He gently placed her in the chair.

"You're in a lot of trouble, Pepper," Trowbridge said softly. "But if you help us, we can help you."

It was the old good cop-bad cop routine (done poorly).

"I don't know anything more than you do," she said.

"Then what are you doing here?" Church said angrily. "With all of this?"

He took his hand and slapped several paper stacks. They flew off the table.

Trowbridge returned to his soft sell.

"Pepper, you need to tell us everything you know about the SOL. They are terrorists, Pepper. And since you are with them, you are a terrorist."

She didn't reply. Her raven hair was out of place. Trowbridge moved around her, and then I saw it.

Pepper was bleeding. Her lip was bleeding. I felt anger and squeezed the gun's handle.

"Start by telling us what this place is," Trowbridge said.

Church was walking down the side of the Heroes. He stopped at James Otis' marble bust. And then, with one quick motion, he kicked its base, and the bust fell to the floor.

SMASH!

The sound echoed in the room.

Church went to the next pedestal, Sam Adams. And just as quickly, he kicked the base, and the bust fell.

He turned to Pepper.

"You are going to start talking now, or you will never leave this place alive!"

His foot kicked the next pedestal, and the bust smashed to the floor.

He now walked methodically over to Pepper, grabbed her by the front of her shirt with one hand, and lifted her out of the chair.

Her shirt ripped from the pull.

I had to do something. I had to help her. But her voice kept ringing in my ears: *"You can save us if you can get out."*

But I was not going to let them do anything more to her.

I peered around the base. Blood was dripping from her mouth, staining the torn part of her shirt.

"You know, Pepper," Church seethed. "Maybe we can be friends after all."

His hand now went to her face, then to her chin. She was trying to hold it back, but I could see the tears.

"Do you want to be friends, Pepper?" Church asked.

At that, Pepper took a deep breath and spit right into his face.

And just as fast, Church smacked her again in the head. This time, she collapsed to the floor.

"Enough!" Trowbridge said. "That's enough."

He grabbed Pepper by the handcuffs and pulled her up. She let out a wincing sound.

He turned her around and said, "Pepper Stillwater. You are under arrest for aiding and abetting terrorists. You are in possession of stolen government property. And you have resisted arrest."

Pepper looked up at Trowbridge.

"Isn't it a little late to be reading me my rights?" she said.

"Rights?" he replied and started laughing. "I am not reading your rights. You don't have any rights, not where you are going."

"We tried to make it work for you," Church said, wiping his sweaty, chubby face.

Trowbridge grabbed her shoulder and pointed her towards the stairs. Church walked beside her, purposely nudging one of the busts on a pedestal. It fell and smashed, like the others.

SMASH!

"I want this place taken care of," Trowbridge barked to Church.

"How much taken care of?" Church replied.

"Burn it. All of it," Trowbridge commanded.

"Nothing is to remain," he added.

The three of them walked up the stairs.

I waited a few minutes, then slowly rose from behind the rattlesnake.

The hall was a wreck. The busts lay on the floor, plaster spilling out from the remaining chunks. It looked like someone dropped a paint can. White pieces turned into fine dust.

And the carefully laid-out stacks were a mess, with papers strewn everywhere.

I walked to where Pepper was standing. Blood was on the table, the chair, and the floor. I felt sick. And then, for some reason, I put my finger on a small crimson dot of her blood and worked it between my fingers.

My fist clenched. I was so angry at myself for not helping her. For crouching and hiding. For being scared. For not stopping evil playing out before my eyes.

I was ashamed of myself.

Walking to the stairs, I heard Trowbridge above.

"You stay here," he said. "I will bring her in. You take care of this place."

I heard the front door open and then silence.

Now Church was heading back downstairs.

He was talking on his cell phone.

"We got her," he said. "We just need him."

I quickly headed back into the chamber and hid in the first place possible—next to the Independent Man.

I leaned against the side wall as Church passed me.

I looked down at my fingers. Pepper's blood was still on them. And the anger and shame welled up inside of me.

Church was walking by the tables, looking for something.

Then he saw what he needed: old newspapers. He started shredding the papers, placing them under a table and chairs.

I realized he was going to light a fire. And a second later, the smell of smoke permeated the chamber.

There wasn't much time to escape. But how, without Church catching me? He was standing near the Heroes section, watching the progress of the flames as they shot up the centuries-old mahogany wood.

I was not going to let him catch me. I wasn't going to let him do to me what he did to Pepper.

Seeing the bust in front of me, my mind decided it was time.

Church had turned back towards the archway, pacing and talking a memo into his phone. He was looking right in my direction but did not see me; he was focused solely on the conversation. He walked past me, talking.

A minute later, he was walking in the other direction, and his back was past me.

The flames now engulfed the room and started the rattlesnakes on fire. The red and orange flames ran up their writhing bodies as the heat and smoke became unbearable.

I grabbed the bust with both hands.

It was of Abel Upshur.

It was heavy, but I felt a great strength that I had never felt before.

I picked it up and snuck up behind Agent Neuman Church.

And drove Abel Upshur into his skull.

Chapter Twenty-Four

"Here individuals of all nations are melted into a new race of men whose labors and posterity will one day cause great changes in the world. Americans are the western pilgrims, who are carrying along with them the great mass of arts, sciences, vigor, and industry which began long since in the East. They will finish the great circle."

"What then is the American, this new man?"

– Letters from an American Farmer, by Michel Guillaume Jean de Crèvecœur (changed to John Hector St. John when he became an American), London, 1782

He fell to the ground like a sack of rocks. Thump! And I watched as the gash in the back of his head oozed blood. I felt a great release from doing this. I no longer felt angry or ashamed.

And I had to get out of there.

Racing to the stairs, I paused and looked back at the Hall. The rattlesnakes were now fully ablaze, and the illustration on the wall had streaks of fire rushing up its center.

My eyes went to The Independent Man.

The statue looked back at me, and then it hit me: the map was in the backpack!

Shhhrrrrrkkkk! A burning ceiling panel fell to the floor.

Where is the backpack?

My eyes darted fervently around the room.

And then I remembered that we left it at the base of the snake on the right.

I covered my mouth and ran to retrieve it, dodging the flames as they shot from the tables.

Reaching in and digging around, it was not there!

"Just look, just look," the voice in my head said.

I peered down and saw it; pressed against the side was the backpack.

The burning snake now started to collapse, the embers falling around the red, glowing base. In a flash, I grabbed it and darted across the room, just as the snake smashed to the ground in a burst of flames.

The heat was now intense, and the smoke thick. I covered my eyes with my arm, crouched down, and ran up the stairs. Smoke filled the professor's library parlor.

Instead of going out the front door, I retraced our steps back out through the smaller basement so as not to be seen.

Running to the Mustang, I suddenly stopped.

"Do not get in that car!" a voice in my head said. So I turned the other way and headed down the hill to the train station. I fast-walked and did not look behind me for fear that Neuman Church wasn't quite dead enough.

Outside the station, I approached a young man and offered him $20 if he would do me a favor.

"And just buy the ticket," I said.

Moments later, he returned with a one-way ticket from Providence to Philadelphia. The SOL meeting was tonight at midnight at the Franklin Institute.

I was on the train and found a seat without anyone around.

I put my hands on my head; they were shaking. The shaking got worse.

"You killed a man," the voice in my head said.

"You killed a government agent."

"They are going to kill Pepper."

"And you."

My whole body was now shaking.

"You killed a man," the voice repeated over and over.

My hand reached into my coat pocket. Yes, the gun was still there. I clicked the safety on.

The last few minutes at Professor Redmand's house raced through my head. Church hitting Pepper over and over. Pepper bleeding and crying. Church intimidating her. Humiliating her.

Why did I do this? Why did I kill him?

"You killed a man. You had no choice."

The train rocked left and right. Then it jerked forward. And stopped.

A terrifying thought went through my head. "The police stopped the train. They are coming to get you!"

The train didn't move. I looked at my reflection in the train window next to my seat. My face was dirty. My hair was matted down.

Then I looked at my fingers.

"Is that Pepper's blood?" I wondered. "Or Neuman Church's?"

"You killed a man," the voice in my head said again as the train jerked forward and resumed its course.

I looked up when the conductor entered the car. He took my ticket and clicked it.

"Have a good day, Mr. Trowbridge."

Trowbridge? Did he say Trowbridge?

I looked around nervously. The conductor had moved down the car.

I looked at the ticket. "Jacob Trowbridge."

Oh yeah, I thought. That must be the name of the kid who bought me the ticket. Talk about a coincidence!

No one was sitting next to me. I hopped over to the window seat and closed my eyes.

"You killed a man."

I propped my head up against the window and nodded off. I was exhausted and scared. I couldn't keep my eyes open.

In a dream, I saw Pepper, the girl I first met in kindergarten. The woman I just spent some of the most exciting days of my life with. The person who was beaten by the corrupt agents.

I saw her standing there, taking the blows from Church. I could see those tears. And the blood.

The train slowed down, and I was in and out of sleep.

"Newark, NJ. Newark, NJ," the conductor yelled. "Next stop, Metro Park."

I couldn't fully wake up. I went back to thinking about Pepper. I was remembering the first time I met her. "Hi, I'm Pepper," she declared, boldly walking towards me as I retreated behind my mother. My mother gently pulled me around to her front. "Go ahead, tell Pepper your name." I stammered, and my face started blushing. Pepper was like an angel, wrapped in light and beaming ...

I woke up from the dream.

The train started moving, and several people came into the car. I looked outside the window, so I wouldn't make eye contact.

A woman crisply walked right up to the seat next to me and sat down.

Out of the corner of my eye, I noticed her jet black hair and the way she moved.

Her head was turned into the aisle. I wiped my sleepy eyes to be sure.

It had to be Pepper!

"Pepper, Pepper," I said eagerly.

The woman turned and looked at me funny.

It wasn't her.

The woman shrugged, stood up, and walked to a seat in the front of the car.

I looked out the window, feeling like an idiot.

The train raced ahead. And just as fast, the happenings of the day went through my head. The underground hall and its secrets. Pepper and her beauty. And my evil. I had killed a man. Not just any man, either. A government agent. Killed him.

That was not right, I thought. There is no justification for murder. Especially the sneak up from behind and kill kind of murder.

"HE DESERVED IT," a loud voice suddenly emerged in my mind. "YOU SHOULD HAVE SHOT HIM WHEN YOU COULD HAVE. YOU SHOULD HAVE SHOT BOTH OF THEM!"

The train was slowing. "Metro Park, next station stop," the loudspeaker barked. "Metro Park."

Where's Pepper now? What are they doing to her?

"You need to get the truth out," Pepper said right before they got her.

But now it was more complicated.

"Metro Park, next station stop," the conductor said again. "Metro Park."

Fear started to grip me again. I knew well that when a police officer is killed, it's not like some Average Joe getting killed. Sure, the cops show up, the investigators move in, the crime scene is established, and the detective is assigned to the case. But then, the story fades from the headlines, and 20 years later, it reappears with the headline "Cold Case Finally Solved," and only after the actual murderer confesses.

That's how it is when an Average Joe or a Professor Redmand is killed.

But if it is law enforcement, there is a whole dragnet of the city and surrounding areas. It's like the president was shot. Every police officer on every city street, and even on city streets not in that city, turns their eyes to the crime and hunts down the murderer until he is found.

That is what happens when a cop is shot. Now imagine a federal agent. Instead of them pouring in from every city street, they pour in from every city in the country. And they get their man.

Fear had now taken hold of me.

And they get "YOU," the voice in my head said.

"Now arriving, Metro Park," the conductor said.

"The next station stop is Trenton, NJ," he added.

The train slowed as it approached the station. I pressed my face against the window, looking for what I did not know.

And then I saw them. There were police officers on the platform. I saw one or two at first, then three, then five.

The train slowed to a stop. As it did, I saw several men in business suits, sharply dressed with perfectly cut short hair.

Federal agents!

The train inched forward into position and jerked to a stop.

"Metro Park," the loudspeaker said. "Final call, Metro Park."

I looked out the window. The police were watching who was getting off the train. There were two officers and one suit at my car's front exit. I could see the same at the back exit. And up the ramp, I could make out the same thing going on in the car ahead.

They were checking the passengers as they got off!

I sank in my seat. The dragnet was on. And this wasn't some remote shack in the woods. This was the train; I was inside, and the cops were inches away.

The last passengers got off, and the platform was empty—except for the officers and suits still visible outside.

Then, walking from the front of the train outside, came the conductor. He was holding several pieces of paper and gesturing with his hand. One policeman and three suits now encircled him as he talked.

The smile on his face quickly disappeared.

The guys in the suits weren't smiling.

Someone came up to me, reached over my head, and deposited a suitcase in the overhead. It was another businesswoman, sharply dressed, in a two-piece gray business suit.

I looked out the window, and they were gone. The conductor, the cop, and the agents had disappeared.

I let out a breath. "Maybe you escaped this," the voice in my head said.

"Hi," the businesswoman said. Her voice had a strange calming effect on me.

"Hello," I replied.

"Oh, what a day," she said, and then launched in on a review of how busy she had been, seeing clients, battling the traffic, and staying cool in the heat. The sort of stuff you talk about with strangers on the train.

I interjected here and there, but then realized THE POLICE ARE ON THE TRAIN.

We kept talking. And because I realized they were walking down the aisle towards us, I went into happy conversation mode.

"And then the air conditioner went off in my car, and my makeup started to melt," she said, describing her morning.

I laughed, nodding my head and slapping my knee. Not too loud of a laugh, and not an exaggerated slapping of the knee.

Just enough to make it look like I didn't have a care in the world.

The police officer was looking to his left and right. With each turn of his head, he held his glance for a moment at each turn, studying the faces of the people in the seat.

"I know exactly what you're saying," I told the businesswoman as the officer came upon us. "Everything, except the makeup part."

She let out a laugh, and I joined in, just as the intense eyes of the officer gazed our way.

As he stared at us, the businesswoman quickly stopped laughing and sat up straight, the way you do when you're pulled over for speeding, and the police officer taps on the window.

I did the same. I stopped laughing, sat up, and turned to him.

"Officer," she said. I nodded.

He had seen us laughing together. Now he sees us showing him respect with our body motions together.

He stared right at me.

Then he turned and looked at the people on the other side of the aisle. As he walked by, I could see the gun in his holster.

At that moment, she started talking again, and, without betraying a single ounce of fear, I nodded as if to agree with her.

That's when I noticed the second man walking down the aisle. He had been only a few steps behind the officer, watching the reactions before, during, and after the policeman had passed each passenger.

"They have to do something with the parkway traffic," I said at the moment the suit was staring at me.

I was nodding my head, "No," as if to express displeasure in our conversation.

The suit walked past us.

"What do you think is going on?" the businesswoman said.

"Not a clue," I said, knowing full well the agent was still observing us.

"They must be looking for someone," she said.

"Yeah, you're right," I said.

There was an awkward pause in our conversation, with the officers standing still and silent.

"I hope they get him," I said.

The police officer and the federal agent turned and walked into the next car. Within seconds, the conductor barked.

"Next stop, Trenton," he said. "Trenton, next station stop."

As the train pulled away from the station, I looked out the window, careful not to press my face against the glass.

I didn't want them to see me again.

In all, there had to be six cops and ten suits who had walked through our car.

Chapter Twenty-Five

"His Britannic Majesty acknowledges the said United States, viz. New Hampshire, Massachusetts Bay, Rhode Island and Providence Plantations, Connecticut, New York, New Jersey, Pennsylvania, Delaware, Maryland, Virginia, North Carolina, South Carolina, and Georgia, to be free, sovereign and independent States and he treats with them as such ..."

– From the 1783 Treaty of Paris with Great Britain, which officially ended the American Revolution. The assertion of being "Free and Independent States" made in the Declaration of Independence was officially recognized in this treaty.

The businesswoman was busy on her cellphone, talking on the speaker phone while sending an email.

"Boy," I thought. "Do I miss that!"

My phone had everything I needed on it. It was always with me, anywhere, anytime. It was what brightened up my mediocre life and kept me in touch with my friends.

Until now, of course.

Then I remembered the burner phone. Taking it out of my pocket, I checked the messages. Besides the half dozen messages from Tory that read "Message Cannot Be Downloaded," there was nothing new.

The businesswoman was talking business, just like the businessmen in the aisle across from us. The people in front of us were talking to each other, not on the phone. They were talking about their respective companies.

"I have budget authority of about six million dollars," one said to the other.

The other one loosened his tie knot.

"Well, I have budget authority up to ten million," he said, unfastening the shirt's top button.

And on they went, almost trying to one-up each other in talking about their jobs. People are funny that way. They invest so much of themselves—their very lives—in their job or career. Listening to them talk reminded me of two boys on the playground arguing about who's father was better.

That's how my life was until a few days ago. Though Pepper had a more prestigious job at a more prestigious publishing company, I still had an impressive-sounding title and made decent money. My whole life was my job, to the exclusion of the world around me.

The old Hackworth Lancaster wouldn't have cared about a flag mystery or a chamber of secrets. Or lies the government told to keep control. He would have read the story online, given it a moment's thought, sent a link to Tory, then moved on to the next story, not phased in the slightest.

My smartphone filled the holes in my life. When I wasn't working for the company, I was texting or emailing. When I got home to my apartment each night and had dinner, I would then sit in my chair and curl up and watch the apps on my phone.

This has been my routine in some fashion since the smartphone was invented. TikToks. YouTube. Instagram. Games. Texting. News. Notes. All at the flick of a finger. And I loved it.

The businesswoman kept talking and texting on her phone, as did the men across the aisle. And the people in front kept one-upping each other.

Drones, I thought. They are drones. Worker bees. Their brains were hardwired to the stimuli of the moment. Talking, texting, and bragging worker bees.

"They are? We are. You are," went through my head.

The train stopped at Trenton. No one got on the train. There were no cops, no agents. Some of the people in my car got up and off.

"Philll - aaa - delll -- phi --- aahh," the conductor said. "Next stop is Philll - aaa - delll -- phi --- aahh."

The elongated way he said Philadelphia made me smile. You could tell he loved saying it that way.

We started to cross the Delaware River, and I immediately thought of the picture of George Washington crossing the Delaware in 1776. There he was, standing proud, in a rowboat with a dozen men, navigating the icebergs.

And there was the American flag, flying in the breeze. Except, the truth was, there was no flag. That was put into the scene 75 years after the crossing. And if there was a flag, it was a 'Don't Tread On Me' flag or the 'Appeal To Heaven' flag.

Then I thought about what the real scene was. George was probably huddled with the men, a blanket covering them from the freezing winds of winter. They were hungry. And not properly dressed for the cold. Some had rags for shoes; others were bleeding from their feet from the exposure to the cold.

That is what the history books say Valley Forge was like a year later for the few men who stayed. Many had dropped their guns and gone home, unable to bear the great enemies they faced: freezing cold, nagging hunger, and the British with their German mercenaries.

Bleeding from their feet.

Pepper was bleeding from her mouth after that creep had slugged her a couple times.

Blood was oozing from his head after I smashed him.

Blood. Blood. Blood.

I looked out the window.

"TRENTON MAKES, THE WORLD TAKES," large letters on the side of the bridge proudly declared.

That's funny, I thought. Trenton hasn't made anything in years except crooked politicians. The sign must have been put up a hundred years ago, when Trenton was actually a major manufacturing center. The city was a major producer of cigars, ceramics, and wire. Those jobs went away and never came back.

The train raced across the Delaware River. And when we got onto the Pennsylvania side, I knew we would be in Philly soon.

I then realized the purpose of my trip. I was to go to the Sons of Liberty meeting that Vaughn Clark had invited us to. I thought of the Sons of Italy, for some reason. Of a wedding reception held at the Sons of Italy hall.

Until a few days ago, the last time I heard "Sons of Liberty" was in grade school. We were taught they were a group of men who caused trouble for the British before the war started. They did the tea party in Boston and other things to disrupt society.

They were rebels *with* a cause.

I bet the British considered them terrorists. Isn't that the truth? One side's heroes are the other side's traitors.

Is that how it is today? Of course it is, I thought. What we call terrorists are heroes in their homes.

I thought about the people in the Middle East celebrating after the Twin Towers were attacked and destroyed.

No, those people who flew the planes into the World Trade Center were terrorists. They were murderers. And the people dancing were ignorant and rotten. Period. There was no equivocating on that. Innocent people by the thousands were murdered that day by evil men. And our government had every right to hunt their supporters down and make them pay.

That was more than ten years ago. But something happened after the Twin Towers came down. Our government started looking inward for possible enemies. It started to take extraordinary measures to *prevent* another tragedy.

At first, these measures seemed necessary. We did not know how extensive the terrorist network was or where they would strike again. I remember that day like no other—that day of helplessness watching the towers crumble and knowing there were innocent people, innocent Americans, being murdered.

Thousands of innocent people. Murdered.

And so when the government took new security measures, no one blinked an eye. Like they said, this was a war.

So they passed laws that let the government crack down. They seized suspects off the streets without all that Miranda rights crap. They monitored libraries and what people were reading. They classified as secret what had been easily made available in the past: maps, facility drawings, blueprints, and general knowledge.

They took over the airports and turned everyone into a suspected criminal. Instead of looking for people like the terrorists who lived in those countries, we all had to be considered suspects. There can be no discrimination, after all.

They make us strip down practically to our underwear, then pat us down for good measure—all just to get on an airplane! We walk through x-ray machines and metal detectors, passing people trained to note our expressions. Our laughs. Our looks.

Meanwhile, other people take our picture and watch cameras as we walk to our planes.

Make one move out of the ordinary, make a gesture out of the ordinary, say something out of the ordinary, and you are flagged for another pat-down, another encounter.

So we learn how to be just like everyone else. How not to cause suspicion. How to submit to the authorities. How not to even joke about something, lest it be considered a threat.

Our children watch us behave like this and listen to our admonitions. And grow up, taught how to be ordinary. How not to stand out. How not to be different.

The train was now flying the fastest it had on the trip, and we passed empty factories, smash-windowed warehouses, and shabby houses all so fast, it was a blur.

"The terrorists won, Hack," the voice in my head said.

Think about it, I thought. With the goal of making us all safe and secure, they chained us. It would be like a parent tying a rope around their child when learning how to walk. The rope is attached to the ceiling so that, when the child falls, the rope will prevent the accident.

But the child needs to fall to learn how to walk. And before long, the child would get used to the rope and consider the rope normal.

The child would then know only how to walk with the rope.

"That's what is happening to us," I thought.

But it was worse than that. Terrorism takes thought. Those evil monsters who attacked us on 9/11 had to do a lot of thinking and planning. They had to discuss their plans with each other. They had to do research.

So, to be absolutely sure they were ahead of the next terrorist strike, the government had to get inside the heads of the possible terrorists. They had to listen to their phone calls, study the web sites they had visited, and review the library materials they had read.

They needed to read the text messages and emails. They had to open their mail. They had to review their credit card purchases and their shopping habits. They needed to know how much money they had.

The train was now roaring, as if the conductor knew we were late and he really had to get there to make the schedule. The scene outside was the same: broken windows, empty buildings, and the slums where the workers once lived. But now we were racing past huge piles of steel, cars, and bricks with dirty buildings next to them. Scrap dealers and garbage collectors. The people who collect all the old useless scrap, bundle it together, and ship it off so new stuff can be made.

I thought of what Trowbridge said.

"When the drone lost her," he had said in the library.

So, I thought, not only do they watch every step our mind makes, they watch every step our feet take as well.

A drone was tailing us. That surprised Pepper and me. But it should not have, because actually, a drone is merely a flying camera. What about the fixed cameras that have popped up everywhere since 9/11?

Cameras on the interstates. Cameras on the city streets. Cameras outside of buildings. And cameras inside buildings. Cameras on police cars. Cameras over our heads for the big picture; cameras just a few feet off the ground to record license plates. Cameras at the check-out counters. Cameras on our front porch.

The All-Seeing Eye, like on the $1 bill. Like above the archway in the Sons of Liberty Hall. Eyes that feed their images back to the monster, I thought.

"Someone is behind those little eyes," the voice in my head said. And if it is not an actual person, it is the Great Memory of a computer storing the information for later retrieval or, worse, for processing by artificial intelligence.

The Great Memory and the All-Seeing Eye.

Not too long ago, the only thing that had a Great Memory with an All-Seeing Eye that recorded and remembered our every move was that of *God*—or so our conscience told us.

Now it is the government, with help from the internet industry. No, not the government. SOME PEOPLE DEEP INSIDE THE GOVERNMENT. They have the powers of the Great Memory and the All-Seeing Eye.

The government has become a god for many. A cheap imitation of God. An angry god.

I remembered reading about the American who was one of the terrorists. He lived in some middle-eastern country. One day he woke up, and "BANG," a drone bomb blew him up. No one knocked on his door, like in the television shows, and said, "Mr. Terrorist, we have a warrant for your arrest."

No one put cuffs on him, dragged him to the police station, booked him, and threw him in jail. No lawyer met with him. No judge granted habeas corpus, which means "show the body," so his family could see him and make sure he wasn't abused by the government. Habeas corpus goes back to before the Magna Charta (the Great Charter) in 1215, a right the peasants demanded because the King had this habit of taking a person from the village, and he or she was never heard from again.

Now the King just blows him up with a drone two thousand miles away. No horses or knights are needed.

"Think about it, Hack," the voice in my head said. Big chunks of the Bill of Rights are dedicated to just these situations: the right to say and write what you want, privacy of our papers, our arrest, trial, and conviction.

But now, the King can just waive all of that off, declare a person a terrorist, and issue the death sentence.

No judge, no jury.

No justice. For an American.

Did the terrorists win? Did they knock down more than the towers? Did they harm the very thing that made America the shining city on the hill? That made us different? Exceptional?

Our freedom and liberty have been sacrificed, I thought.

The train was slowing down.

"Next stop is Phill-ah-dell-phi--- aahh," the conductor said.

I smiled at the businesswoman as he said Philadelphia, how he held onto every part. How unordinary!

The train entered darkness at the subterranean levels beneath 30th Street Station. As we passed the platform and slowed to a stop, I looked for the police or federal agents.

It didn't seem like either was present.

The train stopped. We got off, a flood of people rushing into the darkness, now only vaguely lit by dirty lights overhead on the platform.

I went up the escalator to the main floor. The Philadelphia train station was built with greatness in mind. Like the Twin Towers. Designed by creative genius, untethered, free. Built by American strength, brawn, sweat.

That's how our country was back then.

I walked towards the exit, passing a crowd of people hovering around a television. Another crowd was standing around another TV nearby. I recognized that many of them got on the train in Providence with me and may have family in the area.

I walked up to one of the crowds and was able to catch the some of the news.

"A major explosion in the College Hill section of Providence has killed an untold number of people," the newscaster said.

"City authorities say a gas leak under the street caused the blast, which destroyed several houses."

The video showed a blown-out area, strewn with papers and shards of plaster, mahogany, and marble.

Then I realized it was right where I was, just hours ago.

Professor Redmand's house, as well as his neighbor's, was destroyed.

The newscaster continued, "Confirmed dead was a federal agent injured when part of a building fell on him," the newscaster said.

My mouth dropped open in disbelief.

They were talking about Neuman Church.

Then a familiar face appeared on the screen. It was live from Providence, and the reporter was interviewing a man with messy hair and a dirty face.

"He was trying to save people when he died," the man said.

The reporter looked like she was going to cry.

"He gave his life to help others," the dirty-faced, messy-haired man said.

I moved closer to the screen.

It was Brian Trowbridge, the federal agent.

"So sorry," the reporter said to Trowbridge.

I quickly pulled back from the group, having seen enough.

Thoughts raced through my head in search of an explanation.

Then it came to me.

They always intended to blow up the Sons of Liberty chamber. They murdered Professor Redmand and blew up the only place in this country that held the truth.

My hands reached into my pockets and felt the gun, camera, and phone.

Neuman Church a hero? Liars!

Gas explosion? Liars!

The newscaster repeats what the authorities tell him. Throw in some footage of the scene, and there it is—the truth, brought to you by the government and the media. Now, here's a word from our pharmaceutical sponsor.

Only this wasn't the truth.

I knew the truth.

I walked out of 30th Street Station and into the sun. It was a beautiful afternoon in Philadelphia.

Crossing the bridge over the Schuykill River, there was a sudden urge to ditch my useless burner phone. My luck would be that it didn't receive messages but was still trackable!

Reaching again into my pocket, I grabbed it, then held it over the railing to throw into the water.

No, I thought. Do not throw this away. Instead, keep this phone and write down everything that has happened over the last several days.

I put the phone back into my pocket.

I knew where I had to go and who I had to see ASAP.

My pace picked up into a fast walk.

Then I broke into a sprint.

I had to see Tory now!

Chapter Twenty-Six

"Experience must be our only guide. Reason may mislead us."

*– John Dickinson, speaking at the Constitutional Convention,
from Madison's Notes on the Debates*

"The ferry boat and barge were anchored in the
river, and displayed a variety of colors,
particularly a jack bearing eleven stars."

*– Columbian Magazine, May 1789, reporting on the
inauguration of George Washington*

I walked one block past the Franklin Antiques Bookstore, then cut through the alley to the back door. The Russoff's had a book repair shop in the rear of the building where the money-making magic happened. Mr. Russoff would buy beaten-up First Editons for $10 or $100, repair and rebind them, and then sell them for $100 or $1000, or more.

The shop door was open, so I walked in and proceeded into the bookstore. There was Tory sitting at the counter. And there was his father talking to someone in front of the store. Hanging back, I gave a quick wave to Tory, but he didn't see me.

I tried again. Nothing.

"Tory!" I said in a loud whisper.

He looked up in surprise and knocked over a book on the counter. Then he almost tipped over.

Tory ran to me and pushed me back into the workshop.

"Hack, good Lord Man," Tory said, embracing me with a big bear hug. "Are you OK? You look terrible."

"Thanks," I said.

"What is going on? What is the update?"

I told him about what had just happened in Providence, the Sons of Liberty chamber, and the arrest of Pepper. And I detailed what we knew about Professor Mac.

"And I might have killed someone."

"Who?"

"A federal agent who attacked Pepper."

Tory stood up, his big hulking frame now quickly moving to the door connecting the workshop to the bookstore. He closed the door.

"Did the guy have it coming? Tell me! If yes, then don't say another word."

I just looked at him.

"Hack, that strange guy came in again looking for you, except this time he wanted me to relay the following: *'Tell Hack I know about the flag.'* I have his name and number."

"Tory, we know what the flag is."

"What is it?"

"The first flag of the United States of America when the Constitution came into force."

"Who cares? You and Pepper are in big trouble, and it doesn't seem like it's going to end well."

"Did anybody see you kill the guy?"

"No."

"No cameras?"

"No, but I thought you said if the guy had it coming, then I didn't have to say another word."

Tory smiled. "What are we going to do next?"

"We? That's not a good idea, buddy."

"Hack, I can't sit around while this is happening, you know that," Tory said, reaching into the refrigerator and grabbing a Diet Coke. "Did you get my texts? What do you think about what I have discovered?"

"No, I haven't gotten texts since the first batch. Error messages, but not texts."

I reached into my pocket and pulled out the parchment map. "Oh, and there's this," I said, handing it to Tory. "Pepper said this map was tucked in the flag when Professor Redmand gave it to her."

"Goodness, what do we have here?" Tory said, walking over to a workbench with a large, illuminating magnifying glass.

He put the map under the glass.

"Hmm. Ah-huh. Yup. So this is very old. It is printed on parchment, which is a nice way of saying an animal's skin, probably a calf. Parchment is what the Constitution and Declaration are printed on. Yup. Ummm."

He pulled the parchment away from the light, then held it up to the light.

"Maybe a secret message is on the back," I said.

Tory laughed. "That's funny. No, I'm studying how the surface was prepared for ink."

He put the map down and looked at me.

"You really need to take a shower," Tory said.

"You really need to take your ADHD medicine."

"Hack," Tory continued, "the secret message is here."

He proceeded to describe what he saw.

"So the top are the flags that actually flew in the Revolutionary War including the rebellious stripes with the snake. The map shows the colonies in 1763. And the drawing in the bottom corner is of Benjamin Franklin's grave!"

"What? What?" I asked. "I didn't see anything about Benjamin Franklin."

Tory took his phone out of his pocket and snapped a picture of the bottom right corner of the map. He then zoomed in on the gravestone.

Sure enough, it said Benjamin & Deborah Franklin!

"Why would Ben Franklin's grave be on this map?" Tory asked. "And what do those words on the bottom left mean?"

Eleven bees emerge from their hives, headed by their queen.

These words were nearly invisible to the naked eye.

"It's obvious, Hack. The flag you have is somehow related to Franklin's tomb. The flag being nailed on the map is probably the one now in your apartment. And who knows? Maybe it came from Franklin's grave?"

My head was spinning with these facts, and I was again getting hungry.

"Tory, I'm starving," I blurted out.

"What? I figure out the map, and you just want to eat? Fine, I will run to the Reading Terminal Market and get some cheesesteaks and donuts. You get cleaned up."

"What about your dad? I can't work right now."

"Don't worry about him; he's preoccupied. He's got a real whale on the hook!"

I could hear his father sweet-talking the customer. He was trying to sell a first edition of *Animal Farm* by George Orwell.

252 / Francis Pio

The workshop bathroom was less than I needed, but it worked. And by the time I walked out, Tory was there with the food. The Amish-made donuts were a must if you were going to the market.

"I've already eaten," Tory said as he opened the sandwich, "but I'll find room."

I couldn't stop eating mine and was barely listening to Tory.

"Hack, I think the Betsy Ross story is true, except for the date," Tory said. "That's one of the things I was trying to text you about. And I'll even go so far as to say that your 12-star flag was made by Betsy Ross."

I had finished my sandwich. It was excellent.

"Tory, you may be correct. I saw a picture of her making the flag, dated 1789," I said. "But when we were at the Albany Capitol a few days ago, the tour guide said Betsy couldn't have made it in 1776, when the Stars and Stripes were created in 1777. It's impossible."

"Hack, she made it in 1789."

"What makes you so sure?"

"Betsy Ross was a living, breathing flag maker with government contracts and in service to people like Benjamin Franklin and George Washington. That's just a fact. George even had her make drapes for his Mount Vernon estate in 1774."

He continued. "When I found out that the Stars and Stripes were not flown during the Revolution, I discovered Betsy Ross made the flag used when the British evacuated New York in 1783. That's the flag pictured on your old map. The problem is, there was no big star in the middle ever recorded before 1789."

"What are you saying, Tory?"

"Simply this. William Canby, Betsy's grandson and the source of the legend, intentionally used the year 1776 because it marks the beginning of the Revolution. Camby came up with the story around the 100th anniversary of the Declaration of Independence, which was just a decade after the Civil War.

"He knew a strong, nationalist message would be welcomed, so he changed the date of the flag's creation from the actual date of 1789 to 1776," Tory said.

"He knew the truth would not be welcomed."

"Yes, perhaps," Tory said, biting into his third donut.

There was a long pause in the conversation as we finished the meal. I thought about Pepper and what was happening to her.

"Tory, I need to go to a Sons of Liberty meeting tonight."

"No problem, when are we leaving?"

"You're not going. Nothing but trouble awaits."

"Yes, Hack, I am going."

"Tory, I am already in trouble. You don't have to be."

Tory stood up and walked towards me. He is about three inches taller and about 90 pounds heavier than I am.

"Yeah, I'm going, Hack," he said as he bumped against me.

"Whatever."

We walked out the workshop door, then through the alley to get to the street. I was too tired to walk and put my hand up for a cab. One finally came, and we got in.

"222 North 20th Street," I told the cabbie.

He was a little old man with a Philly's baseball cap on his head.

"Got it," he said, pulling from the curb. "222 North 20th."

"The Franklin Institute."

Chapter Twenty-Seven

"And what country can preserve its liberties if their rulers are not warned from time to time that their people preserve the spirit of resistance? Let them take arms. The remedy is to set them right as to facts, pardon and pacify them. What signify a few lives lost in a century or two? The tree of liberty must be refreshed from time to time with the blood of patriots and tyrants. It is its natural manure."

– Thomas Jefferson, in a letter to William Stephens Smith, 1787, regarding Shay's Rebellion in Massachusetts. If only Shay had learned that the state government granted his demands, he would not have marched—poor communication from Boston to rural areas was to blame.

Tory and I knew the Franklin Institute well and loved walking around it. Their managing director was a regular customer at the bookstore. The Institute originally opened inside Independence Hall in 1824 in honor of Benjamin Franklin, the greatest scientist of the day. One hundred and ten years later, a new building was constructed on 20th Street.

The cab sped to our destination, and I admired the view. Philly had changed a lot in the last few decades. I remembered reading that in the 1980's, there was a debate about ending the ban on new buildings being taller than William Penn's hat on the statue above City Hall.

The article said the ban kept Philadelphia's buildings in proportion. The ban also had a philosophical undertone, almost saying there can be nothing larger or more important than the people as represented in their legislative hall. At first, tradition won the day. But over time, interest waned, and the ban was lifted. Today, the people and their legislative hall have assumed their new role, which is much smaller and less important than the enterprises housed in the towers that seem to touch the sky.

"Here you go," the cabbie said.

"Keep the change," I said, handing him $20.

We were early, and the SOL meeting was at midnight, but I wanted to get the layout of the place we would visit in the dark.

Tory and I walked up the steps and into the Franklin Institute, which is a science learning center complete with a planetarium and other cool stuff.

We were seized by the image before us.

There he was, sitting and gazing. I could feel his eyes surveying the room and beyond.

He wasn't looking straight at us, but over us.

As if he saw something bigger than me, Tory, or the people assembled at his feet.

He was in a rotunda, the center of attention.

It was a statue of Benjamin Franklin.

"He looks bigger than Abraham Lincoln in the Lincoln Memorial," Tory said.

"He was bigger in every other respect as well," I replied. "Without a doubt, Benjamin Franklin is the greatest American ever to have lived."

Then I thought about Franklin's bust in the Son's of Liberty Hall and how it was slightly higher than the others.

And what Pepper said: "Franklin's body wasn't even cold before the nationalists took apart his Pennsylvania constitution."

We moved around the building, noting cameras here and there. Security seemed normal for a museum like this. Various groups of people were touching the exhibits. This was a hands-on museum of learning, especially for students.

Franklin would not have wanted it any other way.

We went to the second floor. I paid close attention to the exits and side doors.

"This place is pretty big. How am I going to find the SOL?" I asked Tory.

He just shook his head.

I also thought about the procedure for actually meeting them. What do I do? Knock on the front door and say, "Hi, I am here to meet the Sons of Liberty."

The smell of food coming from the restaurant down the hall drew Tory's attention.

"I am getting a little thirsty," he said as we walked into the cafeteria. Called Franklin Foodworks, its menu was designed for the students who walked through the exhibits. I didn't get anything. Tory got a Diet Coke.

"Look," I said, "we have to scope this place out once again, but this time keep a careful eye on the security cameras. We need to find some spot to hide when this place closes up."

"Excuse me, excuse me," said a man who I took to be the janitor. He was pushing a dolly full of stacked chairs. Right behind him was another janitor who was pulling a cart of lattice panels, ribbons, and drapes.

I followed them to the main rotunda, where they were setting up a reception of some sort. They deposited the chairs and lattice, then headed back to the storage room to get more.

I looked at the clock. It was 5 p.m., and the Franklin Institute was closing to the public. We were running out of time to find a place to hide.

We followed the janitors back to the storage room, taking careful note of the surroundings. They were oblivious to us and were in a hurry to set up for the party. When they left the storage room, we sneaked in.

The room was full of tables, chairs, lattice, and all kinds of event props. There were rooms in rooms, with walls of chainlink fence. One fenced-off area held one kind of chair, the other another kind, and so on.

This was going to be the place to hide.

Out of the corner of my eye, I spotted what had to be the maintenance office. I walked in, pretending to be looking for directions.

No one was there. But on the wall were working shirts of blue with the words "Franklin Institute" emblazoned on the left breast pocket. There had to be a dozen of these shirts, none with any other name. Looking around to see if anyone had entered the storage area and being convinced we were alone, I quickly grabbed two shirts and threw one to Tory.

He watched me tuck it under the shirt I was wearing, then did the same.

Walking out of the office, we passed an older man sitting in a chair and placing letters on an announcement board. He was putting away the remaining letters on the table, obviously finished with the sign.

He took no notice of us.

The sign read:

Lief-Terbily-Shappines 250th Anniversary
Celebrate! 7pm Seating Opens 6:45

It was the sign for the reception in the rotunda.

The words struck me as rather odd. Apparently, Lief-Terbily-Shappines were celebrating their 250th anniversary. Being a writer, the spellings seemed odd. It must be a company or religious group, I thought.

The janitors returned. The supervisor, who was one of them pulling the empty cart, was talking about the details of the reception.

"We need 200 chairs total and twelve more stanchions," he said in a hurried tone.

The other janitors dutifully loaded the cart with more chairs and stanchions.

"Can I help you?" the supervisor said. He was a tall man, and one of the flaps of his blue shirt hung out of his pants.

"Was going to ask you the same question," I said.

"Whatta you two looking for, work?" he inquired, emphasizing the last word.

"Yessir, yes sir, we are," Tory said in a slightly sarcastic tone only I could detect.

The supervisor looked us up and down. I still felt dirty, despite cleaning up at the bookstore. My hair was matted, and my clothes looked like I had been living in them. Which was true.

"We could use it," the supervisor said. "Go get a shirt and help move these chairs."

We went back to the office and walked to the wall with the shirts, quickly pulling the ones we had stolen from under our shirts. We headed into the bathroom and, upon returning, looked every part the janitor.

We were set! We could stick around playing the part of janitor until midnight, when the SOL meeting was to be held.

Pushing and pulling carts of chairs, setting them up, and returning to the storage room ten chairs at a time was hard work. The supervisor no longer did this chore now that he had us. He sat with the older man next to the sign and talked.

"Even in the janitor's world, there is upper management," Tory joked.

Finally, we were done setting up. The room was arranged as if the wedding were to be recreated, with two sides of chairs and a central aisle. At the front of the room was the lattice work, which I helped assemble with Pete, the other worker. He never said a word while we worked.

"Hey, Dirty Pete," the supervisor barked at us. "The right panel is crooked."

We adjusted the lattice.

Three chairs were placed in front and faced the other chairs, apparently for the bride, groom, and minister. Then we set up the stanchions on each side of the aisles, just like in a wedding.

Finally, the older man showed up with the sign and placed it so the visitors would know this was their party.

Back in the storage room office, the supervisor had changed out of his blue shirt and was punching his time card.

He walked over to me and Tory. "Here," he said, handing us both three $20 bills. "Stick around until the party starts and help Dirty Pete. Once the party gets kicking, you can leave."

"Do you need us to work after the party?" I asked.

"No," he replied. "We don't have to worry about breaking down until tomorrow. I have the regular guy coming back at 6 a.m."

He turned back to me. "Hey guys, thanks for helping out."

We nodded, and he departed.

This was too good to be true! Dirty Pete wouldn't even notice if we stayed past that time.

Tory and I walked back to the rotunda. There was a smartly dressed woman busy readjusting the stanchions, the chairs, the lattice work, and the sign. At first, I thought she was with the museum, but it appeared she was the organizer of the party.

On each side of the aisles were bars, with bartenders readying for the evening's festivities.

Caterers had just finished laying out a sumptuous spread of colorful hors d'oeuvres of every kind. Pinks of salmon, reds of beef, oranges of carrot, greens of broccoli, reds of tomato, whites of cheeses. Carvers were now going to their stations.

Tory was looking at the spread, tempted to grab one. I shook my head. Nothing would blow our cover like the smartly dressed woman reporting the janitors for scarfing the food!

I walked to one of the bartending stations. The bartender was crouching under the bar, dumping ice into tubs.

"Water?" I asked.

He stood up and smiled, then poured ginger ale into a glass with ice.

"Here's some water," he said, winking.

Thanking him, Tory and I walked back to the storage room. Only Dirty Pete was there, watching TV.

"And in national news, a deadly gas explosion in Providence, Rhode Island, killed at least one person but destroyed a section of College Hill, one of the oldest neighborhoods in the city," the newscaster said.

There was Neuman Church's picture on the screen. It looked like his high school graduation picture. I didn't feel any remorse.

"Authorities are saying a federal agent died when he tried to help victims of the explosion," the anchor said. "And now its time for sports; how about them, Philly's ..."

Local news. From death to baseball, just like that, I thought.

All the while, Tory was staring at me, knowing the truth.

The Lief-Terbily-Shappines group started entering the institute promptly at 6:45 p.m. Whoever they were, the event sure attracted a big name crowd. Observing the activities from the second floor, we recognized many of the guests.

There was an NBA basketball player. A civil rights leader. There was a senator from down south.

We spotted an entrepreneur who made it big on social media talking to a well-known news reporter.

The more people arrived, the more we instantly recognized them as people in positions of power.

"Wow, fancy," Tory said.

The police chief of a midwestern city, who was just in the news a few weeks ago, was laughing with a congresswoman. Next to them was a well-known Hollywood actor.

In they streamed. Not everyone was instantly recognizable, but enough were to get me thinking Lief-Terbily or Shappines traveled in some pretty elite circles.

The room was filling up, and the buzz of conversation slowly built until it sounded like a hive of bees.

We walked back to the storage room, and Dirty Pete was getting ready to leave. He didn't say a word; he just dutifully took his blue shirt off, punched out, and left.

The storage room was ours!

And if anyone inquired, it was obvious. We were the janitors serving the party.

Tory laid down on the couch, put his hands behind his head, and shut his eyes.

I sat down at the desk, put my feet up on the table, and closed my eyes.

When I awoke, it was 11:30 p.m.

I jumped up.

"Tory! Tory," I said, waking him up.

"Whaaat," he said, slowly coming awake.

How did that happen?

We looked out into the storage room. Blackness. Dirty Pete must have turned off the lights on his way out.

Carefully, we rose and tiptoed through the storage room, careful not to bump into anything. Everything seemed so quiet. The buzz of the party that could be heard even here is now gone. There was no noise at all, just silence. It was like when you sneak down early on Christmas morning to see what Santa brought when everyone else is sleeping.

I stood up straight and walked to the door. I spotted a janitor's broom next to the door and grabbed it. This prop could help us if we were caught outside.

We walked into the hallway. More darkness, with only intermittent night lights lining the hall.

The Franklin Institute was empty.

A chill went through my body. When everyone was here, we felt perfectly fine acting like janitors and fitting in with Dirty Pete.

But now, it feels like we shouldn't be here.

Where was the security guard? We walked down the wide hallway.

More darkness. The lights were off. The place that was so full of people earlier in the day and partygoers in the evening was now lifeless. Even the exhibits faded into the dark.

We walked to the rotunda. The bars and food tables were gone. The chairs, stanchion, and lattice remained, waiting for the morning crew.

Where is the security guard? No one was at the front door.

We went to the second floor. From here, you could see any movements below.

Where would the SOL meet? The only place seemed to be the deserted rotunda area. I pushed the broom down the hallway, carefully listening for any sound. Tory followed.

There was nothing. I then caught sight of moonlight. It was a full moon. Thin beams of light peaked through the windows, casting shadows off the exhibits.

I started getting scared. Tory walked up and glanced at me. He was scared, too.

This place was suddenly eerie and creepy. Still no sounds.

No movement. Nothing.

We headed back to the storage room to get ready for midnight. The hallways were dimly lit, and the exhibits and lights were turned off.

No one was here but us.

Treaty of Paris, 1783 — by Benjamin West (the British refused to sit for the painting)

SATURDAY

Chapter Twenty-Eight

"I wish most earnestly to see Rhode Island federal, to finish the circle of union ... I am displeased to hear people speak of a state out of the union. I wish it was a part of the catechism to teach youth that it cannot be. I wish to have every American think the union so indissoluable and integral, that the corn would not grow, nor the pot boil, if it should be broken."

– Fisher Ames, July 23, 1789 in a letter to George Minot

"I do not know what will become of you, if your Convention should refuse to join the Union, for you certainly cannot exist alone if the other States treat you as foreigners. Have you specie enough to pay your proportion of the Continental debt, or do you expect to put us off with your paper money."

– From a letter sent by a New Yorker to a friend in Rhode Island, published in the Independent Chronicle, March 25, 1790

It was 11:50 p.m. I was all alone, thinking about Pepper, not knowing what was going to happen next. Just then, Tory walked into the room, returning from the bathroom.

"All quiet," he said.

Maybe the meeting was canceled?

Maybe Vaughn Clark gave us the wrong time and place?

I looked at the clock. It was 11:55 p.m.

Five minutes to go.

"Well, we're not just going to sit here, right?" Tory asked.

At that, we both stood up and headed back to the second-floor overlook of the rotunda. The marble hallway leading to it now glistened with a moon glow. And when we got to the overlook point, there was Benjamin Franklin, awash in moonlight that streamed from the windows above.

It was like something out of an Egyptian pyramid, where the ancients constructed the tomb so that on one special day of the year, the sun would appear through a small hole and light up the sacred object.

Except this was a statue of Benjamin Franklin, and it was a full moon's light.

I studied the floor below. Long shadows were cast off the pillars. Franklin's shine was reflecting off the objects surrounding him.

The only sound I heard was Tory breathing a little heavy from the brief walk.

Something moved. We were not sure what, but it came from the direction of one of the shadows off the pillars.

I studied that area and then stepped back.

The shadows were moving!

We crouched down behind the balcony rails.

More shadows were moving.

It was like the Giant Glowing Franklin had summoned ghosts from the dead.

Soon, all of the shadows were moving and getting smaller.

Tory and I turned and looked at each other.

We realized they weren't shadows.

They were people!

As silent as the moonlight streaming through the windows, people floated to the statue.

Each in their turn, they paid homage to the Great Franklin, turned, and walked to the chairs we had set up for the reception.

Not a sound was heard.

Maybe they really were ghosts, I thought.

Tory spotted something that proved they were not.

It was one of the people we saw at the party earlier. I focused intensely on the others taking their seats.

"Yup, that guy was there, and the person next to him," Tory said, pointing to the back of the room. We spotted another person who was at the party, and another.

"What the?" I murmured.

"Hack, look," Tory whispered, hitting my shoulder. There in the back was the strange man who we met in the bookstore and who says he knows about the flag.

Just like before, the strange man was wearing a large, long black jacket in such a way that it was difficult to see his face. His head and hat were cocked at an angle.

The shadows became people, and the people floated to their chairs. In no time, the seats were filled up with the guests who had been at the Lief-Terbily- Shappines affair earlier in the evening.

DONG! A sharp sound broke the still air.

DONG! It rang out again.

DONG! It was an unseen clock.

DONG! We knew on that one that it must be midnight.

Eight more rings told us this was so.

The room was full of silent people, basking in the glow of moonlight and facing the Great Franklin Statue.

And then, near the front door, three people with flags stood like an honor guard.

Everyone in the room stood up, and the three people proceeded to march down the center aisle, the person in the center a step ahead of the others and holding the flag higher than those on each side.

I recognized the red and white-striped flag in the center. To the left was the yellow flag with the rattlesnake and the words "Don't Tread On Me." And to the right was a flag I had never seen before with thirteen blue, red, and white stripes.

"Wow, this is cool," Tory whispered. "The one on the right is the Franklin Flag that Ben made to save John Paul Jones from being hung as a pirate. Long story ..."

"Shhhhh," I silently said with my finger on my lips.

The honor guard marched up the aisle in a deliberate fashion, pausing every couple of steps. The place was still deathly quiet as they floated to the front.

When they got there, the guard turned and faced the audience. All three flags were slightly lowered and are now fully visible.

The center flag was all stripes and no stars, like the original Sons of Liberty flag, but this one had a rattlesnake striking and the words 'Don't Tread On Me' like the one on the map.

"That's the first American flag for the navy," Tory whispered.

The three stayed in that position for a moment, then they went behind the three chairs and placed the flags in their stands.

Above the flags was a banner with large words in an old, cursive style. The words themselves were on a banner of some sort, stretched out the width of the chairs. The words said, "Life - Liberty - Happiness."

The three people who brought the flags to the front now took the three seats there, facing the audience.

The man in the middle stood. "Sons and Daughters of Liberty, Welcome!" he said.

I knew that voice. I studied the face as best as I could, the moonlight playing tricks with my eyes.

"Give me the flag," I could hear him say.

It was the same voice.

I looked again at him.

Aha! It was Vaughn Clark!

He continued speaking. "Two hundred and fifty years ago, the leaders of our Revolution for Liberty gathered just like this in a ceremony to pledge our lives and honor to the eternal cause."

"And every year since that time, we have renewed that pledge," he said.

"And we shall do so again tonight."

The audience did not make a sound.

"Please," he said, "after the first paragraph. The response is 'I do'."

He began, "I believe that all men and women are created equal, that they are endowed by their Creator with certain unalienable rights, that among these are life, liberty, and the pursuit of happiness."

I knew those words. They were from the Declaration of Independence, updated.

"I do," the audience responded.

"I do, too," Tory responded.

"I knew you shouldn't have come," I replied, shaking my head and smiling.

Vaughn Clark continued:

"That to secure these rights, governments are instituted among people, deriving their just powers from the consent of the governed. That whenever any form of government becomes destructive to these ends, it is the right of the people—IT IS THEIR DUTY—to alter or abolish it."

I knew the words well. They seemed to have been shortened.

"And for the support of this declaration, with a firm reliance on the protection of Divine Providence, we mutually pledge to each other our lives, our fortunes, and our sacred honor."

The people on each side of him now rose.

"Do you so pledge to each other tonight?" Vaughn Clark said.

In unison, the people in the seats said, "I do."

Everyone returned to their seats.

Vaughn Clark remained standing.

"A moment of silence for the passing of a son, Macsen Redmand."

The silence was broken with the playing of the Scottish bagpipes. The somber notes came from a sole bagpiper who stood in the back of the room.

"That's Dark Island," Tory said. "That's the song he is playing."

When the pipes ended, the man sitting next to Vaughn Clark rose and addressed the audience.

"We have been penetrated by dark forces who seek our destruction. This has been an ongoing issue for the last ten years. Unfortunately, all of our efforts to secure private communications and secret operations have failed. For the first time in 250 years, we are not at liberty to conduct our affairs," he said.

He paused and took a sip of water. He looked ex-military, special forces. Clean, cut, and in shape.

"Our Sons of Liberty Hall in Providence was intentionally destroyed. In accordance with procedures," he continued, "the Watcher has established active operations."

The speaker sat down.

Then a person rose from the assembly, walked to the front, and spoke.

"Operations Report. Tests are ongoing for grid displacement and network disability. Ongoing recruitment of elected officials and penetration of government. No report from the Militia Correspondence Committee."

This speaker sat down and was followed by another.

"The Watcher," Tory said. "What's that?"

I couldn't help but wonder: Are these people responsible for the blackouts that have been plaguing the East Coast? For those odd times when the internet slows down? And they work with militias?

We were witnessing the Sons of Liberty in action. Not as some dusty history book club, but the real deal—men and women who took defending their rights seriously.

And I realized Lief-Terbily-Shappines was an anagram for life, liberty, and the pursuit of happiness! That reception earlier must have been the start of their meeting, and this was the end of it—an ancient ceremony that has probably been performed for centuries.

Next up was a report from the Rules Committee and then the Conference Committee.

The ex-military officer next to Vaughn Clark now rose.

"I need to repeat the ancient rule," he said, "that we will countenance no step whatsoever to the disturbance of the public tranquility, nor private peace of any man, nor engage in any one matter or thing under color or pretense of the cause of Liberty, in a separate and detached manner, or without the advice and consent of the President and majority of the Committee. Is this understood?"

"Yes," the audience said in unison.

He remained standing, and after a moment Vaughn Clark rose from his seat.

"We now end our annual gathering," he said. "Go forth as sisters and brothers, Americans all!"

With that, the audience rose, and the three people in the front resumed their positions as honor guard and walked down the aisle and exited.

The striped snake banner was now perfectly visible, lit by the moonlight.

And just as quietly, the chairs emptied, the people floated to the pillars, and they became shadows once again.

I looked at the end of the aisle for the honor guard. But they were gone. I looked at the seats.

Nothing. They left as quickly as they came.

All that remained were empty chairs. And a giant, glowing Franklin.

"What did we just see?" Tory asked. "It happened so fast; the people came and went. It was like a mirage. And they were like ghosts!"

The Franklin Institute was once again empty.

I started to rise when a cold hand grabbed my shoulder and pushed me back down.

It was forceful and deliberate and made me bump and then fall into Tory, who was also starting to stand up.

Tory fell backwards onto the floor.

"Heyyyyy" Tory exclaimed as he fell to the ground with me crashing onto him.

Then a voice spoke.

"It's alright, big boy," a familiar voice said.

I turned and looked.

There before us was a sincere-looking man with blonde hair, staring right at me.

"Good evening, Hackworth. I am glad you were able to join us," he said.

It was Vaughn Clark.

Chapter Twenty-Nine

"Washington got the reputation of being a great man
because he kept his mouth shut."

– John Adams reportedly said to Gilbert Stuart about
Washington at the Constitutional Convention, from The Oxford
History of the American People by Samuel Eliot Morison

Who you calling Big Boy?" Tory said as he rose above Vaughn
Clark, a good three inches taller and half a foot wider.

We would joke all the time about him being a "big boy," and it
never bothered him. But Tory had a way of pretending he was of-
fended as a joke, and if you didn't get his sense of humor, you would
think he was serious.

"Who are you calling Big Boy?" Tory said it again as he towered over Vaughn Clark.

Vaughn Clark backed up. "No offense intended," he said,
reaching out to shake Tory's hand.

Tory hesitated, then gave him a limp handshake as a way of
being standoffish.

"Come with me; there's a place we can sit down," Clark said.

We got up and walked down the opposite end of the hallway.

Clark opened a small, gray utility door with an electrical
warning sign of a guy getting a shock from a bolt of electricity. I
don't know why, but I thought of Ben Franklin and the kite and
how appropriate it was for this sign to be in this building.

The room was small, with electric panels on each side. In the middle was a table. Sitting there was another man, the ex-military guy who was one of the leaders at the just-concluded gathering of the Sons of Liberty.

He had a steely, serious look but gave a nice smile when we were introduced.

"Hackworth, this is Morgan Stonewall," said Vaughn Clark.

Stonewall stood up and put out his hand.

"I'm pleased to meet you," he said, sitting back down. He stopped smiling.

"And this is?" Clark asked, gesturing at Tory.

"Terrance Russoff," Tory said.

Stonewall nodded and said hello. Clark didn't move.

It was dead quiet. I didn't know what to say or where to begin. I didn't even know if I should be here.

Several minutes went by, then Tory broke the ice the way only Tory could.

"Who is the Watcher?" he asked.

They just looked at him and did not answer.

Vaughn Clark turned to me.

"We know about Pepper," he said. "We know what happened."

Did he know I killed the federal agent? The thought terrified me because Vaughn Clark's day job was a New York State Trooper.

The other guy was staring at me.

"Ah...ah," I stumbled.

"DON'T SAY A WORD ABOUT THE AGENT," the voice in my head instructed.

Tory leaned in at the table, giving me a nod that he was going to handle this.

"You know what happened?" Tory asked, looking directly at Clark. "Then you tell us what happened."

Vaughn Clark looked at me, and then Tory.

"Pepper was arrested in the Sons of Liberty Hall."

"How do you know that?" Tory replied.

Looking surprised, Morgan Stonewall turned his head and looked at Vaughn Clark, who avoided eye contact.

There was an awkward pause. Clark tried to answer the question, but I interrupted.

"Where is Pepper now?"

"They took her to the naval brig in Providence," Clark said.

"The what?" I said.

"The naval brig, a military holding prison," he said.

"Military prison? Why there?" I was gaining more confidence in my tone.

"They are holding her as a terrorist," Vaughn Clark said.

I couldn't believe it. Pepper was in a military jail for some stupid flag? For being in Professor Redmand's house?

"Has she been charged with a crime?" asked Tory.

"Not yet," he quickly answered. "Terrorists don't get the luxury of being charged with anything. All the government has to do is say you are a terrorist, and they can lock you away."

"Indefinitely," Stonewall said.

Tory now rose from his chair. Oh no, I thought, he's going to start shooting off at the mouth.

"Yes, it is called indefinite detention, the idea that there is a class of criminals who are so dangerous that they are not entitled to even be charged with a crime but held indefinitely with no jury trial," Tory said.

"But she has the right to be charged, to have a lawyer, to know..." I said.

"Exactly," Stonewall said. "Ever since September 11, our world in America has been turned upside down. With technology, the government is now more powerful than ever to monitor and control the people. If you are labeled a terrorist, they can seize you, take your property, and make you vanish. Or just kill you. Or, just make your life absolutely miserable."

"How can that be?" I said. "How can that happen?"

"Americans revolted against a king who pushed them around and stole their rights," Tory said. "Yet even the King of England adhered to the Magna Charta, which outlined the basic rights of the people."

Morgan Stonewall's steely appearance softened.

"It's ironic that she is being held in Rhode Island of all places. Rhode Island refused to join the Union over rights, or lack of them," he said.

"Please explain," Tory said.

"Because the rights Rhode Islanders possessed in their state constitution were greater than those in the U.S. Constitution, and they did not want to give them up," Stonewall said. "Rhode Island's constitution was identical to the colonial charter the King had given them in the 1600's. All they did when they declared themselves independent was change the word 'King' to 'The People'."

"So?" I said.

"So? So?" His voice was rising. "Rhode Islanders did not want to give up the liberties they had BEFORE the revolution, let alone what they gained by winning it. They were bullied to do so, to join, all with the promise that the new government would play by the rules and would protect their rights and liberties."

"But your friend now sits in a military jail on Rhode Island soil, denied her rights, and treated worse than a medieval peasant in the very state that was founded for exactly opposite purposes," Stonewall said.

"And they want you to join her there," Vaughn Clark said, turning directly to face me.

"Do you still have the flag?" he asked matter-of-factly.

I nodded yes, glad they were finally going to discuss the problem at hand.

"A question about the ceremony," I began. "There were three flags brought down the aisle. One was the famous yellow rattlesnake flag. The other was the flag Franklin made and registered to save John Paul Jones. But the one in the center, with only red and white stripes, and the rattlesnake. What flag is that?"

Morgan Stonewall smiled. "That's our flag, with a bite!"

"The Sons of Liberty?" I said.

"Well, yes," he began. "But more than that. It is your flag and my flag. And everyone's flag. It is the American flag."

"With a snake instead of stars?" I said.

"Yes, indeed," he replied.

I must have looked bewildered because he moved in closer across the table and spoke gently in the tone of a religious leader to a novice.

"Do you know where the red and white stripes come from, Hackworth?" he asked.

"Yes," I said, winking at Tory. "They are the rebellious stripes. The Sons took the solid red British Meteor Flag and shredded it, adding white stripes in between the red ones to express disunion. It was made when the Sons of Liberty organized in the 1760's."

"That's right," Stonewall said. "The symbol was simple: British authority was no more. It was ripped up, and now power resided in the people, each in their own separate colony. That's why the stripes are numbered by the colonies in America."

"Now place the rattlesnake, fangs out and striking with the words of defiance, 'Do Not Tread On Me,' and you have the first American naval flag, ready for war," Stonewall said. "We would have used the stripes-only flag for the ceremony, but we used this one instead, as a way to alert the members that we were going on offense."

Vaughn Clark looked at Stonewall as if he didn't know that.

Stonewall leaned back in his chair and looked at Tory.

"Always remember, the stripes represent the freedom and liberty of the people in their states, not the government. The stripes represent freedom from any authority outside their community. And the little patch in the corner called the canton—that's what represents the government. Note how little of the flag it takes up and how much of freedom and liberty remain," he continued. "The British knew this fact very well, while Americans today don't—that the striped flag is the symbol of revolution."

A silence came over the four of us, a silence like I heard at the Franklin Institute. An eery silence. I thought about Pepper and wished she could hear this.

"Why do the Feds want to hide the 12-star flag?" Tory blurted out. "Because it shows that the Founders considered the new federal government as just another star on the flag, in the image of the states?"

"That's right!" Stonewall answered and smiled. You could tell he liked Tory; he understood Tory. "That's exactly right."

Tory now spoke. "Yes, sir, I have learned from reading old books that there is a distinction between *our country* and *our government*. They are two different things altogether. But any government's first job is to make the people believe they are the same thing, even though they are not."

It was again quiet in the room. With the passionate manner in which Stonewall and Tory were speaking, you would have thought the Sons of Liberty meeting never ended!

"That's why the 12-star flag was hidden," Stonewall said. "Because it screamed the distinction between country and government. Even more, it screamed the distinction between the Revolution and the Constitution."

"The early leaders after Washington knew that the flag could not have such distinctions and that the people must be taught that the government, our rights, our liberties, and our country were all the same thing and all started at the same time," he said. "Otherwise, the people may get ideas..."

"Wow," Tory said.

"Hackworth," Vaughn Clark said. He had not spoken a word in five minutes. "Do you still have the flag Pepper gave you?"

"Yes, I told you I did." Something about his singular focus bothered me.

"Where is it?"

"Hidden," I replied. My answer wasn't sufficient, given how fairly they had been treating us. And it was the Son's flag, after all.

"Hidden, in my apartment," I answered more accurately.

"We need to get it," Vaughn Clark interjected.

"You can have it."

There was an uneasy pause. Vaughn looked at Tory, then at me. His look was hard to decipher. He seemed cold.

"Do you two know why it is so special?" asked Stonewall, with a much warmer appearance.

"We have some theories," I replied.

"That flag you have in your apartment is the first flag of the present-day United States of America, flown when the U.S. Constitution began. It flew on top of the Federal State House at George Washington's inauguration."

I nodded. Pepper was right.

I was beginning to understand. The 12-star flag had a lot of meaning in its symbols, but I had wondered why this one was so important to the SOL. Now I knew. It was actual proof of our true history, which so few are aware of.

"We need to get it," Vaughn Clark repeated.

I thought for a moment, and then a wild idea went through my head: trade the flag for Pepper.

"OK, guys," I said. "Let's make a deal. You help rescue Pepper, and we will give you the flag."

"Done," said Stonewall. "I will make that deal. And just so you know, we were going to get Pepper anyway."

Tory looked at Stonewall and then back at Vaughn Clark.

"Who's in charge here?" he asked Clark, payback for calling him a Big Boy. Clark didn't understand the insult.

Vaughn Clark looked the other way.

"Who's in charge?" Tory asked again.

"Done?" I said. "That easy? I don't think so. You guys say she is in a military prison. How could you possibly get her out?"

"We have our ways, Hackworth," Stonewall said. "What did you see at the meeting tonight?"

"Huh?" I shrugged.

"What did you see?" he repeated.

"A lot of people came to a party—a pretend party—then stuck around for a midnight rendezvous."

"That's right," he said. "What kind of people?"

"A lot of different people: old, young, black, white, and brown. Politicians, actors, and famous people. And people I didn't know."

"Hackworth, what you saw were lots of people from different walks of life with different points of view, who may be rich or poor, or work with their minds or with their hands," he said.

He leaned in. "But they believe in Liberty. In Freedom. Above all else, they are Americans. And they are members of the Sons of Liberty, though many of them are Daughters and have been with us from the start."

Pepper would have agreed.

"And there are a lot of us, around every corner, throughout America," he said, then sat back in his chair.

"Why do you think the government is so paranoid?" he asked. "Because of terrorism? Hardly."

""How so? You said the government spying intensified after the terrorists attacked on September 11," Tory said.

"That's the cover, but there is a deeper reason why," he said. "Once people started using the internet to search, post, email, and text, they left a record of what they were thinking and feeling."

"Some people in power quickly found out what these thoughts and feelings were. And they didn't like it one bit," he added, drawing out these words. Then he continued.

"You see, they found out that a lot of people—many, many millions of people—value freedom and liberty. And not just the kooks in the sticks. But millions of ordinary, every-day citizens in the cities and in the country have a love for American liberty deep in their hearts.

"They found out that the government is not trusted, that many people resent paying their taxes for corrupt purposes, and that people *question their authority.*

"That's how they got onto us," Stonewall continued. "We learned in the early 2000's that they were monitoring us, what we posted, our emails, everything. They tried to infiltrate our meetings. We now know for certain that they have penetrated our leadership for the first time in 250 years."

Stonewall looked at Clark when he said the last sentence.

Tory put his hand up like he was in a classroom. Morgan Stonewall acknowledged him and signaled for him to speak.

"Are you saying there is someone high up in the Sons of Liberty who is working to destroy it?" Tory asked.

"Yes," Stonewall replied. "We learned not to talk on cell phones, not to search the internet, not to even use the U.S. Mail because they are monitoring us and everyone else."

"Before the electronic age, when the government actually followed the Constitution, people were targeted AFTER they did something illegal, and it could be proven before a judge," he said. "Then the judge allowed the government to search a person's papers and property. This was usually the end of the process, just before the person was arrested."

"And it was done on an individual-by-individual basis," Vaughn Clark added.

"But now, in the electronic age, agencies in the government are able to collect ALL information on everyone, then sift through it to find persons of interest. Not individual by individual, but everyone at the same time," Stonewall continued. "And what they found was that some Americans despised the government."

"To not like government interfering with our rights is the American way," Tory said. "There shouldn't have been any surprise to that. People have been writing anti-government screeds since the Declaration of Independence kicked it all off."

We all laughed in unison.

"True enough," Vaughn Clark said. "Keep in mind that you are talking about public acts. Men signed their names to the Declaration, and anti-government articles have a known author and are published for the purpose of sharing ideas with the public."

"Before the internet, the government couldn't do anything about it," Morgan Stonewall said. "Yeah, they could have sicced the IRS on you or had the FBI infiltrate your group, but that again was on an individual basis."

"Today, it is total information awareness. On everyone. All the time. And not just what you post on social media or in a blog. But what you really feel is what you are really thinking. They know everything about you—your predilections, your likes, and your dislikes. They have supercomputers at their disposal to sift through the trillions of messages and searches. And when they identify you or your group, they have special ways to find out what you buy, what you eat, and who your friends are."

"All the while," he continued, "we pay for it. We pay the salaries of those violating our minds and our space. Our taxes bought the supercomputers. The bill you pay to the internet service provider, the phone company, the credit card company, and Facebook. Google, Apple—you might as well be sending that to the government as well, because these companies are their agents. They are government clerks keeping tabs on you, ready to share it when authority clicks its fingers."

"But isn't some of this activity necessary to protect the homeland," I said.

Stonewall pulled back in his seat.

It was suddenly quiet.

"Please don't say that word," he said. "It is un-American!"

"How so?" Tory asked.

"That word is the word of the National Security State. It was never, ever used in the first 400 years of America," Stonewall said. "You know who used that kind of word?"

"No," Tory replied.

"The Nazis. They used Fatherland, close to Homeland. It implies an amalgamation. One unit. You and the entire country, when in reality you have your own home, live in your own state that created a republic with the other states. Homeland is a foreign term, not suited for these shores," he said.

"Think of the words we used to describe our "homeland" in the past. Country, nation, republic, state, county, city, town, village, home—these are the words we use to describe where we live. I love my country, of which my homeland is part."

He paused and then continued.

"Homeland is the government's attempt to make "Your Home" very personal. But like the Nazis, they used words to change the way you think. Your country is something bigger than you. Your homeland is, quite literally, the land around your home."

"Now think about the Department of Homeland Security," he said. "a federal government force that is responsible for the security around your home? Think about it. You provide the security around your own home. Local police provide security in your community, the sheriff in your county, and state police in the state. All of these police are paid for by taxpayers and controlled by local and state authorities. So why do you need another layer of federal police that did not exist for 200 years?"

Tory butted in.

"And now it is taken for granted that they will monitor and molest us at the airport, watch us at the train stations, photograph our mail, coerce our vendors to spy on us, not to mention observe all we do online," he said.

It was getting late. We had been talking for hours. We were all exhausted.

"Where are you two staying tonight?" Vaughn Clark asked.

"I don't know," I said.

"Come with us, Hackworth; you will be safe," he said. "We have a secure place not far from here."

Tory thought otherwise.

"Hack, why don't you and I go to my place instead? We can hook up with them tomorrow."

Vaughn Clark's invitation was sincere, and the danger seemed to be near. I trusted him. I rose, took my blue shirt off, and walked to the office door.

"Come on, Tory, let's go with them so we can get this done early in the morning."

Tory didn't move and shook his head "no."

He gave a distrustful look at Vaughn Clark.

And then he looked at me.

"Come on, Tory," I said again.

With that, he quickly stood and put his shirt back without saying a word.

"When will we rescue Pepper?" I asked.

Morgan Stonewall smiled.

"Tomorrow."

Chapter Thirty

"The early years of my life, which were spent in the little cabin, were not very different from those of thousands of other slaves. My mother, of course, had little time in which to give attention to the training of her children during the day. She snatched a few moments for our care in the early morning before her work began, and at night after the day's work was done."

– Up from Slavery, by Booker T. Washington, Doubleday, 1901

It was already Saturday. Exhausted, the four of us walked out a side service door. On the way, we had to pass the rotunda. The Great Franklin statue was no longer glowing.

In the darkness, I could still make out its form, though the clouds were blocking the moon's rays.

"We want you to join us," Morgan Stonewall said as we got into a brand new, black Cadillac Escalade.

"You and Pepper," he added.

"Join you as in a job?" I asked.

"What about me?" Tory joked. "I know a lot about taking down power grids and hacking the internet."

"No, sorry, those jobs are taken," Stonewall joked. He paused and then turned to me.

"We need to get the word out. We need to help people remember their past. You and Pepper are writers. You know publishing and mass communication."

"We need to help people remember," he repeated.

The SUV pulled up to what looked like an abandoned warehouse on North Broad Street. Lights were on in the building, which had to be 15 stories high. It was an old car factory converted into a warehouse, now converted into office space.

We parked on the side of the building and walked into a little office, connected to another little office, connected to a small living area with bunk beds.

I said good night and jumped into the top bunk. Growing up with my brothers, we had bunk beds. I always stayed on top for fear that when sleeping in the lower one, the top bunk would collapse and crush me. Seeing Tory squeeze into his bunk confirmed my decision.

I shut my eyes and immediately passed into deep sleep.

The last few days were exhausting, and the sleep on the floor of the secret chamber wasn't so good. Images flashed through my head in one dream sequence after another.

Pepper and I at freshmen orientation. Walking hand in hand. The basketball player turned her face toward him. Drinking coffee as the federal agents watched us. Taking a box out of a locker. The sincere man grabbing at the box in the taxi. Fear.

Professor Mac teaching us in class. Pepper laughs at his jokes. Fake laugh. Sitting with him in the park. Looking at the inscription on the State Capitol. Sovereignty. Fear.

Boston. Picnic table. Eating lobster rolls. Pepper surprising me. Black hair. Bright smile. Beautiful. Albany. An angry veteran walks out. Look up. Diner. Vaughn Clark at the table. Fear.

Rattlesnakes. Flags. Independent Man. Marshall. Washington. Franklin. Story. Pepper. I love her. Men talking. Listening.

Hiding. Pepper smacked by Church. Anger. Coward. Fire. Flames. Upshur bust. Smash. Terror. Fear.

Run, run, run. Train. Police. Looking for me. Run. Tory cheesesteaks. Giant Franklin stands up. Smashes walls and ceilings. Run. Hide. You killed a man. Not just any man. A federal agent. Get the flag and save Pepper. Running. Giant Franklin chasing me. They are going to get you. Giant Franklin is going to get you.

Fear. Terror. Fear.

"NO!" I yelled. I was sweating. It was a nightmare. A series of nightmares. Where am I? I looked around the room. It was morning.

Tory's big head popped up as he towered over the bunks.

"Bro, are you OK?" Tory asked and then, looking me up and down and then seeing my sweaty face, said, "Dude, sweat much? What the..."

"Yeah, yeah," I said, turning my back on him, and he retreated below. I didn't want to be afraid. I wanted to confront the fear.

I shut my eyes and tried to restart the dream. But the harder you try to remember a dream, the quicker it runs away from you. Within seconds, I had forgotten it all. And my body was sticky with sweat.

"We want you to join us." That's what Morgan Stonewall said.

"We need to help people remember."

Join the Sons of Liberty? No way, I thought.

Then a voice in my head answered differently.

"You have to join them," it said.

No way, I thought again. I have a good job, and the bookstore work, even if it is mundane and routine. But what about my vow not to return to that life? Right now, I would kill for a little mundane and routine.

"Like you killed that guy?" the voice in my head said.

For the last five years, I would rise early every morning at the same time, to the same alarm. I would walk the same steps to my kitchen and make the same pot of coffee. Take a shower. Get dressed. Walk to work. Do eight hours of what, in the larger scheme of things, was not so meaningful. Interview people. Write stories. Go to lunch and say the same things to my co-workers. Go home and eat dinner. Go to bed and wait for the alarm to ring again.

The same thing, day in and day out. The weekends were a salvation, when I could work at the Franklin Antiques Bookstore, listen to Tory pontificate on this or that subject to rile up the listener, joke around, and get paid. Tory was my escape from monotony. He kept my intellectual curiosity alive.

And between the two jobs, it's how I could afford to live in the city. I was a drone, a worker bee, like everyone else. It was wage slavery, but it was necessary to pay the bills, loans, and credit cards. And sometimes I was happy.

I thought of the people on the train ride to Philadelphia. The smartly dressed businesswoman. The two men one-upping each other on their spending power in the company.

Worker bees. Each one of us has a specific job that isn't too powerful or too challenging. The division of labor was such that if any one worker bee dropped out, the hive would still keep buzzing. You had an important job to do, they told you, but the truth is that you were one of many, and the system was made so that you had no power over the hive. You could leave, and you would be easily replaced.

Every two weeks, they handed you money—a check that would go to the rent, the food, and the essentials. And the taxes. About a third of my paycheck I didn't even get because the hive took the money from me and sent it to various governments. A custom house was built right into the hive, taxing every second of the drones' labor.

I thought about that as I lay in bed. The room was getting brighter as the morning was starting up.

"You awake?" Tory said from below.

"Yeah."

"What a weird night."

"What a weird couple of days. I never got a chance to tell you about the Sons of Liberty Hall. You would have loved it! You could have spent months going through the books, papers, and exhibits. Some stuff must have dated to the 1600's."

"But it all burned down, right?" Tory said. "Just my luck."

"There were stacks of papers on different subjects, like President Eisenhower and the Military-Industrial Complex."

"Ah yes, the cozy relationship between the military and the companies that make the weapons," Tory said. "But did they have anything on the Justice-Industrial Complex? Most of the Supreme Court judges come from Harvard or Yale, the home of Orthodoxy and Indoctrination, who in turn receive billions and other federal privileges. From their ranks, the top jobs in government are filled, and to their ranks they return."

Tory could pontificate lying down, and it didn't take much to set him off. He was on a roll.

"Or the Education-Industrial Complex? Where the truth of our history and duties as citizens are obscured? Education used to be a family and local matter, and most people were done with school after the eighth grade. They knew how to read, write, and do enough math to get a good deal in the market."

"Now, it takes twice as long, and college kids still need to be taught the basics of reading and writing. And it is no longer local, but a sprawling enterprise of unions, agencies, textbook and testing companies, and others who decide what our kids learn and how they learn it," he continued.

"And, Hack, there's the best complex of all—the Financial-Industrial Complex, the famous revolving door between Wall Street and Washington, DC. It started with the Constitution when Congressmen bought up near-worthless Continental money issued during the Revolution, paying ten cents on the dollar, then voted to pay it off at face value with the new Federal Treasury! The profits were poured into new bonds traded on Wall St."

"You're on a roll. Do another one," I said. "The Medical-Industrial Complex."

Tory didn't miss a beat.

"The Medical-Industrial Complex. Same thing. Government and industry collude to ensure the profits of health insurance companies and drug companies while paying tax dollars to their biggest customers: doctors and hospitals."

"Hack, truthfully—no joking—is it all corrupted? People need justice. They need education. They need to stay healthy. But do the institutions, companies, and government serve them or themselves? It starts with the educational system, which obscures our past. If the worker bees knew the truth, maybe they wouldn't go to work but instead would stick around the hive and start stinging their masters. They may even get to the Queen Bee!"

We laughed so hard that I almost fell off the bunk.

"Oh, come on, Tory. It sounds good, but we do very well. You get paid more than enough to afford your taxes. You have all the latest toys. Video games. Streaming. Movies. TV. A nice car. You have the essentials. Good food. Nice apartment. And the hospital you can go to around the corner is one of the best in the world!"

Tory took up the argument. He loved taking the opposing side and pressing hard.

"Yes, I do have a good life, as far as that goes. A good material life. And I am one of the lucky ones, because there are many more people who do not have a good material life," he said. "But is that good material life part of the problem? Are we addicted to it? Slaves to it because it fills some dark hole in our lives?"

"How so?" I asked.

"Well, some are addicted to cosmetics because they refuse to age. They fear the loss of physical beauty and what others will think of them."

Tory shot out of his bunk. Sometimes, he needed to walk to talk. He proceeded to pace back and forth.

"Some are addicted to drugs, alcohol, food, and even social media because they like how it makes them feel—even if it's killing them," he said, turning on his heel. "They are killing themselves, and they like how it feels and how it helps them cope."

"And the worst are the narcissists, for they are addicted to themselves. The modern-day Narcissus not only stares at his own reflection; he takes a selfie and posts it for all to admire!"

"And then gets mad if no one likes it," I shot back.

We started laughing because much of what he said was true, but exaggerated and not all bad.

Tory had a way of joking out the truth.

"Well, here's the answer, Hack. People must better themselves individually. Do it yourself. Lift yourself up. And in America, with liberty and freedom, they have a shot at doing that and being successful if they keep their heads down and work hard. Why do you think so many people want to come here? For that shot to control their own destiny! It's why Franklin thought America would be the envy of the world.

"And he was right. Still to this day people pour into America in search of freedom and liberty," Tory continued.

"It isn't all about materialism and what you have. The richest people can have little money, and the poorest people can be trapped in their mansions. Being rich is more than money. It is not about having more than the other guy. It is about having a meaningful life. Of growing spiritually and intellectually. It is doing the things you want to do and helping others along the way."

"And Hack, that's the secret. All of the complexes want obedient drones to buy into materialism. They want CONSUMERS and not CITIZENS. But you don't have to choose."

"Tory, I like my smartphone; I love it, and all the other toys, I need them. I want them. So what if they are watching me? I can't live without it. I've gone a couple days without my phone, and I'm going through withdrawal. *Seriously!*"

We laughed.

"I like good food and don't want to eat beet soup like a Siberian peasant. I like my apartment and the fact that there's a great hospital nearby. I don't want to stand in line at a second-rate clinic like in Canada. Call me selfish, but I don't want to give it up."

"Hack, dude, it is not an either-or situation," Tory said. "The fantastic lifestyle you and many others enjoy did not happen because the government is corrupt. It happened in spite of corruption. The material prosperity of America existed and exists regardless of anything."

"America, in her original glory, was truly a miracle. It is a miracle now, in spite of it all. What it started, the world had never seen. When America rose, mankind suffered in ignorance. Humans were controlled for millennia by powerful forces of Kings and Empires. Bishops and Church. Peasants and Slaves. Most people were dirt poor, with no rights and no control," Tory said.

He was on a roll.

"But across the sea, change was happening. America attracted the liberty seeker, the desperate, the curious, the believers, the adventurers, and their families, and it became the haven for those who rejected empires, rejected kings, and rejected religious control."

"And in its place, it put its faith in the individual person. It said society's very purpose is to protect the individual's liberty and freedom so he or she may pursue happiness. People who were careful to craft a government so that there would be no kings, no empire, and no central control. That America lives in our true history. And it is still alive. And it can be reawakened from the spell it was placed under. We can help break that spell."

Tory stopped speaking. We could hear our companions had just entered the kitchen.

"You know," I said, jumping off the bunk bed and jokingly shoving him forward. "You really have to get into politics. You'd be huge, Big Boy!"

He returned the push so hard that I fell forward and into the kitchen.

Tory walked past me and towards the refrigerator and said, "Let's see what they have to eat."

There were Vaughn Clark and Morgan Stonewall sitting at a small table, heads down, using their phones.

"Good morning," I said.

"Morning," came the response from them in unison, their heads remaining down.

"You want a bagel?" Tory asked.

"Yes," I said as he put them in the toaster.

There was a pause. Morgan Stonewall looked right at me.

"Have you thought about what we talked about last night, Hack?" he questioned.

"You mean, about joining the Sons of Liberty?" I said.

He nodded.

"I have thought about it," I said. "Given a lot of thought to it."

There was a pause, as in a poker game, when everyone was waiting for you to show your hand.

"Yes, I will join."

Chapter Thirty-One

"The sad truth is that man's real life consists of a complex of inexorable opposites—day and night, birth and death, happiness and misery, good and evil. We are not even sure that one will prevail against the other, that good will overcome evil, or joy defeat pain. Life is a battleground. It always has been and always will be; and if it were not so, existence would come to an end."

– C.G. Jung, Man and His Symbols

There was a knock at the door, and Morgan Stonewall jumped up. He went to it and looked through the peep hole, then quickly unlocked it and let an older man in. Morgan turned his head to the side and listened as that man whispered into his ear.

Within a minute, the man had finished and was instructed to wait outside.

"That was about Pepper," Morgan Stonewall said, returning to the table. "She is going to be arraigned later today in New York."

The sound of her name made me sit straight up.

"She is being charged with theft of government property and seditious conspiracy," he said.

"That's crazy ..." I replied.

I didn't finish because neither of the men were listening to me. Vaughn Clark was busy handwriting a letter, and Morgan Stonewall was stuffing a bag. Finally, they looked up.

"Pepper is not a thief," I said.

"And there's more," Vaughn Clark said as he folded the paper and put it into an envelope. "There is a warrant out for your arrest."

"On what charge?" I asked.

"Same as Pepper, and maybe an accessory to murder," he said, licking the envelope. "Murder... of a federal agent."

I sank in my chair.

Morgan Stonewall went about his work as if he heard nothing.

Vaughn Clark looked right at me. His sincere face had a concerned look.

"Is that true?" he asked.

Tory leaned forward at the table.

"No, it can't be true," Tory said slowly. "Because Hack was with me!"

Vaughn Clark didn't take his eyes off my face. I looked down at the table and then up and into his eyes.

"Even if I did it, I wouldn't confess anything to you!"

"I believe you," Stonewall interjected. "But you need to understand that the Sons of Liberty do not kill people. And we do not take actions by ourselves. Any actions must come from the council and be approved by them. There is absolutely no freelancing. Do you understand?"

I nodded yes. "I heard what was said last night at the meeting."

"Hack," he began, "we aim to protect freedom and liberty in our society. But we cannot accomplish those goals by injuring people or their property. Every single person out there is an innocent person who has a right to live and pursue their happiness. For the Sons of Liberty to interfere with that right, even once, makes our cause meaningless. And we become exactly that which we now oppose."

Stonewall pulled his chair closer to me.

"Do you understand?" he said.

I nodded that I did.

"Then say it," he said.

"Yes, yes, I understand."

Stonewall took out a piece of paper that said SOL Constitution and read a passage:

"That we will, to the utmost of our power, detect, oppose, and assist in bringing to condign punishment, any person or persons who, taking advantage of the public trouble, would make the same a pretext to injure any person in their Character or Property ..."

"Here," he said, handing me the SOL constitution. "Read it. Especially the part about writing lies. You won't be able to do that either."

I took the paper.

"What are you going to do?" I asked nervously.

"About what?" he inquired. "What happened on College Hill?"

"Yes," I said.

"At this point, nothing," he replied. "I would imagine you only act in self-defense, right?"

I nodded.

"Where will I go?"

"After we get Pepper, the two of you will be sent to a safehouse where you can work for us," he said. "And they will never find you."

"How are we going to get Pepper?" I asked.

"You'll see," he said, rising from the table and going to the door. He knocked on it and opened it.

It was the first time I saw someone knock on a door from the inside.

The old man walked back in. Vaughn Clark handed him a piece of paper. He clicked his heels together, as if in a salute, turned, and left.

As he did, a cell phone went off. I was startled, but Vaughn Clark didn't seem to be.

"Yes, yes," Clark said, the phone to his ear. "Thank you," he said, hanging up.

"I thought there were no phones allowed," I said to Clark. "They can track us."

"It's alright, Hack," is all he said. But that didn't make any sense. Either they were avoiding detection or they didn't have to.

"Come on, boys," Morgan Stonewall said, holding the door open. We walked out, and I caught a glimpse of a gun holster under his suit coat. Stonewall was dressed in a business suit, his slim, muscular figure enshrouded in light wool.

Tory whispered in my ear. "He's a cop!"

We walked out onto the side street. The sun pierced my eyes, and I turned away to see myself in the reflection of the building glass. I was dressed in rumpled, casual clothes. My hair looked like it hadn't been washed in a week, which was pretty close to true.

I realized I had not shaved in days. I put my hands on my chin to feel the whiskers.

The guy looking back at me in the reflection of the window looked like a fugitive. I put my hat on to really fit the part.

We walked towards the new SUV. Clark and Stonewall were on each side of Tory and me, almost escorting us to the car. I nervously looked about to see if there were any police cars.

Being a fugitive was new to me. I had never been in trouble with the law. Now I was out-of-your-mind paranoid.

A woman pushing a stroller passed us. I looked down. I did not want to make eye contact.

She passed after the four of us moved to the curb.

Another guy was right behind her, mindlessly squawking on his cell phone. I used to be like him.

Now I feared for my life. Then I thought, Maybe he should fear for his as well. I knew I was wanted. I knew I was being watched. I knew the government was all over me. But this guy didn't know the same people were watching him and very well could some day want him. He didn't know. He should know.

We walked up to the SUV when Tory saw something that startled us. It was the license plate of the SUV.

It was a blue federal government license plate.

"They are cops, bud," Tory said.

I stopped walking. So did Tory.

"Get in, guys," Stonewall said.

The way he said it brought an ominous feeling. Are we stupid? I have been with a State Trooper and another guy who looks like he's in law enforcement, and they both know I am wanted for what happened with the federal agent.

And he has a phone that can be tracked?

We were being set up, I feared. Tory shot me a glance. He had the same suspicions.

We didn't move. Vaughn Clark opened the car door. The back seat was shiny with nothing on it.

Morgan Stonewall pressed in from the back. We were trapped.

"Get in, boys," he said, pressing his hand onto my back.

Tory and I got in the car.

Chapter Thirty-Two

"Those who would give up essential liberty to purchase a
little temporary safety, deserve neither liberty nor safety."

– Benjamin Franklin

The SUV peeled out, making the tires spin on the pavement.
We headed towards the Ben Franklin Bridge.

Benjamin Franklin is honored in so many ways, I thought.
Just like George Washington, he has a memorial in his honor, his
face on our money, and a bridge named after him.

And like Washington, Franklin was betrayed by his contemporaries. The Pennsylvania he helped create through revolution
was dismantled and replaced with one more subservient to the
federal master. Washington's confederated republic would be
chipped away over time as the nationalists gained more power.

"Proceed as planned," Stonewall said. He clicked the phone off
and put it in his pocket.

"OK, here's what we're doing," he said. "First, we get the flag.
Then we rescue Pepper. Time is tight, but doable."

"Oh, and one other thing," Stonewall began. "There is a good
chance Trowbridge is in your apartment waiting for you. But we'll
deal with that when we have to."

"I'll go with Hack and stay outside," Vaughn Clark said, looking at Stonewall, who flashed an odd look.

"That's crazy," I said. "Trowbridge is going to arrest me the minute I walk in there. Come on, you guys know very well. He's a Homeland Security agent, and he will arrest me."

"Trowbridge isn't Homeland Security," Stonewall said.

"Homeland Security is a federal department with agencies in it," Stonewall said. "It was formed after the 9/11 terrorist attacks; it consolidated customs, border enforcement, airport security, and other groups."

"For almost 150 years, Trowbridge's agency was part of the Treasury Department; now it is under Homeland Security," he said.

"What is his agency?" I asked.

"Secret Service," Stonewall answered.

"You see, Hack," Stonewall said, turning around to me and Tory. "The work of suppressing inconvenient truths goes way back to the early days of the Republic. Back then, it was the job of Army and Naval Intelligence and the Postal Inspection Service. After the Civil War, the Secret Service took on some of those duties."

"The people who protect the President?" Tory asked.

"Yes," Stonewall responded. "They were one of the covert groups that conducted many of the things we now associate with today's FBI, CIA, and NSA. The FBI is the oldest of the three, dating back to the early 1900's. The CIA was created out of the World War II Office of Strategic Services. And the NSA was begun in 1947."

"These agencies serve many important purposes and do good work," Stonewall said. "And sometimes, not so good work."

"What I don't get is you," Tory said to Vaughn Clark. "You are a New York State Trooper and a Son of Liberty? They don't go together."

Vaughn Clark laughed.

"Of course they do," he said. "Remember I told you the Sons are bigger than you can imagine? Well, it's true. Our members are in every branch of government and in all sectors of society. You can be a federal agent and love liberty!"

We were now talking about the mission at hand. I was to be wired up, go to my apartment, act surprised if Trowbridge is there, and then engage in a conversation that tells Vaughn Clark to show up. Otherwise, if Trowbridge is not there, just get the flag and get out.

"I'm coming with you," Tory said.

"Not a good idea," Vaughn Clark responded. "Let's not make this more complicated."

As simple as the plan sounded, I was afraid I couldn't pull it off. I was also afraid Trowbridge would attack me because of what happened to his partner.

"Tory has got to go. I need him there," I said.

Stonewall turned and looked at both of us. Then he stared at Tory, waiting for a reply that never came.

"OK," he said. "You can go."

The SUV was now slowing down. We were getting close to my apartment. Clark turned the corner and passed my row house, looking for a parking spot.

I swallowed hard, afraid.

This wasn't going to end well.

Chapter Thirty-Three

"A true Friend is the best Possession."

– Poor Richard's Almanack, 1744, from the Franklin Institute

The SUV circled the block and then pulled up to the street corner opposite my apartment. It was one of two units in an old row home. Parked nearby was another SUV, very much like the one we were in. Blue federal government license plates were on it as well, and it looked empty.

Vaughn Clark handed me a small black box with two wires connected to microphones. He told me to take my shirt off. The smell of sweat came off it. I hooked the box to my belt in the back. He then reached over and attached the microphones to my undershirt. I put the shirt back on, embarrassed by the odor.

"Talk," Vaughn Clark said.

"Huhh?" I said.

"Say something," he replied.

I then realized he wanted to test the listening system.

He put his thumb up, signaling it was good. I leaned forward and saw another black box, only this one was bigger, and it was connected to an ear piece that was in Vaughn Clark's ear.

Seeing him give a thumbs-up gave me confidence.

"Let's go over this one more time," he said. "You are going into your apartment to get the flag. That's what your primary mission is. If Trowbridge or anyone else is in the apartment, you need to let us know."

"How?"

"Just say, 'He's here' and we will move right in," Vaughn Clark said. "I will go with you and wait outside your apartment."

"Now let's test it again," he said.

"He's here," I said.

Clark gave the thumbs up.

Tory put his hand out and grabbed mine. Then Tory made the thumbs-up sign.

"Let's just do it," Tory said.

The cell phone rang. I wiped my palms on my pants. I was sweating.

"We're a go," Clark said in the microphone. He watched the apartment building intently and pointed to a man on the street corner.

"I'm not sure who that is or if he's involved," he said.

"What happens if he shows up?" I said. The tone of my voice betrayed my nervousness.

"Calm down," Stonewall said. "We will take care of him."

We all watched the agent on the corner. Just then, one of the other SUV's doors opened, and two men in business suits got out. They walked towards the man on the corner.

"Time to go," Vaughn Clark said. "You can do this, Hack. Do it for Pepper."

"Good luck," Stonewall said, and the locks on the doors popped up.

Tory and I slid across the seat and opened the door. It was a cloudy day, but it was brighter outside than the tinted-window life

I emerged from. I got out, straightened my shirt, and pushed the black box down a little. It was scraping my back. Tory was right behind me.

"Test, test," I said.

Vaughn Clark gave me the thumbs up again, then pointed to the apartment.

I took a deep breath, and we walked across the street.

"Do it for Pepper, do it for Pepper," I kept repeating to myself.

A cab went whizzing by me, blaring his horn. Tory jumped back. He was beeping at the guy in front of him.

My apartment was straight ahead. An older man was standing on the corner. He was sharply dressed in business attire and on his phone. He looked right at me, then turned and walked across the street.

I put my key in the door, and it opened. Tory and I entered the hallway.

I paused and listened. It seemed like we were alone.

We took a few steps and stopped again. Empty. Just like it always is, like the thousands of times I've walked through that door.

Maybe this will be the last time, I thought. A chill went through my body, and I stopped. I didn't want to walk this plank.

"Do it for Pepper," the voice in my head said.

"Do it for Pepper."

I straightened up and took a deep breath. Tory looked at me like he was ready to fight. He was a street kid who knew how to take care of himself in physical confrontations.

"Dear Lord, please help me," I said. It was the first time I said those words since being a child and asking God not to let me have any bad dreams.

This was like those days. I was afraid of bad dreams. But this nightmare was real.

We walked into the living room and gasped. My apartment was destroyed. The furniture had been slashed, and the tables were overturned. My books and papers lay strewn about the room. The whole place was trashed. Methodically, purposefully trashed.

I walked to the back sliding doors that opened into a small, semi-enclosed garden of weeds, thorns, and thistles. I opened the sliders to let fresh air in.

The front door slammed shut.

"Well, well, well," a voice said. "Look at this. The chicken has come home to roost."

I knew the voice from Professor Mac's house. I knew that voice from the interview here in the apartment several days ago, even though it felt like a year.

I turned.

"Don't move," Trowbridge said, "or I will spray your brains onto the wall like you did to Neuman Church."

"He's here," I said into the microphone. "He's here."

In a louder voice, I exclaimed, "I didn't do anything to Neuman Church."

"Come, both of you. Against the wall, hands above your head," he said, waving his hand while holding the gun steady and walking around the couch.

While turning, I spoke into the microphone again.

"HE'S HERE."

Trowbridge walked to a chair and flipped it over. He didn't take his eyes off of me. And now he started on Tory.

"Hey, boy, who are you?" he asked Tory.

"Put your hands up," he yelled.

He now walked closer, keeping the gun trained on me. He reached forward to check if I was armed.

Where was Vaughn Clark? Did he hear me? Why isn't he here?

Fear gripped me as Trowbridge began searching me. Oh, no, I thought, he's going to find the wire.

He patted under my arms, then around my waist. I could feel the wires press against my body. He reached into my shirt and yanked out the black box and wires.

"What's this? Ha! You're wearing a wire. So that's why you were mumbling."

Tory and I froze, our backs to the wall and hands up.

"Are you expecting someone to show up?" he said. And then he started laughing—a horrible, cruel laughter—as he crouched down and picked up the black box and microphone.

"I'll take it from here," he laughed into the microphone, then threw it back to the ground.

"We were set up, Hack," Tory said.

"Hahahahha!" Trowbridge laughed. "Haha. Setup? A setup? You think?"

I started to smile as well, expecting Vaughn Clark to walk in right now.

"You think this is funny, boy," he said. "Well we will see who laughs last."

Suddenly, a sharp pain burned on the side of my head. He pistol-whipped me, hitting my head with the butt of his gun.

I nearly fell, but regained my balance. I could feel Tory getting ready to fight. Everything was starting to get blurry.

"Where's the flag?" he growled.

"You will give me the flag right now, or you will die," he said.

"And you," he said, pointing the gun at Tory. "You try anything, and I'll blow your black head off."

He pointed the gun at me and then Tory.

My head was pounding, half from the blow and half from my rapidly beating heart.

"Fine," I said. "I will give you that stupid flag."

It was like he wasn't listening to me.

"Your girlfriend finally admitted you have it," he said.

He dragged out the word "finally."

"What did you do to her?" I said.

"The same thing we are going to do to you, Mr. Lancaster," he said. "Now don't waste my time. Give me the flag, or I will give you another knock."

I stumbled into the kitchen and was confronted with more of a mess. The cupboards had been spilled out onto the floor, with the table smashed to pieces. I couldn't get to the refrigerator hiding spot because of the carnage.

"It's over there," I said, pointing to the refrigerator, which was half pulled out. They must have checked behind it, but couldn't find the hidden panel.

"Well, then you better get cleaning up," he growled.

I started to pick up the cans, purposely moving slowly to regain my composure. The reality sunk in: either the microphone was broken and they didn't hear me, or Tory was right; they set us up.

"Come on, get moving," he ordered.

Trowbridge lurched forward and grabbed me by the hair. Holding his gun with one hand, he pulled me up by the hair and pulled my face to within inches of his.

The gun was now pressing into my cheek, where he had hit me before. The top of my head screamed in pain.

This was it, I thought.

"Get the flag now," he said, pushing my head down.

Finally, the debris was cleared away. I put my fingers on the edge of it and pulled. The refrigerator easily slid out.

I walked into the empty, dark hole. Looking up, I saw the small hook and unfastened it. I reached in and pulled out the small package. Walking out, I handed it to Trowbridge.

He didn't take it. He just stared at the package.

His face was no longer enraged. He had an excited look—like that of a child—right before he opened the big Christmas present.

"No, no, over here," he said, gesturing with his gun back out into the living room.

I walked in front of him, expecting a bullet in the back of my head. Tory had his hands down, but he was still up against the wall. He slyly smiled and nodded.

"Sit!" Trowbridge said.

"Now open it," he barked.

I carefully unwrapped the dishcloth and revealed the old wooden box in the shape of a triangle.

With the gun to his side, Trowbridge leaned in to inspect the old flag box. I pulled it open to reveal the first flag of the United States of America.

He was watching my every move.

He had a look of anticipation.

"Unfurl it," he growled.

I opened the flag up and held it so he could see it. For a moment, I could not see him.

But I could hear his devilish sneer.

"Yes, yes," he said. "There it is, the 12-star flag. Also known as the Constitution Flag. Washington's Flag. The Sun of Liberty. The Hidden Star. The Fallen Star. Ha!"

I held it up for several minutes. I looked at the arrangement of stars. Eleven stars circled a slightly larger twelfth star. The eleven were for those states that joined the Union. The twelfth was for the new federal state, created by the Constitution. The confederated republic of George Washington, made real in symbols of cloth by him, Benjamin Franklin, and Betsy Ross.

For a moment, I forgot my circumstances and admired it. The red and white stripes of the Sons of Liberty—the flag of freedom and liberty—with the blue seal of government taking just a little of the top left corner.

"Wrap it up," the voice on the other side of the flag demanded.

Taking great care, I started to neatly fold it. This was a national treasure, to be once again concealed and returned to obscurity.

"You will never understand, Mr. Lancaster," he blurted out. "This flag is an enigma. A fluke. It should never have been made. And its secret will never be revealed."

I tucked the flag back into the oak box and closed the lid.

"You just don't get it," he said, grabbing the box from my hands and placing it on the floor.

"An enigma?" Tory asked the man, who was still holding his gun. "A fluke? George Washington and Benjamin Franklin made this flag. They didn't intend for it to be hidden."

"Oh, yeah," Trowbridge said. "Then tell me why, during the time he was President, the star representing the United States was removed? He had to approve this change."

"So you are very wrong," he continued. "Washington himself changed the flag."

I didn't answer him. I never thought about that. Obviously, something happened that necessitated the change. But I didn't know what it was. Could he be right?

"You don't know that," Tory said. "If we had Washington's diaries, maybe light could be shed on this subject."

"Oh, the diaries," Trowbridge laughed. "Those stupid diaries are in Professor Redmand's imagination. There are no diaries."

"Of course there aren't," I said. "Because they were gotten rid of the same way you got rid of Professor Redmand."

Out of the corner of my eye, I saw, almost in slow motion, Tory preparing to strike. Sure, he was a big boy and not in the best of shape. But he was athletic nonetheless. He was constantly practicing on me all of the self-defense moves he learned on YouTube.

I could see he was slowly coiling his leg.

And then he struck.

Like lightning, Tory's foot came out and snapped the gun out of Trowbridge's hand. The agent's mouth dropped open in shock. And then, as if he were a big ballerina, he spun around and, with his other foot, kicked Trowbridge in the head.

Tory fell to the ground, then returned to his feet, crouching a little. Trowbridge stayed erect for a moment after the big blow and then collapsed onto the floor.

"Whoa! Did you see that?" Tory laughed.

It was like he was surprised it even worked.

"That was unbelievable!" he exclaimed.

I slowly walked over to Trowbridge's limp body, then looked up at Tory.

And we both started laughing, a release of the pent-up fear that was inside us.

Trowbridge was out cold.

We kept laughing.

"Did you see that?" Tory said. "Gotcha!"

"Yes, yes," I replied.

And then we both stopped laughing, realizing our predicament wasn't over.

The room was very quiet.

I put my finger to my lips.

"If they set us up, they're going to come for us," I whispered.

"Yes, Hack. Indeed," said a voice that came from the sliding doors.

I knew and trusted that voice. We turned around.

There was Vaughn Clark pointing a gun at us.

"Where is the flag?" he asked.

I pointed to it, shocked. Vaughn Clark walked over to the table and picked it up.

"Thank you for your assistance," he said.

He walked over to Trowbridge, who was curled in a ball on the ground.

He pointed the gun at him.

Pshh. Pshh. The gun banged.

"Why? Vaughn what?" I was sputtering a question.

"Dude, what is going on?" Tory asked, shocked at what he saw.

Vaughn Clark spoke very calmly and very sincerely. "We had to kill him."

And then, after pausing, he continued.

"Just like I am going to have to kill you."

"But why?" I implored.

"This was all a big mistake. Professor Redmand should never have given that flag to Pepper," Vaughn Clark said. "That flag cannot exist, nor can anyone who knows about it."

Vaughn Clark raised his gun to me, but in a flash, Tory spun at him to knock the gun out, using the same maneuver that worked just seconds ago.

I fell to the floor as a shot was fired.

Tory came crashing down in front of me, the face of a fighter in combat. His eyes were fire as he stared at me with a closed jaw and his lips in a slight smile.

And then his face started to withdraw.

His smile stopped, and his bright eyes faded.

"He got me," Tory said, his hand over his heart. He turned his hand so I could see that it was covered in blood.

In the distance, I could see Vaughn Clark come into focus.

"No, Tory, hold on; it's going to be OK," I said, reaching out to hold his head.

It wasn't going to be OK. Tory didn't move. His eyes were staring at me, but he wasn't there.

Tory was dead.

"I love you, man," I cried, putting my hand on his face. "Oh, Tory, I love you."

Vaughn Clark lurked in the distance and now slowly raised the gun up and pointed it at me.

There was a pause. I shut my eyes.

Pshh. Pshh. The gun banged.

And I tightened my closed eyes, feeling the bullets ripping into my body and seeing Tory's vacant stare in my mind's eye.

Deathly silence hung in the air.

And then I waited a second and realized the truth: *nothing happened to me.*

I looked up and saw Vaughn Clark staring forward, mouth open, standing straight up. Then he fell to the ground. Behind him at the sliding door was Morgan Stonewall, holding his just-fired gun.

Morgan Stonewall killed Vaughn Clark!

"Hack, are you alright?" Stonewall asked.

"I am," I said. "But Tory isn't."

I reached out to his open, vacant eyes and closed them.

Tory had a slight smile on his face.

I grabbed his head and hugged him. "God, please take care of Tory. I love you, Tory."

Stonewall put his hand on my shoulder. He didn't say anything. I knew from his touch that he had been in a similar position, perhaps many times, when your friend and brother tragically left you forever.

There was a somber quiet that filled the room. Three dead men lay in my apartment, a scene of bloody violence.

My eyes went to the large, lifeless hulk of my best friend, lying in a bloody mess.

Stonewall put his hand on my shoulder again.

"We have to get out of here," he said. "We have to get Pepper."

That name refocused me. I shot up from the chair and walked over to Vaughn Clark's body. He was holding the old flag box. I gently pulled it from his hand.

"Let's go," Stonewall said.

Chapter Thirty-Four

"The price of freedom is eternal vigilance."

– President Thomas Jefferson

"Experience has taught me, in fact, that no man should be
pitied because, every day in his life, he faces a hard,
stubborn problem, but rather that it is the man who has no
problem to solve, no hardships to face, who is to be pitied."

*– My Larger Education, by Booker T. Washington,
Doubleday, New York, 1911*

Stonewall handed me a handkerchief to clean the blood from
my face. I wiped the tears from my eyes, then placed it against
my jaw where the gun had made a cut. I hurt inside and out.

We walked quickly to the SUV.

"What's going on?" I asked. "I don't understand."

"You will," he said. "And very soon."

In a matter of minutes, we were at Penn's Landing, named for
the spot where William Penn landed, even though he actually
landed near present-day Chester, but the city bought the name.

Stonewall parked the SUV in a garage. And then he pointed at
a sign that said, "This Way to the Marina."

"Marina? I thought we were going to New York."

"We are," Stonewall said. "By boat."

"Boat...," I could not get the words out, still in a state of shock
from Tory's murder.

At this point, I just followed his lead. The last hour was more than my brain could process. My head and heart throbbed. I realized the bottom line was saving Pepper.

We walked the marina's main deck and came to a corner, then made a right and walked to the end of the dock.

I stopped in my tracks. Stonewall stopped and turned around.

"What's wrong?" he asked.

"That boat. I've seen that boat before!"

And true enough, it was the same sleek, black boat Pepper and I saw in the Charlestown Marina. It was solid black and looked half yacht and half submarine. Sleek-cut windows made it look like it was a miniature warship. It was at least three times the size of Pepper's cousin's boat we stayed in.

"That's how we're getting to New York," Stonewall replied.

We walked up to the ship. You could see its sophisticated array of radar, sonar, and boom instruments twirling on top. Next to it was a small flag—the Rebellious Stripes with a Rattlesnake—snapped in the breeze. In the back was a two-person mini-boat, ready for deployment.

"Follow me," Stonewall said, as we ascended a small set of steps to board the ship. In a flash, we were inside the central room, which had multiple computer screens, keyboards, and instrumentation I had never seen on a boat before. There was a young man dressed in sailor whites who was intently watching one screen. He kept working and did not recognize my presence.

"You can sit here," he said, pointing to a side, padded bench. "There's someone I want you to meet."

As he said those words, the boat silently departed the slip and slowly moved out into the river, steadily gaining speed, heading for

Delaware Bay. I couldn't tell who the captain of the ship was. No one gave the order to depart, and no one was looking forward at the water.

At that moment, on the other side of the galley, a dark figure emerged from the deck below.

I pulled back.

It was the strange man!

The one Tory and I met in the bookstore. The one I saw enter this boat in Boston. And the one who told Tory he knew about the flag was later at the SOL meeting.

I still could not make out his face. His head was at an angle, and his hat was tilted so as to block my view.

In dramatic fashion, he took his hat off. Then he took off his dark glasses and a scarf that covered his neck.

As he took it off, I began to recognize him.

"Yes ... Hack," he said.

"Yes, Hack, it's me."

That voice. I knew the voice well, but I still wasn't sure.

"Hack?" he said.

And then I saw the bushy eyebrows.

How could this be? I stammered, unable to speak.

"Great Caesar's Ghost!" That's what Perry White said to Clark Kent when something shocking happened, and that's all I could think.

A ghost, indeed!

For standing before me was a man I believed dead, who now was among the living.

"Professor Mac!" I declared, frozen in my tracks.

"How is this possible?"

He finished taking off his costume, walked over, and put his hand out. I grabbed it, and then he pulled me in and hugged me.

"Professor Mac," Stonewall said, "we had three casualties."

We all sat down.

Stonewall continued. "You were right. It was Vaughn Clark. He is the government spy sent to destroy us. Or, should I say, he was. He ended up killing Trowbridge. He also killed Hack's friend, Tory."

"The one from the bookstore?" the Professor asked.

I nodded yes.

"I'm so sorry, Hack," the Professor said. "He was a smart, funny guy."

I looked away, convinced that all of this baloney about the flag is why Tory is dead.

"What's going on, Professor Redmand?" I asked, barely holding back tears.

The boat was now increasing in speed, and the shoreline was no longer visible. I still did not know who was piloting it.

The Professor walked to my side of the ship and sat next to me on the bench.

"We were infiltrated by the government," he said.

"We?"

"Yes, we. The Sons of Liberty. For over 250 years, we were impenetrable. We were a secret society of patriots who believed in life, liberty, and the pursuit of happiness."

He paused and looked out the window. The sun's rays sparkled off the ocean's waters.

"Sometime around 2001, forces within the government had achieved total information awareness. They were able to know everything, about everybody, any time they looked. As society became more digital and computer-based, and with the rise of smartphones and social media, they were able to create dossiers on every single American.

"And when they found us—the group that had given their very flag to the Revolution—they were threatened. Because free and independent people tend to resist. And their surveillance showed them that there were millions of Americans who actually thought they were free and independent. And it terrified them," he said.

Professor Redmand got up and walked to a small counter with a sink and glasses.

"What do you want to drink?" he asked.

"Water, please."

He handed me a bottle and grabbed one too, and then continued his story.

"So they made the Sons of Liberty a target. They infiltrated our state and city chapters. They were easy to spot, the fools. How? Because they advocate violence as a solution. And anyone who knows the Sons of Liberty knows we do not destroy people or property to further our goals," Professor Mac said.

"Ummm," I interrupted. "What about the Boston Tea Party?" The so-called Tea Party in 1773 was when Sons of Liberty dressed up as Indians and dumped tea into Boston Harbor, resulting in a harsh crackdown by the British.

"That was an early form of economic sanctions," he said, briefly smiling. "Seriously, Hack, we have known about their infiltration for some time, but we allowed them to continue so we could monitor their tactics. It seemed all they wanted to do was excite the Sons to violence. That way, they could clamp down and stigmatize us."

"About a year ago, we knew they had penetrated our leadership. Now, they had to be stopped. The Sons are patient and don't overreact, but we also have mechanisms to strike—powerful tools that require the strictest authorization, that can punch them in the face and remind them, we're still here!"

As he said the words "powerful tools," I looked around this central room. The computers, the sailor in uniform, and the steps to the deck below. The display of our ship's movements appeared on a digital GPS map in real time, with a large display of ship speed and time at sea.

The rapid speed at which we were now traveling made me realize this was a military vessel with potent capabilities. But there were no visible guns, missiles, or bombs. I sensed that this ship possessed more powerful weapons than any of those, and perhaps it was more effective.

It was dawning on me: could the electrical and internet outages of the last few days be linked to this ship?

Professor Mac was quiet, watching me as I looked around.

He then continued. "If not checked, the Feds would ultimately destroy us, turn us into a 'Proud Boys' or some radical militia group, and imprison us. Fortunately, we are as strong today as we were when we threw tea into the harbor. Probably stronger.

"So we moved into action. And took every opportunity to expose them. When Pepper came to me about the flag, it seemed like the perfect bait," he said.

"You mean all of this bad stuff that has happened is a result of you?" I asked, feeling betrayed. "You should have warned us."

"Oh, I did," Professor Mac said. "I warned you both numerous times. But the cat was out of the bag, and something was going to happen regardless."

"Well, if the cat is the flag, you're the one who let it out!" I said. A part of me felt like the good professor was really the evil professor. Seeing him in this quasi-military setting made me think (for just a minute) that he was the enemy.

"True, but Pepper was already involved," the Professor said. "She knew about Washington's missing diaries. It didn't matter. They had already learned many of our secrets, including the location of our hall. Everything was vulnerable."

I stared at him, listening. "One of my friends is dead, and one is in prison because of this. That's a heck of a price for freedom, isn't that what you would call it?"

The boat was now racing to New York, faster than any vessel I had ever been on. Most surprising was the lack of engine noise; this ship must be electric.

"The key, Hack, is that we fix this now. We rescue Pepper and take care of the flag."

"But it won't be so easy to bring Tory back," I said, then asked where the bathroom was. Morgan Stonewall escorted me to a spacious sauna room with a shower. I took off my clothes and turned on the shower. The warm water hit my face, and for a moment, it was the only thing on my mind. My emotions were numb. I still had a hard time believing Tory was dead or that Professor Redmand was alive.

And I realized that Pepper or I, or both of us, may meet the same fate. I could see Tory's dead eyes opening. *Oh God, I prayed. Please take care of Tory.*

I finally exited the bathroom. The shower was healing. And for the moment, no one took notice of me. I looked around at the ship. Instruments and stations lined the walls, each with a chair. All that spinning sonar and radar array on top wasn't for catching fish. This ship seemed to have a more sinister purpose.

Morgan Stonewall walked up and handed me a cup of coffee.

"You're going to need this," he said as we sat down. "And Hack, I know you've lost your friend, and I know what that is like. I have had my best friends cut down in battle, and it is a hurt you never get over," he said as we sat down.

"If it means anything, Tory is the one who exposed Vaughn Clark. Remember when he asked him the question, "How did you know Pepper was in the Sons of Liberty Hall?" It was obvious that the only way he could know that was if someone in the room called him."

I looked up and remembered. Neuman Church told someone on the phone that Pepper was there. He must have been speaking to Vaughn Clark. There is no other way he could have known. I certainly didn't tell him.

The boat abruptly slowed down. Then stopped. I looked out the window, and there were the skyscrapers of lower Manhattan. We were here! I looked at the computer board, and it read:

Distance Traveled: 197 nautical miles

Average Speed: 50 knots

"Wow, that's fast," I said. "Too fast; double what most ships can do."

"We're here," the man staring at the computer screen said. He was wearing a white shirt with a coiled rattlesnake emblem.

"Full stop and stabilize!" Stonewall barked.

"Prepare craft for launch."

A whirring sound now filled the room.

"Aye, aye," the sailor replied.

Stonewall continued yelling orders.

"Is Alpha activated?"

"Affirmative."

"Is Omega activated?"

"Affirmative. They are waiting for your command."

"Standby."

The whirring sound dissipated, but a very low-level hum remained.

A window slit now opened, and Stonewall peered out, holding high-powered binoculars.

Professor Redmand walked up from a lower deck and came towards us, holding a cup of coffee. This boat is bigger than it appears.

"I feel really bad for your friend," he said, looking out a window slit at Lower Manhattan Bay. "It was a high price to pay to identify the intruder. But if Vaughn Clark had any more time to mess up the Sons of Liberty, centuries of work would have been destroyed, we would be jailed, and the fight for liberty would be lost."

I relayed to Professor Mac the conversation we had with Vaughn Clark about tipping points and how they ultimately lead to revolution.

"Tipping points is exactly the rationale he was instructed to promote. By whom, we are not sure," the Professor said.

"What do you mean?" I asked.

"The tipping point argument was told by other plants in our city chapters as a way to radicalize them," he replied. "Once they convince you about the 'tipping points', the next step is armed violence."

"So, you're saying the Feds are trying to incite violence?"

"Yes. Indeed."

"Why is this flag so important?" I asked, looking up.

"It's simple. It contradicts the official narrative of when the USA began and who created it."

"Why does that even matter? We are what we are today, despite any old flag."

"It's not any old flag," Professor Mac said, becoming annoyed. "It is literally the first flag of the USA, the symbol of the Republic's birth."

Morgan Stonewall turned from the computers and spoke. "We can talk about all of this stuff later; right now we have to focus on the mission at hand. With Vaughn dead, we need you to play a critical role, Hack."

He placed an odd-looking handheld device on the table. It was a block with a thick antenna and two fat dials.

"This is yours," he said, pushing it toward me. "It is a secure radio phone that cannot be tracked and that scrambles all voice communications."

Weary from what had happened just hours ago, I could barely focus on his words. Sensing this, Stonewall got up and poured another cup of coffee.

"Wake up, Hack," he said. "In a couple of hours, we can have Pepper on this boat and this boat out in the ocean—if we are successful. *If you are successful.*"

"Sure," I said, grabbing the cup and taking a big gulp. "What do I have to do?"

Stonewall laid out the plan. I would be dispatched on the smaller boat to the upper New York Bay and dock at a spot in lower Manhattan that was especially made for the Sons. From there, I would walk to Fraunces Tavern and wait for instructions.

"Fraunces Tavern has always been our safehouse," Stonewall said. "They know you are coming and will assist when you come back with Pepper."

"What do you mean by a safehouse?" I asked.

"Just what I said. The tavern has been a meeting spot for the Sons of Liberty since the beginning and is now owned by the Sons of the Revolution."

"Let me finish the plan, Hack," Stonewall said as Professor Mac put his finger to his lips as if to tell me, "Quiet!"

"At this very moment, Pepper is being arraigned at the Thurgood Marshall United States Courthouse. When they are done, she will return to the Manhattan Detention Complex. Both of these locations are within a mile from the tavern."

I nodded. "OK."

"At the designated moment, when the bus is transporting her back to the jail, we are going to turn New York off."

"Turn New York off?" I asked.

"Please let him finish, Hack," Professor Mac pleaded, a look of disappointment flashing in his eyes.

"Yes, turn New York off. And when it's off and the bus is trapped in traffic, we are going to wait and make everyone else wait. Then we will rescue Pepper. Once we know the exact location, we'll radio you, and you'll go to the street, locate the bus, and stand behind the emergency backdoor. We will open the door, Pepper will be given to you, and you will return to the tavern with her."

"Just like that, no problems?" I said skeptically. "Get the... forgive me for not believing you!"

Morgan Stonewall nodded and frowned. "I understand."

Then he continued.

"Hopefully we will be able to get her chains off in the bus. If not, our people in the tavern will take care of the chains and give her new clothing. Then the two of you will go back to the water, get on the attack boat, and return to the *Reprisal*."

"Return to what?"

"The *Reprisal*."

"This ship is called the *Reprisal*?"

"Yes, indeed," Professor Mac said. "Named after one of the most famous ships of the American Navy."

"Do I need this?" I asked, placing the revolver Pepper gave me onto the table.

Morgan Stonewall looked at Professor Redmand, who gave a quick nod.

"Yes, take it," he said. "You may need it."

"ZERO HOUR—IT IS TIME!" cried the sailor behind the computer screen. Suddenly, two more sailors came on deck and sat at their stations.

Professor Mac put his hand on my arm. "Godspeed, Hackworth Lancaster. Please come back with Pepper!"

Godspeed. I remember learning that this term was used by sailors to mean success with divine protection. I appreciated the sentiment.

Stonewall and I got up. The computer screens were now fully lit, and the three sailors were busy on their keyboards, talking among themselves.

Stonewall handed me the radio. "Don't mess with the dial. You are locked in."

I couldn't help but remember that just a few hours ago I had another communication device, but no one came to help me.

"Does this work better than the one this morning?" I snarked at Stonewall.

He pretended not to hear me. I kept staring at him, forcing a response.

"Yes, this one definitely works," he said. "I eliminated the bad part."

We walked out on the lower deck, where the smaller boat was. Stonewall called it an attack boat, and I could see why. A small turret suggested it could be armed, but it wasn't. On the right of the front seat were several black boxes.

Like the *Reprisal* itself, this craft was difficult to describe. But I wasn't afraid to take it out, having spent many summers at my uncle's lakehouse messing around with boats.

"Why can't you just bring me to the upper bay?" I asked.

"Because there is too much interference from the buildings that will not let *Reprisal* do its job," Stonewall replied. "And, out here, we can't get caught."

"Get in," he said.

I jumped into the boat, which was lowered slowly into the water by an elevator-like deck. Gradually, the boat became buoyant as the deck became submerged.

I turned the key, and the engine roared.

"Hack, good luck!" Stonewall said. Both of his thumbs were up. I steered the boat towards the upper bay and hit the gas. In a flash, I was on my way.

The upper bay was not far off, and then I spotted something I hadn't seen since my father took me and my brothers to see it when we were young.

It looked different than I remembered—smaller. Was that because I was older and seeing it from a different perspective?

There, a giant in her greenish dress, holding a torch, looked over my head.

I held my hat and looked straight up, tipped it to her, and then raced past Lady Liberty.

Chapter Thirty-Five

"The chancellor advanced to administer the oath ... and Mr. Otis, the secretary of the Senate; held up the Bible on its crimson cushion. The oath was read slowly and distinctly, Washington at the same time laying his hand on the open Bible. When it was concluded, he replied solemnly, "I swear --so help me God!" Mr. Otis would have raised the Bible to his lips but he bowed down reverently and kissed it.

"The chancellor now stepped forward, waved his hand and exclaimed, "Long live George Washington, President of the United States!"

"At this moment a flag was displayed on the cupola of the hall, on which signal there was a general discharge of artillery on the Battery. All the bells of the city rang out a joyful peal and the multitude rent the air with acclamations."

– from George Washington, A Biography by Washington Irving, originally published 1856-59, edited by Charles Neider, New York, 1976

My dad had taken us to the Statue of Liberty when I was about ten. It was there that we learned it was a gift from the French people to the Americans. The French name for the statue translates to "Liberty Enlightening the World." It depicts the Roman Goddess of Liberty holding a torch in her right hand, and in her left hand is a tablet with the date of the Declaration of Independence.

As a small boy, she really did look like a colossus, but today she is dwarfed by the nearby skyscrapers many times her size.

In the dusk, she looked small and irrelevant compared to the lights now starting to sparkle in lower Manhattan.

To those lights, I sped.

Pushing up on the throttle, the boat was now hitting the light waves, skipping as it went faster and faster. The wind blew through my hair, and I felt just like when I was in the shower earlier—a cool numbness. My emotions were numb. But I knew I couldn't dwell on what happened this morning. I had to bury those feelings for now.

I looked at the front of the boat and saw *Reprisal* neatly engraved on the side. The original *Reprisal* took Benjamin Franklin from Philadelphia to France in the fall of 1776. He would stay in France for the entire war, orchestrating critical French money, soldiers, and the navy.

Franklin knew a secret. He knew the French would do anything to kick Great Britain out of North America, like Great Britain kicked them out a decade before.

Franklin also knew that bringing the war to British shores would certainly help the cause. The *Reprisal* dropped him off in France and then went north and attacked British shipping. Later, John Paul Jones would arrive in a ship, referencing Franklin's Poor Richard's Almanack—the *Bonhomme Richard*.

I kept thinking about this as a way NOT to think about what happened to Tory.

I let back on the throttle, looking for the yellow flag marker to park the boat at. In the British Navy, the solid yellow flag was used as the Quarantine Flag. If you came upon a British ship flying this flag, you immediately turned around for fear of catching the deathly illness yourself!

I didn't see anything, and the water was choppy. The Brooklyn Bridge was now visible on the right, so I knew it was getting close. A big splash smacked the edge of the boat and slapped me in the face.

"Whooaaa!" I exclaimed. The cold water really woke me up.

I looked again for the yellow flag. Yes, there it was on a very small deck connected to stairs. The flag wasn't flying. It was wooden and nailed to a headwall that surrounded a large, dry culvert pipe.

I cut power and then started again slowly, towards the yellow flag. The smell of sulfur hung in the air, courtesy of a chemical plant in Elizabeth, New Jersey. There wasn't much traffic on the water at this time of day, except for a Circle Line tourist boat heading to the Statue of Liberty and a garbage scow heading to who knows where.

I docked on a small, floating pontoon deck anchored to the headwall. A steep wooden staircase brought me up to street level.

"Now landed," I said into the radio.

Fraunces Tavern was no more than two blocks away. I had been there before and knew its amazing story. Not only is it still in business, but it also served as Washington's headquarters and the principle offices of the Confederation Congress after the Revolution.

But the thing I remembered most were the oysters, which I hoped to have now.

I walked into the colonial brick structure that resembled more of a mansion than a commercial enterprise.

A young man behind a small lectern greeted me.

"Do you have a reservation?"

"Yes,"

"Name?"

"Morgan." It was the name he told me to use.

The young man looked down and then at me again. He picked up his phone and said, "He's here." In a matter of seconds, I was sitting at a table for two, with a menu and water now being poured into my glass. The waiter spoke.

"We know you're in a hurry, but do you want something to eat in the meantime?"

"A dozen oyy... wait. Two dozen oysters, a sampler of your best sellers."

"Fine. So we will bring you a selection including Malpeque's from Prince Edward Island, Rappahannocks from Chesapeake Bay, and Moon Shoals from Cape Cod," the waiter said.

"Great," I replied.

"Absolutely," he said, sharply turning and walking out of the dining room.

I grabbed the radio from my coat pocket.

"In the tavern," I said.

"Standby," the voice returned.

"ETA 40 minutes."

Huh, I thought as I read the history of the tavern. It served as the offices for Treasury, State, and War before and after the Constitution was ratified in 1789. It made sense that Washington was inaugurated in New York because that's where the Confederation Congress and executive offices were.

The oysters came and were devoured. And just as quickly, the radio came on.

"Standby. The bus is preparing to leave the courthouse. Standby."

Pepper was being held at what was known as "The Tombs," a city jail facility in lower Manhattan now called the Manhattan Detention Complex. I couldn't think of a worse name for a jail to stay in. She would be returning there after appearing at the courthouse.

The waiter came and asked if I wanted anything else.

He picked up the emptied platter and said, "The bill is taken care of."

"And when you come back," he said, turning and looking me in the eyes. "Use the side street. There is a set of street basement stairs that will be open."

"Thank you."

I was nervous, but not like in the past. It was a numb nervousness, where you're scared but just going through the motions.

The radio squawked.

"Alpha in 60 seconds. Standby."

I had no idea what that meant, but didn't move. I watched the clock tick on the wall, noticing it was an old colonial clock, the wind-up kind, and not needing electricity.

And then, one minute later, "SNAP!" The lights went out, and the power was off. You could hear the grumbling, for this had become a common occurrence.

You could still see without light, but it was darkening—not yet twilight.

Several customers were informed that payments could not be processed and that cash would be preferred if possible. More grumbling could be heard. Old-fashioned credit card machines—the manual, unconnected kind—were now brought out.

I waited for instructions that didn't come. Is this a setup again? Suddenly I thought about Pepper. I could almost feel that she was nearby, like she was talking to me. "You can save us," the distant voice said in my head.

I thought about her, the last time I saw her. And touching the blood she left on the table. I thought about Tory, but blocked it and stared at the clock.

Twenty minutes went by, and nothing from the radio.

And then it squawked.

"Go to Baxter Street and look for the bus. Copy?"

"10-4. En route now," I replied.

I jammed the radio into my pocket and headed onto the street. The relative quiet of the tavern was drowned out by the noise and confusion on Pearl Street, which was packed with people.

Two men were arguing and yelling at cars locked in place. No traffic was moving and hadn't moved for the last half hour.

Two other men were talking. "The whole state is shut down," one said. "They think something happened with the transmission lines from Canada."

"No mobile phones, no internet," the other said. "Even backup systems have been hit."

I was walking now, looking for Baxter Street, which was not that far away.

The noise intensified, as did the crowds. The streets were not made to drain skyscrapers full of people at the same time.

Car horns, ambulance sirens, loudspeakers, yelling police officers, arguing pedestrians—noise, noise, noise. A coffee house fight breaks out over the last croissant.

I turned onto Worth Street and then saw Baxter.

My heart was racing. There was a bus, a two-tone colored corrections bus, stuck on Baxter Street.

"On Baxter. Bus spotted," I said on the radio.

"Proceed to the back of the bus," the reply came.

The noise was loud as ever, with car horns beeping. It was starting to get darker outside. The streets were not as packed on Baxter as they were on Pearl.

At that moment, the scene rapidly unfolded before my eyes.

There were two NYPD police officers walking in front of the bus. I could also make out two other men standing on the street parallel to the stopped bus.

I had to move quickly. Swallowing hard, I walked onto the road, passed stopped cars, and then came to the back of the bus. A small car was behind it. I waved to the driver, turned, and stood in front of his car, facing the bus.

"Here's some water for you guys," the cop said to the bus driver, knocking on the folding bus door and holding up two large bottles of water. The two men who were on the street were now crouched on the side of the bus, and I could see one of them had a rifle.

The bus driver refused.

"No, we're OK," he said.

The cop responded. "We heard the power will be out over night. You will not be OK, and this may be the last chance you will have to get some water."

And then it happened so fast—a blink of an eye. The bus door was opened, and just as quickly, the cops with water and two men on the side were on the bus!

"Hey, stop, what the..." the driver exclaimed. The bus rocked as the corrections officers inside were subdued.

"If anyone moves, you're dead," shouted the guy with the rifle.

Then it was quiet. A head appeared at the back of the bus, looking through the dirty rear window. It was the police officer (or better yet, the SOL fake cop), and he gave me the thumbs up.

"The chains. The chains. Unline the chains NOW!" the fake cops yelled.

The guards on the bus quickly did what they were told, with no resistance.

And then the cop reappeared in the back door window. Another figure was beside him, and I knew it was her.

Swoosh came the sound as the bus' back door was opened.

There, standing in an orange jumper with dirty hair and the look of a broken spirit, was a hunched over Pepper. The fake cop took his hand and gently raised her head so she could look out the door.

And she did. And we looked at each other in a way we hadn't since we were five years old—when we were innocent and excited to meet. I looked up and saw her countenance quickly change. She started to stand up straight. She took her hand and wiped her hair to the side.

Her eyes opened a little.

And she smiled.

"Are you ready down there?" the fake cop yelled.

Before I could answer, Pepper, in her orange jumper, jumped out of the bus and into my arms. She didn't wait.

We hugged, squeezed, and cried out, "I love you," almost in unison, and then laughed. For a moment, all the action, all the noise, all the problems—they didn't exist, and it was just Pepper and me.

"Hey, buddy!" the fake cop yelled. "GO!"

I suddenly remembered we had to get back to the tavern; we both turned and started running, retracing the steps that brought me here.

The back door of the bus was slammed shut, followed by a loud explosion that sounded like a gunshot.

KA-BOOM!!

That sound reverberated off the buildings.

The noise drew attention away from the Sons slipping away from the scene.

We raced onto Pearl Street, turned a corner, and bumped right into a real NYPD officer coming in the other direction.

"Hey, you two, HEY, hold it right there," he yelled after we passed him.

Pepper looked at me, startled. I grabbed her hand, and we ran across the street and into an endless crowd. Turning back, it looked like we had lost him.

We kept running, working our way through the crowd and back to the tavern. Finally, we made it to the side of the building and down the street stairs into the basement, the doors closing after we entered.

"Here are some clothes for you to wear," a woman said, handing Pepper a shirt and pants. She quickly changed into them.

The woman led us to a small, well-appointed room with bottles of water and snacks on the table. "You must wait here until it gets darker," she said.

We grabbed the water bottles and fell back on the couch at the same time. The adrenaline was wearing off.

We just stared ahead and didn't say a word to each other.

The woman led us upstairs with her flashlight and then through the front door.

It was getting darker out, and without any lights on, it was a little more difficult to get around. Fortunately, the car headlights offered some help against the darkness, and we made our way to the boat.

"Hey, stop NOW!" The order came from across the street from the real cop, whom we thought we had gotten away from.

"STOP NOW!" he yelled.

"We ain't stopping now," I said to Pepper, and we took off, running to the boat dock. We found the stairs and raced down them to the dock landing and boat.

We pressed ourselves against the headwall, looked up, and listened. Nothing but a distant church bell rang eleven times.

Then our gaze slowly came down to us staring into each other's eyes. She had several bruises, including a big one on her cheek. She tried to talk, but she couldn't. Her bottom lip was trembling.

We kissed and hugged tightly. And then I grabbed her head and pressed it to my chest.

"Pepper," I whispered. "I love you, Pepper," and she nodded her head. She didn't have to talk. The motion of her head told me she loved me, too.

"I let go of you once," I said softly. "And then again. And I let them arrest you."

She was still nodding and crying.

"I will never let you go again."

Betsy Ross makes the first flag of the United States of America, 1789
Modified from the original The Birth of the Flag — by Henry Mosler

SUNDAY

Chapter Thirty-Six

"Three can keep a secret, if two of them are dead."

– Benjamin Franklin

"This is a copy of a 1786 design that has a slightly
different flag design. The earlier print is described as
having 13 dark stars arranged 4-5-4 on a light canton
and 13 dark and light stripes. (This one) has 12
five-pointed dark stars on a light canton arranged in a
square of eleven with one in the center."

*– "L'Hommage de l'Amerique a la France" Fabric Design Print
(detail) French; 1790; Original in the Smithsonian Institution*

A powerful flashlight made its way onto the stairs. It then shot a beam into the upper bay and slowly moved on the water.

The cop who was pursuing us was on street level, looking around. And then he started scanning below.

"Get on," I said, pointing to the boat. Pepper jumped in. I tried to unhook it, but the rope was caught on the deck cleat.

"Hey, you hold it right now," he yelled. "Now!"

I yanked and yanked on the rope, but it was caught.

"Stop now or I'll shoot," he threatened, as he began to come down the stairs.

I jerked it again. Now the rope slipped out and was free of the cleat. I threw it in the boat and leapt into the front seat.

Pssshhee, a bullet whizzed by our heads.

"Stop now," the cop yelled, standing halfway down the steps.

I hit the throttle hard, and we blasted off.

Pssshhee another bullet whizzed by.

Pssshhee and then another.

Very quickly, we were out of his gun's range.

It was so dark that I didn't know if there was anything in front of me. The boat had lights, but they only penetrated the darkness for a few feet. Still, I raced back towards the Statue of Liberty.

The entire island of Manhattan was dark, except for the backup lighting still on in some of the skyscrapers. It was a half light and not enough to chase away the darkness.

But there on the right side she was, draped in light both on her and on the shore behind her—bright, beautiful light.

The lightning that ran down Franklin's kite is now made useful in the illumination of Lady Liberty and the little island she dwells on.

The boat raced away from the dark financial district to her radiance and then past her. It was here that I was instructed to notify the *Reprisal* that we had cleared the upper bay.

"Entering lower bay," I said on the radio.

"10-4," the radio squawked back.

I let up on the throttle, and we slowed. Pepper was holding onto my waist when she quickly let go and turned around.

"Hack, look!" she said. It was the first words she spoke since jumping out of the bus.

And before us, we watched New York turn on again. First slowly, but the light gained against the darkness as the electricity pulsed through the city. Soon, its light would once again overpower Lady Liberty's torch.

We approached the *Reprisal.*

"Ready to board," I said on the radio, and quickly several sailors appeared on the deck.

"This way, this way, this way," one said, pointing to the back of the boat. They lowered a deck into the water as I positioned the boat to return home.

"Hit it hard until you're on, and then let up," he said.

He said it again, pointing to the spot.

I did just that. The boat flew up the deck, stopped, and the platform began rising up to the main deck.

"Maximum Sun!" Pepper yelled.

"Professor Mac!" Pepper yelled, pointing at him. Morgan Stonewall was at his side.

Pepper was shocked. "Professor Mac!"

We jumped off the attack boat as the Professor approached.

"Let me look at you," he said, hugging her. She pushed back.

"You're not dead!"

We laughed.

"No, not yet," he said. "Come inside; we'll fill you in."

And that is what we did after settling into the center galley. Pepper was told everything that had happened since her arrest. We were all eager to explain, until it came to Tory.

"Tory's dead," I said, my voice shaking as I held back tears.

"Oh, Hack," Pepper said, grabbing my hand. "That's terrible."

Morgan Stonewall filled her in on the gruesome facts, starting with the Sons of Liberty meeting right up to her rescue.

She looked around the room, taking in the computer stations.

"How do you fake a death?" she asked Professor Mac.

"It's easy when the police are SOL," he replied.

"Who is the Watcher?" she shot back.

It was like she was channeling Tory, because I remember him asking the exact same question. Tory never got an answer.

"He is," Morgan Stonewall said, pointing to the Professor.

The Professor made a slight bow. And then he spoke.

"The first Watcher was Paul Revere, who watched for a signal in the Old North Church. If he saw one lantern, it meant the British troops were marching by land. If he saw two lanterns, it meant they were coming by sea. The Redcoats were heading to Lexington and Concord, where the Sons had the guns and powder stored."

"One if by land, two if by sea," Pepper said.

"Well, Paul Revere—the Watcher—did not just ride a horse to alert the Minutemen," the Professor continued. "He also built a gun powder factory to supply the state's army. And later, he commanded forces for the Massachusetts Navy."

"From then until now, the Sons of Liberty have had someone watching. The Watcher's job is the same as then. To look for signals and take action," Morgan Stonewall said. "Like we did today."

The *Reprisal* started to pick up speed. Her hull was so angled as to make it glide. It appeared to be made of molded titanium. You could not see any connections or rivets, but you could feel it gracefully split the water.

"Now, let us go and eat," he continued, leading us to the deck below, from where I had seen Professor Mac earlier emerge. There was a nice kitchen and galley. The food was already prepared and on the table, with cheese, olives, crackers, tuna fish, hard-boiled eggs, smoked salmon, onion, bagels, cream cheese, capers, and more.

Pepper made a large bagel with salmon, cream cheese, red onions, and capers. You could tell she was famished.

I started to talk, but the Professor put his finger to his lips and nodded. He wanted to give her a chance to speak first.

Finally, she did.

"Where are we going now? And what's going to happen to us?" she asked.

There was no answer. Our hosts looked down at the table.

"We can't go back to Philly," she said. "That's the first place they'll look."

"Actually, Pepper, we are going back, but just for a moment," Professor Mac said. "We have to put the flag back where it belongs. It's the only place it will be safe."

"Which begs the question, Professor," she said. "How did you get the flag? And what exactly is it?"

"Slow down, I'll tell you the facts. But eat up, Pepper."

She reached for some nuts and olives. Both of us were now looking directly at him, listening intently.

"When Ben Franklin first proposed a union among the colonies in 1754, it didn't take long for every colony's legislature to vote "No." Twenty years later, when the newly independent states created the Articles of Confederation, it would take the states more than five years to approve and join."

It was like we were back in Professor Mac's classroom.

"And do you know how long it took for the states to ratify the Constitution?"

He didn't wait for an answer.

"Just a matter of months. Not decades. Not years. But a mere couple of months."

He picked up a bottle of water and drank half of it. For an old man, he was pretty spry.

"When the Constitution was drafted, its proponents got smart. They took the vote out of the hands of the state legislatures and into special ratifying conventions elected by the people of that state. But the people didn't quite understand, and not many voted—only 160,000 out of 640,000 eligible voters cast a ballot. In just a matter of months, the nationalists were able to stack the conventions, and the Constitution was approved.

"When the ninth state convention approved it, the Constitution kicked into operation. In the past, every state had to agree before that could happen. Now, only nine would make the Union," he said.

"By the time of Washington's inauguration, 11 states had joined. North Carolina and Rhode Island refused. This caused a big problem. The new United States would need a flag, but it would only have 11 stars, plus a 12th star for the United States itself."

Professor Mac looked at us to make sure we understood.

"You were right, Pepper," I said.

"You see, in the 1780's, the American states were all the rage. They had won independence, and each had its own constitution. The King of England negotiated trade treaties with each one of them separately. They were the envy of other nations, who saw promise in a system that did not have kings and queens but was based on ideals of equality, life, liberty, and the pursuit of happiness," Professor Mac said.

"Mankind had seen nothing quite like the thirteen united States of America, each with its own constitution and bill of rights," he continued.

"Franklin and Washington knew there was a hard problem: they needed a new flag. But what were they to use? They both believed that a new republic was about to begin, and they could not use the old Confederation flag. So, Franklin and Washington met with Betsy Ross."

"Tory was right," I thought. "Poor Tory."

"The Betsy Ross story is a half-truth. She did make the first flag, but in 1789 and not in 1776. And she knew both Franklin and Washington very well," he answered.

"Ben, George, and Betsy settled on the 12-star flag, with the star in the center representing the new Republic and each star having five points. She made several flags for Washington's inauguration and the start of the U.S. Constitution."

"And the first flag, the one that flew on top of Federal Hall, is the flag I gave you."

Pepper looked at me and nodded.

"The first flag of the United States of America we know today," she said.

"That's right," Professor Mac said. "Now the story gets interesting. Rhode Island was the last holdout and was finally bullied, against its will, into joining the new United States. And with Vermont next in line, it became obvious. The USA wouldn't need its own star. It could revert to being the sum collection of stars who joined," he continued.

"The new federal government needed the people to associate it with the Revolution and the start of American independence. The problem with the 12-star flag is that it was different from the originally specified, and by now well known, Thirteen Stars and Stripes."

"Yes, I understand," she said.

"The 12-star flag is a stark reminder that something changed on April 30, 1789. It marks when we went from being *the United States of America in Congress assembled* to just the United States of America.

"A year later, Franklin died. Washington would die ten years later, leaving his diaries, journals, artifacts, and the 12-star flag to his nephew Bushrod Washington, who in turn gave them to John Marshall, who was working on a biography. Marshall was the Chief Justice of the Supreme Court," he said.

"Marshall was the third person to understand the secret and the only one living," the Professor said. "He was the last Federalist in office and spent his entire 35-year career empowering the national government at the expense of the states."

"At some point, he realizes the diaries and flag contradict his rulings and undermine his legal theories," he continued. "So the simple solution was to destroy the evidence."

"Enter Robin Spurlock, Marshall's right-hand man, butler, and slave. He instructs Spurlock to burn the diaries and the flag. But Robin Spurlock disobeys his master because he sees an important historical artifact being wrongly destroyed.

"Instead, he gives the flag to his closest friend and fellow slave, Hercules," Professor Mac continued.

"Hercules was the acclaimed master chef for Washington, both at Mount Vernon and in Philadelphia, when Washington was President. At that time, Pennsylvania law provided that slaves held for six months in the state would become free citizens. Despite Hercules being sent back home periodically to skirt that law, eventually he escaped. Washington would ultimately free him in his will."

"Spurlock gave the 12-star flag to Hercules, who, in turn, contacted his good friend Tobias Lear. Lear had served as Washington's private secretary for many years. Lear was by Washington's side when he died. Hercules and Tobias had a special box made to preserve the flag, and then they hid it secretly in Philadelphia."

"Tobias Lear, why does that name stick out in my head?" Pepper asked.

"Because Lear was the fall guy for Marshall," Professor Mac said. "Marshall was telling people that Lear was responsible for the missing diaries, when it was Marshall who made sure they disappeared."

"What do you think were in his diaries that he did not want known?" Pepper asked.

"Great question, Pepper," he replied. "Who knows. But there must have been something about the new Republic, the new flag, and the new star in the middle."

"In 1816, the Supreme Court granted itself powers forbidden at the Constitutional Convention," Professor Mac continued.

"The Virginia Supreme Court refused to abide by the decision, and the 12-star flag would explain why. That 12th star is like the other stars: the federal star is equal to one of the state stars, and each is in its own space."

"After the decision, Lear killed himself," he said. "I can only imagine how he viewed the treachery of Marshall."

"How did you get the flag?" Pepper asked.

The professor was tapping his fingers together.

"I was a young and brash historian, and in researching my doctoral thesis, I discovered a very strange map," he said. "The one I gave you with the flag."

Pepper nodded.

"That map made me very curious. It was printed on old parchment, and it was trying to tell a story about the American States. Well, I cracked it," he said. "That map shows where Hercules and Tobias Lear hid the flag. And so I figured it out and retrieved it from the graveyard."

He looked down for a moment and paused.

"Realizing what I discovered, I contacted a colleague who put me in touch with the Sons of Liberty. I gave it to them when I joined, forty years ago."

"And now we're going to put it back."

Chapter Thirty-Seven

"As we approached the harbor, our train (of people) increased, and the huzzaing and shouts of joy seemed to add life to this lively scene. At this moment a number of porpoises came playing amongst us, as if they had risen up to know what was the cause of all this joy. We now discovered the shores covered with thousands of people -- men, women, and children -- nay, my I venture to say tens of thousands."

– Elias Boudinot writing to his wife on accompanying George Washington across the Hudson River from New Jersey to New York for the inauguration.

The *Reprisal* was now at top speed, and I knew it wouldn't be long before we were back in Philadelphia. The Professor asked Pepper where the map was, but I had already reached into my inside coat pocket and placed it on the galley table.

"I was young and dumb," the Professor said, picking up the map. "I should have not pursued it. Fortunately, the Sons were watching."

He looked at both of us. Morgan Stonewall was called upstairs and left.

"Did you figure it out?"

"Figure what out?" I asked.

"The map? It tells you where the flag is hidden," he said, laying it down on the table.

"Was hidden," Pepper added.

He now held the map up so we could both see it and explained its parts. The map was a record of the past. It shows the flags of the Revolution that Americans fought under. Benjamin Franklin's snake and slogan are under the flags. The snake is broken into parts by state, but when combined, it becomes dangerous. Join or Die—they could win together, not alone.

"It took me a while to find the source of the Eleven Bees quote on the lower left of the map," Professor Mac said. "I traced it to the French Embassy in New York in 1789. French General Count de Rochambeau had a celebratory display for the inauguration with that quote, which will be key when we get to the grave."

"The image on the bottom shows where it is buried," he said. "The dotted line originates in New York and ends in a graveyard."

"Yes, yes," I said. "Tory magnified it, and it is Franklin's tomb."

"Exactly! Excellent detective work. Very good," the Professor said. "And that's where the flag will return."

Pepper had been very quiet, regaining her energy but also beaten down by the last few days. I could tell she wanted to ask him a question, and I thought I knew what it was.

"Professor," I said. "You said in Providence that what is taken for the truth is often a lie. And that thought a lie, is often the truth."

I was working up my courage. I didn't want to insult him, but there was something that bothered me, Tory, and Pepper.

"Yes," he said.

"Then why did *you* teach lies?" I asked.

His bottom lip pushed on the upper one, and he nodded.

He looked at both of us, and we sensed he had regrets.

"Fair enough, good question," he said. "And for the record, I didn't teach lies. I helped expose them."

He looked at both of us as if we were interrogating him.

"First, keep in mind that it's only recently that we can collect all of the facts and have access to all of the sources. Historians rely on narratives, and unless they are disproved, stick with them. Unfortunately, some teachers pick sides."

"Yes, and..." Pepper said, but the Professor stopped her.

"What are we supposed to teach kids about their past? That it is their duty to rise up and fight their government? The greatest fear of those in power is that the people will understand that truth and be motivated to change the established order," he said. "Is that really our job as teachers?"

We both stared at the Professor.

"We never teach the fundamental right and duty to revolution as stated in the Declaration because Americans are crazy enough to actually believe it," he said. "Our system achieves revolution at every election without any blood shed."

"Teaching individual rights empowers the people and begets more individually minded people," he said. "Groups are easier to manage. That's why the establishment divide us—by race, sex, and religion—into groups. The victims and the victimizers. It keeps our eyes off of *them* and their nefarious activities. It keeps us angry at each other. And it was wonderful when there were just three television networks saying the same thing. It helped promote uniformity of opinion."

"The internet has smashed that; technology has atomized us," he said. "And there is great power in the individual. Do not buy from people you oppose! That was one of the Sons of Liberty's most successful tricks during the Revolution. Don't give them your money; get others to join you, and they usually cave."

"But Professor Mac," Pepper started, "isn't the historian's job to let the chips fall where they may? And not be advocates of one narrative or the other?"

He laughed. "You heard the saying, The Victor writes the history? Well, who pays the historian, but the victor?"

The boat was now slowing. We were nearing Penn's landing.

"Americans are special people," Professor Mac said. "We brought to this New World the Roman and British ideal of liberty under law. We then lived with natives who enjoyed liberty without law. And we were constantly reminded what the opposite of liberty looks like—slavery, in all its hideous parts."

Pepper turned to me and smiled. He was confirming to us what we had already learned.

The boat now stopped, and I could hear the order to anchor. We were back in Philadelphia.

"So what did we do? We created a place that puts the ideals of equality, liberty, and freedom first. Not something absolutely guaranteed. But something to strive for, something to work towards, something to perfect. A destination we never fully arrive at but keep trying to get there.

"And we have been a work in progress ever since. Not perfect, but what is? As long as you understand the ideals and keep trying to reach for them," he said.

Pepper looked at me and then back to the Professor.

"Americans, their Declaration, and their constitutions changed the world," Professor Mac said. "And we are still changing it."

"But what about now?" Pepper asked. "With surveillance capitalism, where they know everything about you and what you do on a computer, where they read our texts and mail, violating our constitutional rights? I guess today we're changing the world for the worse."

The Professor laughed. "And to think I was going to miss being a teacher. Ha! No!"

"Pepper, the technology used to spy on us is the same technology that empowers us. The elite's greatest fear is not being able to control the narrative. And with computers, phones, and social media, it is impossible to control," he said.

"Fight your battles with words, ballots, not bullets; that's how you do it. You're free to live as you want. Don't like something? Then stop using it and organize boycotts against it. Use the technology to oppose it," he said.

I couldn't resist challenging him.

"You just turned off New York City's internet and electricity and hijacked a prison bus! You command a sophisticated military-style ship! How is that fighting with ballots?"

"Ha Ha," the Professor said. "Excellent! Your answer is right in the Declaration of Independence. When you face absolute despotism, it is your *duty* to oppose it."

"The Sons of Liberty are facing absolute despotism. For the first time in 250 years, these forces illegally pierced our privacy, spied on our operations, infiltrated us, and instigated violence to destroy us—all in violation of the Bill of Rights!

"We have to act or we perish," he said. "Just like we've done before, many times, for two and a half centuries. We must stand up to tyranny, there is no choice."

We were taking in his words as the boat made a whirring sound and the bilge pumps were activated.

"Freedom isn't doing what you want; freedom is not having to do what you don't want," he said.

Morgan Stonewall came down the stairs.

"We've anchored. But now we must move quickly. There is a warrant out for Hack, and Pepper is a fugitive from the law. I say they stay right here, and we do the job."

He looked at the Professor for his decision.

"No, it's night. We can do this in the darkness. Hack, get the flag, and let's get this done," he said. "You two have earned it."

In minutes, we were on the street, headed for Christ Church Burial Ground, the final resting place of Benjamin Franklin. I held the old flag box and map with one hand and Pepper's hand with the other. With the moon blocked by clouds, it was dark but not pitch black. The streets were empty.

We arrived at the cemetery. Standing behind an iron fence, the Professor pointed through the bars. There was Franklin's tomb, with a large stone covering his and wife Deborah's graves.

A small plaque outside the cemetery had his epitaph:

The Body of B. Franklin, Printer;
like the Cover of an old Book,
Its Contents torn out,
And stript of its Lettering and Gilding,
Lies here, Food for Worms.
But the Work shall not be wholly lost;
For it will, as he believ'd,
Appear once more,
In a new & more perfect Edition,
Corrected and amended By the Author.

We read the epitaph together, silently and in reverence.

"The truth is, Benjamin Franklin is the Father of our Country," the Professor said. "He was the first to push for union, learning its principles from the Six Nations of the Iroquois Confederacy. His fame as a scientist and inventor made him a global personality while he was alive. His charm and diplomatic skills won the French over to our cause. He was a philosopher, publisher, author, and postmaster known worldwide. He was a celebrity before there even was such a thing."

The Professor was searching his jacket for a key to the gate.

"His invention of the bifocals, lightning rod, and stove helped all in society, rich and poor, and were given without profit," he said. "We all know he grabbed the lightning from heaven, but did you know he mastered the winds in making the first maps of the Atlantic gulf stream?

"Ah, here it is!" He held up a large, old skeleton key and walked to the gate.

"Franklin was of the Enlightenment, a polymath. He started the first abolitionist society to end slavery and supported the residence law that freed slaves in Pennsylvania like Hercules. He was a genius who walked into Philadelphia dirt poor and barefoot and left as the First American, greatest to ever have lived."

He placed the key into the lock and turned it. The door to the cemetery opened with a gentle snapping sound. A slight squeal could be heard as the gate was pushed back.

We walked to Franklin's grave. A whooshing sound in the trees, followed by the hoot of an owl, announced our arrival. Another owl appeared and let out a hoot, as if they were guarding the sacred grounds.

Hoo Hoot. Hoo Hoot.

A stillness now enveloped us.

Professor Mac asked for the map and pointed to the flag pictured just above the grave image.

"See those dotted lines," he said. "They show exactly where the flag is hidden."

We could make out the dots leading to the main post of the cemetery stone wall.

Professor Mac then said the barely visible words on the map:

"Eleven bees emerge from their hives, headed by their queen."

Pepper just stood there, then turned to me.

"These words were displayed at Washington's inauguration and explain the 12-star flag most succinctly," the Professor said. "But more importantly, they are the critical clue to where the flag is hidden."

I walked over to the post.

"Look for the 11 bricks under the slightly larger 12th brick," the Professor said.

Suddenly, Morgan Stonewall raised his hand.

"Quiet," he said. "Someone's coming."

We all tried to fade into our surroundings when there appeared on the opposite street, a man dressed in a trench coat. The man stood for a moment and then resumed his way down the street.

Hoo Hoot. Hoo Hoot, the owls cried out.

We waited until Stonewall signaled that it was all clear.

I walked to the post and looked at the bricks. Sure enough, there was one larger brick with eleven holding it up, then a line of much smaller bricks to frame it out.

"Hack," the Professor said. "Take the flag box and put the triangle flat against the 12th brick and push."

I did as he said, but nothing happened.

He walked to me.

"The corners have to line up," he said, nudging the box a little to the left.

Hoo Hoot. Hoo Hoot, the owls cried out again.

I did as he said and pushed in hard. Nothing happened.

"Not so hard. Gentle," the Professor said.

I tried again and gently pushed on the flag box, and then the most curious thing happened.

The entire brick flipped, taking the flag box with it.

In literally a blink of an eye, the 12-star flag, which had caused so much trouble, torment, and death, was returned to where Hercules and Tobias had placed it so many lifetimes ago.

Chapter Thirty-Eight

"The stars upon it were like the bright morning stars of God, and the stripes upon it were beams of morning light. ... And wherever this flag comes and men behold it they see in its sacred emblazonry no embattled castles or insignia of imperial authority; they see the symbols of light. It is the banner of Dawn."

– Henry Ward Beecher

The sun announced itself with a purplish blue sky. It was the same color as the twilight at the Rhode Island Capitol in Providence days ago when this all began. Now the color was yielding to light and not darkness.

It was the early morning hours. Professor Mac locked the cemetery gate, and the four of us walked back to the marina, Pepper and I hanging back.

I felt lighter without the old flag box in my jacket.

I grabbed Pepper's hand and held it.

We didn't talk for a while. Just walked.

She squeezed my hand tight.

Finally, I broke the silence.

"You know what I told you in New York. Well, it's true. Losing you and then getting you back when you brought me the flag, and then losing you again when they arrested you," I said in a rambling, exhausted way.

"Yes," she said.

"I realized I would never let you go again," I finished, stopping and turning her to me.

Looking into her eyes, we came together and kissed.

"Promise?" Pepper said.

I waited to see if she was going to say more, determined not to interrupt her. She just looked at me.

"I swear it," I replied. "And you know what? I'm not going back to that old world. We're going someplace new, together."

She nodded.

We kissed again, turned, and headed past the *Reprisal*. Neither of us acknowledged Stonewall or Professor Mac as we walked away from them.

"Hey! This way to the ship," Stonewall barked.

We kept walking away.

"Guys, this way," he yelled.

"Pepper, Hack!" Professor Mac cried out.

But we didn't stop. We kept walking away.

Where were we going?

We didn't know.

At this point, we didn't care.

We were together.

Dawn had arrived.

And we knew it was going to be a better day.

www.ingramcontent.com/pod-product-compliance
Lightning Source LLC
Chambersburg PA
CBHW071156020726
47502CB00002B/433